MESSENGER

MESSENGER

A Sequel to
Lost Horizon

Frank DeMarco

HAMPTONROADS
PUBLISHING COMPANY, INC.

For information write:

Hampton Roads Publishing Company, Inc.
891 Norfolk Square
Norfolk, VA 23502

Or call: (804)459-2453
FAX: (804)455-8907

If you are unable to order this book from your local
bookseller, you may order directly from the publisher.
Quantity discounts for organizations are available.
Call 1-800-766-8009, toll-free.

ISBN 1-57174-013-9

Printed on acid-free paper in the United States of America

Dedicated to:

His Holiness the Dalai Lama, admirable representative of his people, a man upon whom hatred has no hold.
> Having,
> of all mankind,
> reason to be bitter,
> the Dalai Lama lives serene.
> He smiles.

And to Danny Lliteras, author of the Llewellen trilogy:
> *In The Heart of Things*
> *Into the Ashes*, and
> *Half Hidden by Twilight*,

who encouraged and prodded me by word, example, and friendship.

And to the memory of my brother Joe, 1949-1979.

Contents

PART ONE

❄

In A Quiet Place

November, 1962

Chapter One.

Chance

At the time, I thought in terms of accidents and coincidences and meaningless chances. So for a long time I took the results of my flight as I had always taken the events of my life, good or bad: as something that had inexplicably happened, something to be managed as best I could without thinking much about what it meant. I never worried much about meaning with a capital "M": All the Meaning I knew was that things happened. I had neither the time nor the training nor energy enough to look beyond appearances, and anyway I was only 26. How many people worry about Meaning at age 26? Only the long months that became years changed my perspective. To use one of my favorite analogies, the river of my life moved out of rapids into a calm, steady flow, and gradually dropped the silt that my turbulence had carried. As the silt dropped to the bottom, I began to see clearly for the first time.

All of which is a fancy way of saying that gradually I came to accept the fact that too much coincidence can only amount to meaning.

To confine the argument to its simplest terms, consider merely the geography involved. Tibet is about as big as the United States east of the Mississippi, more or less. How long are the odds against landing near any one particular house in all that territory? Particularly if, instead of however many people live east of the Mississippi these days (100 million? More?) the same amount of territory has only a few million people scattered within it. And then suppose that the only way to get you into that spot is to have you sent up in an airplane over some particularly inaccessible territory because suddenly there's a war on. And then, on top of all those unlikelihoods, suppose that just when you're more or less over the right place, something inexplicable happens. . . . You get the idea. It's the kind of business that tends to shake your belief in Chance.

✻ 2 ✻

In the Fall of 1962 Red China, which had occupied Tibet a dozen years before, suddenly used that territory to launch an invasion of India. Only three years before, the Chinese had put down a revolt in Tibet, in the course of which the Dalai Lama had fled the country. Did this sudden attack promise further Chinese moves southwestward? They sent me up to see what I could see.

"They" in this case means the U.S. Air Force: In 1962 I was a 26-year-old Air Force Captain stationed at Peshawar, Pakistan. I was one of several trained to fly the still very hush-hush, if notorious, U-2.

[I wonder: Will any but historians even remember the U-2? It's all ancient history by now: the reconnaissance flights out of Peshawar over the Soviet Union, the uncompleted mission of Francis Gary Powers in the Spring of 1960, the disruption of the Paris summit conference, all that? But it was big news, once, and certainly it changed my life.]

Well anyway, at that time we were still operating U-2s out of Peshawar (although officially we were out of that business), and here was a mission pretty nearly ideally suited for that particular plane. The U-2 was a spyplane, none better. Designed for high-altitude reconnaissance. Built like a sailplane (a glider) with enormous wings on a small fuselage.

When Francis Gary Powers had been shot down, deep in Russian territory, two and a half years earlier, he'd been hit, we were told, by a new type of missile with greater range. But we also heard the contradictory rumor that the only reason he was hit was because he had for some reason flamed out — lost power. In either case, we were pretty sure that the Chinese wouldn't have anything capable of shooting me down. Also we had hopes, and reason to believe, that the training of the Chinese radar operators wasn't always what it should be. With great good luck I might pass undetected, and even if I were seen (so my briefing officer reassured me) they ought to be unable to hit me.

The Chinese had launched invasions in two places. Were these attacks merely designed to pressure the Indians into making border concessions, or were they the forerunner of a full-dress intervention, as in Korea and Tibet in 1950? Given enough information on supply trains, road improvements, observable troop placements, etc., intelligence thought they could make a pretty good estimate of Chinese intentions. A series of overflights could get that information. So they loaded up my camera, and one fine morning before dawn in the autumn of 1962 they sent me up on a trip that was supposed to carry me from Peshawar right over the roof of the world: over India's Jammu and Kashmir, over the Karakorums into Sinkiang to check out the main road running into India from Kashgar (though I was to go nowhere near Kashgar), then east along the road toward Keriya and into Tibet, checking out things along its main road (Gartok and Gyangtse particularly), then east to the area around Lhasa, then to the Salween . . . .

But I never got even as far as Gartok.

* 3 *

I was pretty sure then and I'm entirely sure now that the Chinese never got me on their radar. Either they didn't have the equipment or they weren't using it, or their operators weren't well-trained — or maybe they saw me as a blip where there couldn't be a blip and so ignored me. Whatever the reason, I never saw the Chinese Air Force, and I can't believe they wouldn't have scrambled at least one or two fighters, if only to see how close they could come on the off-chance of a lucky shot if I made an error of judgment or the plane malfunctioned.

I went up from Peshawar about an hour before dawn and crossed over Jammu and Kashmir provinces in darkness, not by accident. (India and Pakistan were still bitter enemies at the time, with Jammu and Kashmir disputed territory, arbitrarily divided between them along the cease-fire line of their 1947 war. Though Pakistan was a U.S. ally, my superiors had no wish to alienate neutral India, particularly since China's attack had presumably served to discredit India's anti-American, pro-communist foreign minister, V.K. Krishna Menon.) Of course, darkness is no defense against radar: I wonder, now, if the Indians did see me on my way. Even if they did, they were not very likely to want to warn their adversary of an impending violation of Chinese airspace.

At any rate, by the dawn's early light I was beyond the white Karakorums, streaking almost silently toward Moji and Guma, my built-in cameras busily whirring away, shooting some terrific scenery, which is all that bit of country is, from Peshawar right up to the Kashgar road at the edge of the Takla Mahan desert. First there is hilly country, then mountains, then higher mountains, then the glacier-covered Karakorum mountains, and then more mountains, and then more mountains on the Chinese side.

But I'm not going to indulge in picture-painting beyond remembering what a terrific clear morning it was — blue-black cloudless sky, all that corrugated scenery passing below, absolute silence except for the subdued howl of the engine.

I followed my flight plan down the road from Jammu and Kashmir as close to Guma as I was supposed to get, and then eastward, flying parallel and south of the road past Moji and Khotan, cameras working steadily. When I saw the Yurang Qash river below I turned toward its source, brought myself over more glaciers, and then I was flying over Tibet.

* 4 *

But not for long.

I was a trained pilot, good enough to be entrusted with a sensitive mission in an airplane whose recent notoriety assured widespread publicity if it got into the news again. That airplane was well-maintained by professionals who knew that the life of a friend, or anyway of a colleague, depended on how well they did their jobs. Given the sensitivity of this particular mission, I have little doubt that the bird received particularly careful attention. Naturally, I had done a pre-flight inspection. All the gauges indicated everything normal.

So why, all of a sudden, did I completely lose power? Within the frame of reference I then lived in, no reason was to be found.

But it happened, and when such things happen your immediate impulse is not to say, "This can't be happening so it *isn't* happening." Instead, you say, "Oh my God, now what?" — and you try to figure our what to do. If you're driving down the road and your car's motor quits, you don't spend time telling yourself "I just had the car checked over and nothing was wrong so it *can't* be stalled," you get off the road and put the hood up.

Which is difficult to do when you're 55,000 feet above ground level.

Elementary pilot training: Aviate, navigate, communicate. Regain or retain control. Find a place to land and do your checklists and your restart procedures. Finally, if necessary, send out a Mayday and bring it in.

Well, the ship was under control; skip to number two. Find a reasonable place to land. What you are supposed to do is find a good place and then circle over that place as you lose altitude. What you *aren't* supposed to do is put off finding a place to land, hoping for a better place just out of sight. But there sure wasn't a whole lot to choose from down there — particularly from a vertical distance of 55,000 feet! So for quite a while I just let it glide while I frantically flipped switches and tried everything I could think of to get that flame re-lit.

Now as it happens, gliding is what the U-2 does best. As a matter of fact, it was designed as a sailplane specifically to allow pilots to prolong its 2,200-mile cruising range by shutting off the engine and gliding. So to hope to be able to re-start was reasonable, particularly given the great height I was starting from. When I flamed out I was close to the U-2's 70,000-foot ceiling, which left me 55,000 feet or so to fall before I'd begin to get hemmed in by terrain.

And that is what I kept telling myself, all the way down. Another minute and I'll do something that will get a response. A little lower and whatever's frozen up will thaw and let the engine whisper itself back to life. A little more thinking and I'll come up with a bright idea that will work. And all the while I fed myself these little confidence-builders, down I came. I came down gradually, extremely gradually, but down I came. There came a moment, as the peaks below slowly rose to meet me, when I began to need to devote at least some of my attention to not flying into something. Imperceptibly, the air I sailed through was no longer an ocean, but a sea surrounded by an archipelago. Gradually it became a series of bays and lagoons separating peninsulas. Finally it became a river, and I found myself sinking down between narrowing shores. But still I gave my navigation no more attention than was needed to keep off the rocks. My full attention went to trying to regain power.

When I finally gave up hope that I could get the engine lighted again, I realized that I had delayed looking for a landing spot perhaps too long. I was very low; an end could not be long delayed. No matter how recklessly close I steered to the rocks beside and beneath, I could find no updraft to buy me a little more time. Too early in the morning.

I had to decide quickly: Ride it in, or eject?

I couldn't see even a hundred-foot stretch that was anything like smooth or level. Everything was great jagged boulders and upended rock. There wouldn't be any soft landings. But I was already too low to eject, probably: Parachutes need a certain amount of falling-room to slow you down. Drop from too low and you might as well just jump out without one and hope to land on your feet. Besides, ejections are tricky. It isn't like the days of fabric-covered biplanes, when all you did was climb out and drop off. Instead, the cockpit you sat in was mounted above a rocket. If you had to bail out, you moved the canopy out of the way (if you could!) and then fired off the rocket. With luck you got a great kick in the pants and it kicked you out of the plane — away from the tail surfaces — the parachute opened and you went from there. But if your luck was bad. . . . We'd all heard stories of malfunctioning ejection rockets firing slightly wrong and shearing off somebody's arm for them on the edge of the cockpit. Ejection beat certain death, but didn't necessarily beat a hard landing. The decision was left to the pilot's judgment.

Not much to choose. The ground below was such an un-believably bad place to land, being the side of a mountain: jagged, tumbled, boulder-strewn. But then I saw something a little further on — and here is where I began to see the inade-quacy of words like luck, and the extraordinary extent to which we are guided (when we are not officiously overriding that guidance) by something beyond our conscious selves.

From the moment I had flamed out, I had concentrated my conscious mind strictly on getting the engine restarted. Since I had no intention of landing if I could possibly avoid it, I merely — unconsciously — prolonged my descent as the mountain ranges rose to meet me, steering away from immediate hazards without making any attempt to steer a particular course. By the time I had lost enough altitude to be forced to maneuver be-tween mountain walls, my position was the end result of drift and — and what? Unconscious guidance?

Certainly everything I had done was logically defensible. What reaction could be more natural, more automatic? Nobody in the situation I was in was going to come in one minute sooner, or ten feet higher up in the mountains, than he had to. Nobody, slipping down into the lower atmosphere, would pay as much attention to steering as he would to figuring out how to re-ignite his engine. It was all perfectly natural. But the end result was that in the middle of that twisted frozen wilderness of unrelieved rock that now hemmed me in on both sides, I looked directly ahead and saw a haze where there should have been no haze, and my heart leaped as I thought, incredulously, "Heated air! A thermal!"

Did I care what caused a thermal current so early in the morning, so high in the Himalayas? I did not, and I did not waste any time speculating, either. A thermal current, if I could get to it, could mean life. Sailplane pilots use them all the time, even tiny thermals like the ones caused by little patches of black asphalt: parking lots, say, or country roads. If I could nose into that updraft — whatever was causing it — I could gain a few dozen feet, circle back into it, gain a few more, and keep it up for maybe several thousand feet. Obviously I couldn't regain enough to get me out of the mountains, and I could hardly expect a convenient trail of thermals to lead me home, but one thermal would buy me time, and who could say that at any moment my engine might not re-light?

I'm tempted to wonder what would have happened if I'd reached it. How long would I have circled and circled, trying to restart my engine? I'd have had to come down before dark, at the latest, no matter what the ground looked like. But I suppose I would have seen the valley and headed in, so maybe it would have ended up more or less the same. Of course, it's possible that I might have finally gotten the engine to fire, in which case I'd have gone happily on my way, breathing a sigh of relief.

But wondering "what if" is a relic of another way of thinking that sees life as chance and coincidence and hairbreadth escapes.

Anyway, I tried hard to reach the thermal, but I didn't have even a hint of air current to work with: The day was as still, even for early morning, as I have ever seen it. All I could do was watch the ground come rapidly up to meet me, while the haze was still miles ahead. Finally I had to admit that no miracle was going to allow me to reach that current, and I started looking around seriously for a place to set down. I was far beyond looking for a "best" place; I was settling for the least worst.

And at very nearly the last minute I found it: a place some avalanche had swept clean of at least the largest outcroppings. It wasn't level, of course — I couldn't expect that — but it might not kill me immediately. I was down to my last few score feet of altitude and nothing else offered. It was a yes/no situation, and what choice did I have? I ran through my emergency landing checklist, shutting down electrical power. [This would have been the time for a Mayday, but not this mission.] The U-2's detachable wing-supporting wheels had been dropped in Peshawar, as soon as I'd become airborne. The only undercarriage left were nose- and tail-wheels, so I was in effect coming in "wheels up." Just as well. That much less sticking out to snag something and flip me over.

I cut the fuel switches, brought the ship around into its final circle, and flared it in.

* **5** *

It wasn't the best emergency landing ever made, but it didn't last too long, it didn't kill me or break any bones, even, and the fuel tanks didn't ignite and wrap me in flames. Any and all of which might easily have happened. It could have been a lot worse.

For a long few seconds I sat numb, dazed from a Ricky Ricardo sequence that bongoed my helmeted head back and forth against the side and front of the cockpit. But then I remembered the fuel tanks, and I scrambled to force the canopy back, get out of my harness, and make my way, on legs that seemed to have turned a little wobbly, out of the plane and out among the rock a little distance away. When I figured I'd gone far enough, I sat down and took a good look at the wreck that had been a flying machine three or four minutes before.

It looked, as we used to say, a little second-hand. The tail-wheels had been ripped away. The undercarriage from just aft of the cockpit was battered and broken up, the thin metal crumpled like so much tinfoil. The left wing was sheared off 20 feet or so from the tip; most of the right wing (60 feet or so), though still attached, was tortured almost shapeless. The tail surfaces were twisted a good 30 degrees out of true. Looking at it, I shook my head in disbelief. The cockpit had been protected, even though everything aft was a wreck.

A good landing is one you can walk away from.

After a bit I remembered that the fact that I'd been able to get out and run to safety didn't demonstrate that I hadn't broken anything, wasn't bleeding, etc. So I checked myself out as well as I could without taking off my flight suit and exposing myself to the early-morning high-altitude November cold. I found nothing broken, nothing bleeding.

Later I realized that I was probably in a mild state of shock, sitting on that rock ledge waiting for flames or an explosion. Neither came, but after a while my mind started functioning a little better, reminding me that although I was alive for the moment, I did have a problem or two to begin working on.

Standard operating procedure after a crash is to stay with the airplane, rather than rushing off hoping to reach safety. The theory is that wrecked airplanes are a lot easier to spot from the air than footsore, half-dead, arm-waving aviators.

But my case didn't seen to fit the rules, for the same reason that had stopped me from sending out a distress signal. In the first and most obvious place, the people likely to "rescue" me I didn't care to be rescued by. That attitude may seem impossibly idealistic — give me liberty or give me death — but at 26 it came naturally. I decided easily I'd rather die in the mountains than under interrogation, or in a prison cell.

Besides, I needed merely to absorb the appalling immensity around me. In the clear early morning air, I could see many miles of mountains and valley. In all that extensive moun-tainscape, not a tree, not a bush, hardly a blade of grass. Not only no sign of civilization, no sign of human life. Who — even the Chinese Air Force — looking down on all that immensity, would be able to find one dot of an individual and his crumpled airplane? No, the fact was clear: The only chance I'd have would be whatever chance I'd make for myself. Since I didn't care to stay and be captured, or (more likely) stay and die unnoticed, there wasn't any alternative but to start walking.

Walk all the way back to Peshawar?

Well, to India, anyway. Jammu and Kashmir couldn't be more than — 100? 120? — miles to the west. Say 150 miles, at the outside. In level country, with minimal provisions, three to 10 days, depending on how well I walked and where exactly I started from. Without provisions, in this broken terrain, with the Chinese Air Force and ground forces to consider. . .?

But what choice did I have?

By the time I had worked all this out — my mind was working extraordinarily slowly — I was reasonably sure that the U-2 didn't intend to scatter itself and me all over the landscape in delayed reaction to the trauma it had just suffered, so I proceeded back to see what I could find that might be useful on a little jaunt through the countryside.

I didn't find much. Most of the useful things were in the pockets of my flight suit: sheath knife, a big bar of concentrated chocolate, salt tablets. Water, though not much of it. I did unclip the first-aid kit and distribute its contents in two zipper pockets, though I had a feeling I'd soon begrudge the extra weight. I took my oxygen mask, of course. The emergency flares I left, after trying unsuccessfully to imagine a situation in which they'd be useful.

Then, as I thought I was ready to start, the first breath of wind began to rise, and I suddenly remembered that I was overlooking the question of what I was going to do when the nighttime temperature plunged. My flight suit would help a bit, as would my parachute, which I could make into a sort of sleeping bag. But on this exposed rock, I'd freeze. If not the first night, the second, or the third.

Mentally I retraced the route that had brought me to that place, looking for terrain that promised snow I could burrow into, or dirt. Then I remembered that I'd arrived by way of China, and in fact had no idea at all of the lay of the land between India and the rocky ledge I stood on. The only guarantee was that it would be impossible terrain, the most forbidding north of Antarctica. And with that, I about lost my courage, appalled by the slimness of my chances.

* **6** *

Then came intervention.

I suppose you could make a plausible argument for coincidence again, or could say it was the natural mental leap to make, starting from the awareness of cold. I don't care to argue the point. The fact is, until the wind began to rise, my only thought had been of walking west for as long as my strength held out. In the back of my mind was the enormous difficulty I'd have getting past the guards at the border; still, I thought, I could deal with only one thing at a time, and clearly the first thing to do was to be on my way. But that wind threw my mental gears into neutral. For a long moment I stood, not only irresolute but unthinking. And into that mental gap a small thought — an urge, rather — inserted itself. It told me, "Go toward the warmth." I had suddenly remembered the thermal current I'd been anxiously making for, not half an hour earlier.

Needless to say, that made no sense at all. Even assuming that the thermal did signal some kind of heat source — a fair assumption — I had no way to judge what that source might be. A stratum of black rock that absorbed heat and threw it back? Not likely, this early in the day. Volcanic activity, maybe? What difference did it make? I needed water, food, and progress toward freedom, and while I couldn't see any prospect of the first two anywhere, the third clearly enough lay to the west, while the source of that thermal lay farther east, or east by southeast.

Suppose I found the heat-source and it proved suitable to warm myself on? So what? What would I have gained? One night's warmth?

No, it didn't begin to make sense. I set my mind on the west, and actually took a few steps in that direction before slowing down and coming to a halt. A voice within was crying insistently that I must make for the warmth. I started walking again, ignoring the voice, striding step, step, step westward, trying to concentrate on the terrain ahead, watching where I placed my feet, very much aware that a sprained ankle would end the play. Again, this time after a few hundred feet of progress, the internal clamor brought me to a halt.

Looking back from the perspective of all these years later, I realize that my life was saved at this point by two aviators (one dead) whose books I'd read as a teenager. For at that self-divided moment, I doubt I'd have found the courage to follow that inner voice if I hadn't found an argument to use against my arrogantly rational intellect. At 26, the product of an Air Force education and my parents' attitude toward life, and the attitude I saw all around me in society, I was accustomed to following reason, or what passed for reason, rather than instinct. What could not be logically demonstrated did not exist, or at least was not a trustworthy guide. To blindly follow a hunch in the face of reason would have struck me as a variety of betrayal. Without arguments, I'm fairly confident that I would have continued obstinately walking westward, in which case I'd now be dead many, many years. But again, this is a useless "what-if" argument.

My life was saved because I listened to the inner voice. I listened because I suddenly remembered two things I had read half a dozen years before. So, clearly, I got off the Tibetan altiplano in November, 1962, because a high-school boy read two books on aviation. And since those two books were only beads on a string of books he devoured, it would be equally true to say that my life was saved because I developed a love of aviation and of reading. So was my life saved by that high-school boy? By those who taught him to read? By Charles Lindbergh and Antoine de St. Exupery?

When you have to cast the net so widely, isn't it simpler and just as accurate to say that my life was saved by the *pattern* of my life? And doesn't that amount to saying (since that pattern was certainly not determined by me) that it was saved by life itself, or by the source of life? So it seems to me.

As I stood undecided on the side of a mountain in Tibet in 1962, overruling instinct with reason, I remembered Charles Lindbergh in 1927, and Antoine de St. Exupery a decade later. Two memories popped up, unbidden by me, and tipped the balance, reminding me from other men's personal experience that not everything that can be trusted is found in science and logic.

Lindbergh in May, 1927, at night, over the North Atlantic, out of his mind with fatigue and the need for sleep, seeing visions, no longer sure what was real and what was hallucination. All night (he said later in *The Spirit of St. Louis*) his cockpit was crowded with other presences, spirits who told him things. But when his conscious mind regained control with the coming of day, the presences faded away.

Illusions?

Hallucinations?

Sure — except that after a day and a night of semi-conscious dead reckoning, he reached Ireland within *three miles* of his intended landfall. He wasn't prepared to attribute the result to luck, or to skill. It was obvious to him that more was involved.

St. Exupery, lost in the North African desert after a nighttime crash landing. His logical mind, which knew more or less where he must be, told him to walk eastward. But his instinct, which he could not find strength to ignore, to fight, or to overwhelm, sent him walking northwestward. Even as he walked, he was convinced that he was walking deeper into the Sinai Desert. Still he walked. At more or less the last moment, he was rescued — and learned that (due to an unsuspected headwind) his airplane had crashed hundreds of miles west of where he'd thought he was. If he'd followed logic, he'd have been lost. Instead, he had followed an inexplicable certainty, and had been saved.

He had been saved, to write a book that would be read by a teen-age boy. Saved, to save my life some 30 years later. The strength of my own inner voice had brought me to a standstill, but the memory of what had happened to the two aviators tipped the balance. Reluctantly, still not believing that what I was doing was anything more than delayed-action suicide, I retraced my steps to the plane, swatted it half-heartedly on the nose as I went by, and started walking toward the haze of heat I'd seen a few minutes before I'd run out of time.

* 7 *

No point in saying much about my little hike. No chance of losing my way, with the valley having narrowed to little more than a mile wide at the level I was at. No need to climb up, no reason to climb down, so I followed an imaginary contour line. No sign of human habitation to steer toward (or avoid); no vegetation to consider; not even any particularly difficult or advantageous terrain to traverse. Nothing to do but hike, being careful not to turn an ankle or risk a fall. Find a sustainable pace and stick to it. One foot, then another. Keep moving toward the source of warmth, whatever it might turn out to be. Use oxygen whenever the alternative seemed to be inability to continue, but remember that it is more precious than gold.

And so I trudged all day toward the east, unable to see any haze or source of haze, telling myself that by continuing on I must come to the source.

* 8 *

If I had had a sidearm, there might have been an argument with tragic consequences. As it was, I raised my hands and did as I was told.

I don't suppose I need to apologize for my lack of alertness. I'd gradually sunk, as I walked and walked, into almost a semi-conscious state. I'd been walking all day, I was hungry, I was tired, I was cold. Also, I had every reason to assume I was alone in that empty country.

With darkness coming, perhaps in a few hours I would have welcomed even Red Chinese soldiers bringing the promise of years in prison. But I can't say that I welcomed the sudden sound — coming straight out of hours of isolation and silence — of a shell being jacked into a rifle chamber.

My reaction (amusingly, from this safe distance) was entirely divided. The sudden, *very* familiar sound reached right down into my instincts, bypassing my brain entirely. The first thing I knew, by the time my mind returned from wherever it had been wandering, I was lying prone, flattened down on the rocks, trying to present a smaller target. Seeing this, my mind listened again to the sound I'd heard, and scoffed: "Not a shell being jacked into a chamber, of course, not out here. Sounded extraordinarily like that, I'll give you that, but certainly not that."

And so I was starting to climb wearily back to my feet when I saw the man and his rifle. The rifle was aimed at my stomach.

I froze, one knee and hand on the ground, for all the world as if I were getting ready to scrimmage. Then, as I moved to stand up, I heard him jack another shell into its chamber. Except that you can't jack two shells into the same chamber, and anyway he hadn't moved. In another delayed-reaction sequence, I realized that the sound (echoed off the walls around us) had come from behind. I very slowly turned my head, to see another rifle trained on me, the rifleman standing perhaps 200 feet away, a few feet higher than the contour I'd been following. I must have walked right past wherever he had been hiding.

I put up my hands and watched the second man make his way down to me. What choice did I have?

Of course, I expected the worst. Downed in Red territory, coming off a spy mission, American. . . .

The men were Tibetan, I supposed. At least they didn't look like Chinese, and certainly weren't Westerners. Both were young, both were calm and confident. Well (I thought), at least they didn't look like they had itchy trigger-fingers. One small point intruded and offered an absurd comfort: On neither fur hats nor coats could I see red stars, nor any military markings whatsoever. But logically I knew they had to be Reds.

They made no attempt to search me, but fell in behind me and motioned me to continue on in the way I had been going. They followed—thus, I thought, leaving the position unguarded. (I later learned that other sentries remained, two of whom began quickly to retrace my steps as far as they could before nightfall.)

We proceeded only a few hundred feet before I rounded a bend and saw the valley laid out before me, a great space several miles long and perhaps a mile wide at its widest, a mile below the level of the surrounding plateau, looking like it had been punched down by God's own chisel. At the bottom of the valley — incredible sight after a day of unrelieved brown and grey — I could see living green. Above, as I looked to the far horizon, there was the haze of warmth and moisture I'd seen so long ago, so short a time ago.

The way led down, and my guards made it clear by gestures that we would travel it, quickly, before sunset, roped together like mountaineers.

Was I in a position to object? I let them rope me, one before me, one following, wondering if the ropes I saw were always left in the little overhang from which they'd been taken; wondering what they proposed to do if I objected; wondering how well they could manage the descent with rifles slung across their backs; wondering if I should try to grab one of the rifles and turn the tables; wondering what in the world I would do if I succeeded. Since I'd have to descend anyway, I decided to bide my time.

Well, we made the descent uneventfully, though the sunlight faded fast. The warmth increased as we descended until, about halfway down, I had to unzip my flight suit partway and they had to shed their heavy fur overcoats. The heat grew more intense until, at the valley floor, it resembled Biloxi, Mississippi, in the summertime, which was pretty astonishing given the altitude and season, not to mention the contrast with my long day's chill experience.

* 9 *

To my surprise, they did not unrope us: The valley floor was not the end of our journey. It being full night now, my guides — guards — lit torches, and on we went for another mile or so, threading our way through dense vegetation that I couldn't in the darkness identify: something under cultivation, though, that was clear enough. Then we were climbing again, a long climb, not nearly as difficult as the descent we had made, but longer. We climbed and climbed until we were back in coolness, then in cold that made me zip up my flight suit again, cold that put them back into their overcoats.

I was tired, by this time; dead tired. I tried to ask them to go slower, or halt for a rest, but they paid no attention to my gesturing. The lead man pulled, the one behind prodded, and the trussed animal in the middle — namely me, as Daisy Mae used to say — was forced to stay on his feet and keep pace. Self-rationed whiffs of oxygen were about all that kept me on my feet.

Unfamiliar journeys always seem to take forever, and this one was travelled by torchlight, at forced pace, with silent companions, at the end of a long day of walking which had followed a crash landing at the end of a flight over enemy territory. If all that hadn't been enough, I'd been up since 3 a.m. The climb went on and on, and I stumbled through it like a blind mule treading corn.

When finally we stopped — they stopped — and they unroped us, the effect was peculiar. It was as though we'd gone for a hike for the hell of it, and had stopped completely at random. The place where we were was nothing but a level spot on the trail. The little circles of torchlight showed me exactly what they'd been showing me since our climb started: rock on one side, emptiness on the other. We were perched on the side of the mountain, on a trail that was none too wide, none too obvious.

We had already followed the trail forever, apparently toward no goal in particular. Weariness overcame discretion. I determined to sit, regardless. I sat, letting my head sag between my knees, half-expecting a blow from a rifle butt. Instead, I heard them exchange a few words, then one put his hand on my shoulder, speaking urgently but at least not barking orders. When I looked up at him, he pointed upwards, a little to the side of the trail leading up. I shook my head wearily. I knew I'd have to give in, but every second off my feet was worth fighting for. He spoke again, even more urgently than before, pointing to the path and flicking his fingers upward. But — having finally stopped — I felt like I could never start again.

I expect that they wouldn't have put up with that for too long: soon enough they'd have pulled me to my feet and encouraged me along. But they were saved that inhospitable effort. The gibbous moon came up suddenly over the horizon, and in its light I suddenly could see what the guards had been pointing to, beyond the circles of light their torches provided.

* **10** *

Standing there, what did I see? An immediate impression of bulk, of solidity. Several buildings, all connected — or else one building, built in increments over time. The faintest impression of color, unverifiable in the pale moonlight. A sense of impermanence, arising perhaps from the fact that the buildings perched so near to so sheer and catastrophic a drop.

I must not forget, as I am tempted to, that overwhelming every other impression was an unmixed astonishment. Dragging myself down and then up mountain trails, roped like a horse and helpless as a bunny, I'd had no energy for speculation about where we were going. Probably I would have guessed at a sentry's shelter: an army tent, perhaps. Some temporary structure of metal or plastic or canvas. And on the valley floor. Certainly not stone buildings, and certainly not halfway up a mountain.

Yes, certainly astonishment came first.

But hard on the heels of astonishment came bewilderment. And apprehension was not absent.

* 11 *

My guides gave me little time to gather impressions. As soon as they saw my eyes widen, they helped me to my feet and half-pulled, half-prodded me onward. Within three minutes of the time I first saw the buildings, I was standing inside the entrance to the first of them, a small room lit by an oil lamp on a table. There one of my guards unslung his rifle, leaned it against a corner, and disappeared through a doorway.

The other took off his fur hat but stood holding his own rifle, quietly watching me. Watching, I suppose, for any sign that I was going to grab for the one his companion had left. But I was a long way from having ideas like that: I was tired and apprehensive and a long way from home, and I knew the difference between reality and a TV western. Instead of making a play for the rifle, I looked around the little room.

Reception room, I figured. I didn't know what else it would be good for. Smallish, maybe 6 by 10, with a few stick chairs for furniture and two walls' worth of hooks, mostly in use, for coats and hats.

At first, expecting my vanished guide to come bounding back with someone in authority, I paced up and back. But I quickly tired of this, and the long minutes in which nothing happened soon lulled me out of the alertness my new surroundings had revived in me. I eased myself down into one of their chairs. The room was little warmer than the outside, though the absence of wind was a comfort.

My guard did not sit down, nor change positions from the spread-legged, flat-footed stance he'd assumed when he took off his hat. His alertness reminded me, as if I needed a reminder in surroundings so strange, that I was a prisoner whose fate was perhaps even at the moment being decided.

But tension can be sustained in the absence of incident only so long and no longer. As one minute followed another, I began to lose the struggle for consciousness. The chair felt so good after a day's hard walking. The room seemed so human—so welcoming, almost—after the mountainside's vast indifference. The day had started so early and had gone on so long. . . .

I fell asleep where I sat.

* 12 *

Of all the experiences life commonly provides, I can't think of any more disorienting than being awakened out of a sound sleep only recently entered. I could have used 10 hours' sleep. I got perhaps 20 minutes' worth.

My alarm clock proved to be a man, apparently in his mid-50s, surprisingly enough a Westerner: that is, a white man.

"Sonny," he was saying, shaking my shoulder, "sonny, can you wake up? Sonny?"

I don't know where I'd been, but it was somewhere far. I struggled, for a moment, to place this man's voice and face among the gallery of officers at Peshawar or Eglin or Keesler. By the time I realized that I couldn't do it, I was awake.

"Sonny, I know you're tired, but you have got to wake up."

I shook myself, feeling how slow my movements were. "Okay, okay. I'm awake now."

"Here, have some tea, it'll wake you up a little. Warm you some, too." Behind him I saw another man, an Oriental, with a tray on which was a teapot and a cup.

Warmth and liquid: Either sensation would have been welcome singly. Together they were irresistible. I had two cups in quick succession, burning my tongue in the process, while the man looked on benevolently. "Come on, now," he said as I reached out for another, "let's go where we can get more comfortable." With that, he picked up the tea tray and led me through the door.

I was still half-asleep: I didn't have the mental energy to keep track of the passages we traversed. By the third or fourth doorway, I was hopelessly confused, and probably couldn't have found my way back to the entry. I figured there was a good chance we were heading for the interrogation chamber.

We stopped in what seemed at first to be a small room with four easy chairs, illumined by an oil lamp hanging from a wall. A second look showed me that it wasn't a separate room at all, but one alcove of many that formed a much larger room. A third look showed me that the walls were lined from floor to ceiling with books. Interrogation chamber? We were in a library! I laughed, and laughed again at the surprise on my companion's face.

"Sorry," I said, laughing again. It was an effort to stop.

"Have a seat, there, sonny," he said, and I wasted no time doing so. He put the tray on the table and poured us each a cup. "You probably got plenty of questions, and I'll be glad to answer 'em, but I figure you could use a night's sleep first, am I right?"

I yawned. "You are. I'm dead on my feet. Can you give me some idea where I've wound up?"

"Sure, I'll give you the whole story before you're a day older, don't worry. But if you don't mind, we got a couple of other pieces of business to get through. First off, my name's Henry Barnard." In retrospect, I remember him watching me intently, to see if the name meant anything to me. But maybe that's just memory-tacked-on-after-the-fact.

"George Chiari," I said, and — somewhat absurdly — we leaned toward each other from the chairs we sat in, and shook hands.

"George Chiari," he said slowly, meditatively. "Eye-talian, is it? Glad to know you, George. Where are you from?"

"Southern New Jersey. You?"

"Ohio, little town called Yellow Springs, not so far from Dayton."

"Been there," I said promptly. "Wright-Patterson."

He looked at me blankly.

"The Air Force Base."

"Oh, sure," he said vaguely. "Well, now, George, before we let you get your beauty sleep, we got to know something about what to expect next. You didn't come all this way into the hills walking, so I expect you were in an airplane, and that means you crashed it somewhere."

My thoughts went something like this: He's a kindly looking man, and a fellow American. But he could be a front for the Chinese. Pretty nearly has to be. Or is that too suspicious? Too much suspicion can mislead just as much as too much credulity. But go slow.

"For what it's worth," Mr. Barnard said casually, "the two that brought you in weren't the only two watching the passes. Already, there's two more headed back the way you came, to see what they can see."

Of course they would find the U-2. "Well, I flew in, sure," I said.

"Chinese bring you down?"

I couldn't see any reason not to answer that one. "No, nothing like that. I just flamed out."

"You what? Oh, your engine stopped ticking over?"

"Uh — right. I don't know why, either. I was a long way up and I had a long time to get it going again, but no luck."

Mr. Barnard smiled at me, smiling with just the corners of his mouth. "Maybe you and me got different ideas about luck. Seems to me you could have come down in a lot worse places."

"Speaking of which," I said slowly, "tell me about this place. I've got sense enough to know I'm in trouble, and I'm not going to do any talking about my mission, but I *would* like to know what I'm up against."

Mr. Barnard sat back, absorbing that. "You think this place is run by China." He sat there thinking. "I reckon it would look like that to you. You figure you're over enemy country, anything underneath has got to be someplace you'd just as soon be someplace else. And we're down here, surrounded by enemy country ourselves, and we figure anything comes down on us has pretty near got to be more of the same. So now you and me, we got to convince each other we're both that lucky. How do you suppose we can do that?"

I sipped some tea and tried to decide what I thought. "Well," I said, "even if I *was* with the Chinese, you couldn't do much about it, could you? But you want to figure me out this minute. It makes me wonder what your hurry is."

He shook his head decisively. "Suppose you *are*, there *ain't* any hurry: our goose is cooked. But if you ain't, it makes a difference if you were followed or not."

"Why?"

"If nobody's looking for you, it's worth our time to cover your tracks completely; we'll get your airplane off the ground and out of sight, so it won't be sitting there for somebody to stumble on. But if they are liable to keep looking till they find something, we got to leave it there and take our chances. We want 'em to stop looking just as soon as possible, and hope they don't find us before they find your airplane. Course, they won't find a body to go with the plane: That ain't going to help any."

"You're telling me the Chinese don't know about this place, after however long they've been in Tibet? A dozen years?"

"I imagine they got other things to do than look under every rock in the whole country," he said quietly. "If they had any idea there was anybody here, I reckon they could find us quick enough — but if they figure there ain't anybody here, and they don't hear any different, and they don't have any special reason to come looking, why *should* they find us?" He stabbed a finger at me. "Even in the States, there has got to be odd corners here and there where folks could live for years and never be found out; places wild enough, and off the beaten track enough. And if the folks living there had reason to want not to be found, they could do things to improve their chances: camouflage the tops of their buildings, be careful with their fires, you know. And even if somebody started looking, think how many years it would take to search every square mile of Alaska, say. Or British Columbia."

"I suppose," I said, bemused. "But in 12 years, not even one airplane?"

"I didn't say that, exactly. All I said was that they don't seem to have found us yet."

It was late and I was tired. Finally I took his word for things. After all, clearly they *were* there, and if they'd been working with the Chinese, they would have had no reason to pretend otherwise. Certainly I was in their power. I told him I hadn't seen another airplane all day, and had seen no sign that I'd been spotted by anyone.

By the time I got through answering his questions — including questions I couldn't answer very well, like the hazards to watch out for in disassembling wrecked U-2s (by whom? and with what tools?) — I was again falling asleep. When Mr. Barnard led me to a tiny room (a monk's cell, had I known it), I was more than ready to take off my boots, lie down on the hard cot, cover myself with blankets, and cease to make the tremendous effort required to hold myself awake. I'd started the day in Peshawar. I'd flown, crashed, hiked, climbed down and up and answered questions. Curiosity and apprehension were no match for exhaustion.

Chapter Two.

The Monastery

Late the following morning, Mr. Barnard found me lying in bed staring up at the ceiling, wondering how long the trek back would take. Provided the place wasn't an elaborate Chinese trap, I figured I'd stumbled into probably the only place in Tibet that would help me get back over the border into India or Pakistan. I figured they'd give me provisions, and maybe even a guide. Working our way by night, moving with someone who knew the terrain, I figured five nights, maybe. I couldn't get over the good luck that had brought me safely here. Assuming that the place was what it seemed.

And suddenly there was Mr. Barnard at the door. "Well," he said, beaming benevolently down at me like a Buddha with a mustache, "when I looked in on you a while back, you looked like you were working hard on catching up on your sleep. How are you feeling now?"

I stretched and sat up in bed. "Pretty good, considering. A little stiff from all that walking yesterday."

He nodded. "Sure. Did you have trouble figuring out where you were when you woke up?"

"Yeah, I did. I woke up and saw this tiny room, all this stone and all, and I said '*where* in the hell is this?' I sort of woke up expecting to be in — where I should have wound up yesterday."

He nodded again. "Well, it ain't where you expected to be, that's sure. But you could have done worse."

"Oh, I know that. Even if I *don't* know yet where I am or what I'm involved with here."

The corners of his eyes wrinkled, and his mouth shaped itself into a wry half-smile. "I told you I'd answer questions, and I will. But I reckon you're going to have to choose. Do you want to hear where you've wound up, or would you rather have breakfast first?"

That was an easy choice: I was 26, and I'd always been a hearty eater. Mr. Barnard laughed out loud when he saw my face. "We missed the regular breakfast, George, but I reckon we can rustle up something on our own. Come on."

I put on my shoes and followed him into the corridor. We went down several corridors and wound up in a moderate-sized kitchen. No refrigerator, no freezer, but a large wood-fired cookstove and many wooden cabinets of food and utensils. No one was around, but the stove was hot — was kept hot all day, as I later discovered, except in mid-summer. I sat on a stool in one corner while Mr. Barnard padded around fixing us some breakfast.

"What I'm going to make is called tsampa. Roasted barley meal. I like to think of it as oatmeal. It ain't, but it's maybe close enough. Anyway, it's breakfast. If you'll look in one of those drawers there, you'll find a knife, and the bread is over in that cabinet. Cut us a couple slices, would you?"

He knew what was on my mind. Without turning around from the stove, where he was stirring what did look like dried oatmeal into water, he started to answer the questions I hadn't asked.

"The fact that we didn't meet anybody between here and your cell — your room, I mean — don't mean the place is deserted. We keep our own schedules, and right now pretty nearly everybody else is tied up."

"And how many people is that, all together?"

"Well, there's about 60. Fifty monks and seven postulants. And some servants, but they come and go."

"So this is a monastery, then?" The bread loaves were heavy, solid. They resisted the knife.

"That's what it is."

"In the middle of Tibet."

"Yep."

"Has it been here long?"

"Pretty long. Since long before I got here."

"Isn't that a little —"

"Strange?"

"Well, strange, but — isn't it . . . I mean it's sort of unbelievable. Don't the communists object?"

He turned toward me and smiled sardonically. "I imagine they would if they happened to know about it. So far they ain't found out."

"I don't understand. The Chinese have been in Tibet since — when? 1949?"

"Close enough. 1950. Twelve long years."

"And they haven't found this place?"

"Does it look like they have? We ain't exactly on the beaten track, you know."

"No, but still. Twelve years!"

Mr. Barnard shrugged. "Twelve so far. With luck it'll be quite a while yet." He turned and saw my skeptical expression. "George, it's like I said last night, maybe you don't remember. Suppose this place was in the middle of Alaska somewhere, or Greenland. How long do you think it might be before somebody official came stumbling onto it?"

"Well —I just did."

"Yeah, you did, and you're the first. And since you won't tell them, and *we* sure won't, how do they find out? And if they don't know we're here, why should they come looking? There sure ain't much *else* around for them to come looking for. We figure to keep to ourselves a good while yet." He turned back to stir the pan. "That's why we're so interested in picking the pieces of your airplane off the mountain, and why I wanted to be sure you hadn't been spotted: Once you know something's in a certain area—no matter how big the area—you're going to find it. So for us, the big thing is to keep 'em from ever having a reason to start looking."

"I guess that makes sense."

"Sure it does. It's just a matter of being careful and having God on our side."

"Well, being a monastery, you ought to." We smiled at each other. "But you don't look like my idea of a monk, Mr. Barnard. Or should I say Brother Barnard?"

He spooned the tsampa out of the cooking pan into two wooden bowls, left the spoon in the empty pan, poured water into the pan and put it back onto the stove. "Makes it easier to clean," he said, reading my mind by watching me watch him. He brought the bowls to the table I was resting my elbow on, and pulled up a stool. "Spoons in that drawer behind you, George. I don't look much like a monk? Well, that won't come as big news to anybody around here. How do you like your first taste of tsampa? Taste like oatmeal?"

"Not very *much* like oatmeal. A little, maybe."

He nodded as though I'd confirmed an old suspicion. "It's been a good while since I've had any of the real thing, and I couldn't remember if the taste was close. But I had a feeling maybe it wasn't." Without a pause he continued. "Just because a place is a monastery don't mean everybody in it is a monk. You ain't one, for instance. And neither am I. But most everybody else here is. Except there's some servants here, too, but like I said they come and go."

"Come and go *where*? Oh, down to the valley, I suppose?"

"Right. Some of the younger men take turns working up here a few weeks at a time, except for a couple who stay here. But don't worry about that, it ain't important. I aim to give you the nickel tour when we're done here. Probably it won't look like much, next to what I suppose you're used to. And when you come right down to it, what a body's used to is pretty near everything, ain't it?"

* 2 *

It didn't take long to show me around.

"You see, they made it pretty easy to get from one building to the next. Lots of the monks are old, and in the winter they don't hanker for any extra dose of the weather. And, at that, there ain't so much of the place."

Nor was there. A large room he called the refectory, which was clearly a dining hall. The connected rooms (or, viewed another way, the one large room divided into alcoves) with walls lined with books, a small part of which I had seen the night before. (I saw now there were pieces of statuary on various tables.) Various rooms that appeared to be galleries of a museum of sorts, many of which we did not enter. Two smallish rooms apparently set aside for the playing of musical instruments. (How had they brought a piano into this inaccessible building halfway up a mountain in northwestern Tibet?)

We'd already seen the kitchen. He brought me past a pantry, past the "facilities," past several bath rooms — rooms for bathing — and past a little infirmary. We looked into a sort of chapel that was without ornamentation of any kind, and we passed rooms that he said were servants' quarters, monks' cells and meditation cells. We entered none of these.

Down the hall, and to my surprise we were in a workshop filled with various hand tools, most of which I could not identify. "I spend a good deal of time here," Mr. Barnard said. "Lots of the furniture here I made: that bed you slept in last night, for one."

He opened the next door and I gasped with surprise and pleasure. We walked into a little room half-full of flourishing plants. He smiled broadly at my delighted reaction. "My special hobby," he said expansively. "I planned it and built it onto the outside of the building."

"It's terrific," I said. The entire south wall was panes of glass, and within a room not more than 8 feet by 15 he had packed an incredible number of vegetables and flowers.

"This here is where we get our salads in the spring and fall," he said. "It'd take too much to heat it between mid-December and mid-February, but it's nice to have, and in the winter it still makes a nice place to sit, daytimes."

The room was chillier than the other rooms had been, but the incoming sun was beginning to warm it. I looked through the window to the rock formation on the other side of the chasm we perched on. The contrast between the sheltered room and the barren mountain was comforting, but almost overwhelming. Somehow it reminded me of our isolation. "I'll bet looking at the sky from here is a treat," I said after a minute.

"Yeah," he said comfortably, "but it wasn't any treat getting all that glass up here from outside, I can tell you."

"No, I guess not." I wondered (but did not ask) how they *had*.

The greenhouse room was the end of the tour. I told Mr. Barnard that the cluster of buildings seemed small for 60 people.

He shrugged. "Like I say, it's all in what you're used to. When I was a boy, there was a Trappist monastery out in Kentucky and the folks there didn't even talk, let alone go visit places. At least, that's what the story was, and people pretty much believed it. I never could see living that way, but it does appeal to some. Every man to his own tastes, I say. Besides, the monks here have the valley if they ever want to get out and about."

I couldn't imagine anyone choosing such a life. I wondered if I'd get any insight into that mentality before I got away.

* 3 *

Mr. Barnard's room was much like mine, except that it had obviously been lived in for some time. Two small Chinese-looking pen-and-ink sketches of great delicacy were hung on one wall. A small two-shelf bookcase contained perhaps 50 books and what looked like a bound manuscript. A small wooden wardrobe occupied one corner. Instead of a bed, a bedroll neatly tied in another corner. Nearby lay some cushions about three feet square and nearly a foot thick in the middle. Otherwise the room held only a wooden armchair (which, it turned out, Mr. Barnard had made in his workshop) and next to it a little table two feet high bearing a glass oil lamp. I thought the room austere.

"Austere?" Mr. Barnard laughed. "You wouldn't call it that if you got a look at the monks' cells. You wouldn't find all these cushions, for one thing."

He sat in his chair and I sat on the floor, leaning against cushions propped against the wall, an arrangement surprisingly comfortable.

"We got other places to sit and talk, George, and it won't be long before you get to know 'em all. Except for the meditation cells and the monks' own cells, you'll be able to go pretty much wherever you want. It's just that today it would be better if we didn't run into anybody until they been warned we got a new face. When you're as old and set in your ways as some of the brothers are, you appreciate it if people break surprises to you kind of careful. That's why I took you around just when I did: I knew there wasn't liable to be anybody around. But if we're going to talk, this is the place for it, at least today. I gave you the nickel tour, now you get the ten-cent history so you can see what you're involved in."

"That's fine with me," I said. "I can't understand how this place survives in the middle of Chinese territory."

"Well, that ain't the strangest part of the story, I can tell you. You comfortable there? This is going to take a while."

* 4 *

"There's some things you ought to know right off. First thing, this ain't some last-minute addition to the landscape. It's been here since the 1700s. Longer than that, if you count the oldest parts of the buildings. They were part of a lamasery, back time out of mind. But the 1700s is when the abandoned buildings started to get fixed up and rebuilt and turned into a monastery."

"A Christian monastery?"

"Right. Catholic, in fact. And that's the second thing you need to know. The rebuilding was done by a monk out of Luxembourg, name of Perrault. He'd wandered into the valley, half-dead."

"Wandered?"

Mr. Barnard grinned at me. "I know. Don't seem like it would be very easy to just wander in, does it?"

"Especially not in the 1700s."

"Right. But that's because I'm leaving out half the story. He was traveling with others, all the way from Peking, and by the time they got into the neighborhood the others had died and he wasn't far from dead himself. The only reason *he* didn't die was, he got lucky. At least, luck is probably what *you'd* call it. Anyhow, he could see clear enough that, as hard as he'd found it in, it was going to be worth his life to try to wander back out again. So he didn't even try. He stayed, and spent his time converting the natives in the valley from Buddhism and Lamaism to Catholicism."

"I wouldn't think he'd have much luck at that."

"Oh, you'd be surprised. He sounds like he was one of those iron-willed folks that once they set their minds to something, they just keep at it. And it ain't like he had any real strong opposition. This place couldn't *be* any more isolated, and it ain't like the natives had Buddhist missionaries dropping in as rein-forcements. Old Father Perrault did okay on converts. Besides, it ain't like he was the first. Tibet used to have a Christian community, you know, even in Lhasa."

"Did it?" I shifted positions. "I didn't know that. I thought Tibet kept foreigners out."

"They did, but not everybody. And they didn't work all that hard at it. Mostly they relied on all these mountains."

I didn't need to be persuaded on that point. The row after desolate row of mountains I'd seen from the air were fresh in my mind. The idea of trekking across the bleak terrain was not attractive. Which reminded me: "But Mr. Barnard, how did *you* get here? You didn't come on foot!"

He waved the question aside. "That's getting ahead of the story, George, but I'll tell you this, and it's going to surprise you: Most of the monks here came in from outside. I'm the only American here — was till you showed up, anyway — but a good number of the others are from Europe. Couple of Chinese."

I couldn't make sense of that. "From Europe. How did they all get here?"

"Oh, lots of ways. Some got lost, and some got invited, and three got Shanghaied and stayed on."

"So they didn't all come at once."

"Oh, no. Mostly one at a time. The most that ever came at one time was four, and that only happened once."

I shook my head involuntarily. "That doesn't make sense. That many Europeans got in here, one and two at a time, and the Chinese never found out about it?"

"Oh, that was a long time before the Chinese came to Tibet. Came *back* to Tibet, I suppose I should say."

I pushed back into the cushions, scratching my head. "But — before 1950? And after the war, I suppose?"

"Only a few . . . . Oh, you mean the second war, I reckon. No, nobody since 1931. I was one of that last bunch, in fact."

Mr. Barnard looked to be in his 50s, at the latest. "You were hardly out of your teens, then. And you've been here ever since?"

"You're still ahead of the story. I'm trying to give you an idea of the history of the place."

"Okay," I said, smiling, "I'll shut up."

He met my smile with another. "You don't have to shut up, you only got to remember that you're talking to an old man, and old men are better at talking than at listening. And they like to tell their stories the way they got them in their mind. Anyway, like I was saying, back in the 1700s Father Perrault got himself some converts and he rebuilt the lamasery, turning it into a monastery. And the world turned around some, and eventually he died, plenty old. But before he did, he'd set the place on its way, and it ain't deviated much since."

"Meaning?"

Mr. Barnard's eyes had drifted to considering the ceiling; they returned to me. "You understand, I'm leaving things out. Important things, but this ain't the time to go into them. I'm just trying to tell you enough to give you the general idea. No point in trying to give you the whole story in one day: We got loads of time for that."

I thought he meant several days, perhaps a week or two. I was prepared to stay that long. I stretched out a leg and burrowed sideways against a cushion. "I still don't get it. What's the point in maintaining a monastery behind communist lines? Why didn't you all just pick up and leave a dozen years ago before the Chinese got here?"

Mr. Barnard paused. "Sonny, that's a real good question, but I can't give you the answer just yet. We saw it coming, but we couldn't move. There wasn't any place to go."

"Couldn't you have gotten to India or Nepal or somewhere?"

He shook his head decisively. "Uh-uh. The way wasn't open to us, take my word for it."

I didn't understand, but dropped it.

"What I'm trying to get across to you is that this place goes way back, and those of us living here got a responsibility to keep it going. I may not be a monk, but I'm still part of the place. That ain't so hard to understand, is it? It's just basic loyalty."

"Sure," I agreed. "And besides, it's your neck."

"Right. That's why we're going to all the trouble of rounding up the pieces of your airplane and getting them out of sight." He looked at me, searching my expression as he dropped his bombshell. "And that's why we got to ask you to stay with us till Springtime, George."

I didn't get it.

"Too close to winter. It could snow any time." He said it as if the conclusion followed too naturally to require explanation. Looking back now, I suppose that was a piece of very subtle manipulation, directing my attention away from the hand putting the pea under the shell.

"So it might snow," I said, taking the bait. "So what? It'll just make it a little harder, is all."

He shook his head decisively. "Uh-uh. You mean you don't see it?"

I didn't.

"Two things. One, having to fight your way through snow means there's that much more chance the Chinese catch you, and catch whoever we send out with you. You get hit by a bad storm at just the wrong time and you're buried, snowed in maybe a day or two from the border. How long can you survive without a fire? And if you *build* a fire, how long till somebody sees it you don't *want* seeing it? That's one thing. And even if you don't get stopped by it, still you're leaving footprints. You see?"

"The footprints would lead them right to me — if they see them in time."

"Yeah — but we're kind of more concerned that they'd start asking where you headed out *from*."

I nodded. It made sense.

"Like I said, we don't ever want 'em to start looking for us."

I ran my fingers through my crew-cut, thinking. "Of course, if they didn't happen onto my tracks right away, the next snow-fall would cover them."

"True enough," he said, nodding in turn. "But nobody here is real inclined to take the chance. You can see why."

"I can. But I don't much like the idea of holing up here all winter. Let me get out of here now, today, while we still have a good chance there won't be any snow. I figure five days will do it. Three, if I'm extra-lucky."

Again he shook his head. "George, no. You're still all stiff from yesterday, I can see it in the way you were walking. You really think you're in shape to hike out of here? Besides, it's too big a risk. There's only so many places to cross over in the winter. Don't you think they're all watched?"

"Yes, but —"

"But?"

"Mr. Barnard, my flight is already overdue. They probably put people out looking for me."

"Over Tibet?"

"No, not over Tibet; and not over China. But where it's safe to go, they'll go. And that means some of them may wind up risking their lives looking for me. And if I don't show up in a few days, they're going to think I'm in prison, or dead."

"And if you try to get over the border and get caught, that's just where you *will* be, one or the other."

"But I can't just sit here and let them look for me!"

"Why not?" He asked it calmly, simply.

I found it hard to make a convincing answer. "Well, for one

thing, it isn't fair to the guys who'll be looking. And suppose they send another U-2 this way and the Chinese see it?"

"U-2? That the number of your airplane? What if they *do* send another one? The Chinese missed *you*, who's to say they see the next one?"

"Yes, but what if something happens to that pilot?"

"That sort of thing happen to your airplanes real often?"

"No, not often, at all. But if it happened to me, it could happen to somebody else."

He nodded. "Maybe so."

"I owe them better than that."

"Well, maybe, or maybe you could look at it like the best thing you could do is lie low and let 'em think you got killed. Then they won't fret over you maybe being a prisoner."

That stopped me. I looked past him at the carpeted wall behind him, considering it. "That isn't what would happen," I said finally. "They'd list me missing and wonder if I was sitting somewhere in China."

Innocently, casually, he asked if they'd be able to find out if the Chinese had captured me. I considered some more. I couldn't see how.

"Well, neither can I. I can't see your bosses calling up the Chinese army and saying, 'By the way, have you picked up any of our spies lately?' and the Reds telling them one way or the other. So how are they going to hear about you?"

"You're making my argument for me. That's why I have to get back. Until I do, they won't know *what* happened."

"No, I don't suppose they will. But tell me this one thing, George. Which do you suppose they'd prefer? You out of sight for the winter, but safe, or you slapped into prison because you got impatient and got caught trying to get across before it was safe?"

Thus neatly turning the "duty" argument against me. The pattern on the wall hanging was fairly elaborate. It looked like a Persian rug I'd seen once.

"You see how it is?"

I sighed. "Yes, I suppose I do, Mr. Barnard. You really think the chance of snow makes it that much riskier?"

"I do, George. And not just me. So do the folks who live here, the ones whose families have lived here forever. They know these mountains like you and me never will. None of them would risk it on their own judgment." He added as an afterthought: "They'd do it if we asked 'em to."

"Okay, I said, "I give up. I'll wait till Spring. But it's hard, Mr. Barnard. It's hard."

He shot me a hard, probing glance, and his face softened a bit. "It ain't just your Army friends you're thinking about," he said.

"Air Force," I said automatically. "No, it isn't just my friends."

"You left somebody behind? Don't tell me if you don't want to."

"No, it's all right. My family, of course. They'll get a notice that I'm missing and when I don't show up in a couple of weeks, a month, they'll figure I'm dead."

Mr. Barnard was watching me carefully. "Yeah, probably they will. But if you show up again in the Spring, they'll know you ain't, so what's the odds?" Quietly he added, "You're pretty young to be worrying so much about family. Someone else?"

I nodded. He didn't press me.

≈ **5** ≈

I had carried her letter zipped into a pocket of my flight suit. I have it before me now.

Dear George,

Yes, I agree with you, Peshawar is a long way from Washington, D.C. And yes, of course I miss you too. I miss our long phone calls! And I miss—oh, so many things. Do you remember, back in college, how we used to go to the Sunday concerts at the National Gallery of Art and sit on folding chairs under their little trees and listen to string quartets? And then go out for ice cream afterwards? I thought about that last Sunday. I went, but it wasn't the same.

And I remember so many other things from that year, your senior year. We were really happy, George. It wasn't just what people say later when they look back and say "oh yes, we were young, so of course everything seemed wonderful." WE, you and I, WERE HAPPY. Happier than

I have been since, and you too, I think. I suppose it's getting out of school that changes things. You don't have as much time, you have to think about making a living, you get involved in different things. And before you know it, you don't have as much to talk about as you used to. Maybe we should have gotten married right away. Maybe you were right. But I thought: If I don't finish school NOW, who knows what will happen? If I start having babies right away it might be 20 years or more before I can go back and finish, and by then who knows if I'll have the time and the energy and the money and the motivation.

George, I know you know all this, I'm just rambling on to myself. And of course my parents wanted me to finish school first. But suppose I wasn't two years younger and we'd graduated together. Would it have been the right thing to do?

George, I DON'T want to hurt you, and you know I do love you — I've loved you for five years, since our second date, if you want to know. But sometimes you make me want to cry out loud: "Where did my poet go?"

Do you remember we would sit on the mall and you would read to me? *The Wind in the Willows? Great Love Poems?* All that poetry of Keats and Shelley and Auden and Eliot and dear Archibald MacLeish and Robert Frost? And Yeats, who I rarely understood? Do you even *remember* that you wrote poems too? Some of them were excellent, George. Publishable, I thought. They showed that aware, sensitive side of you that you were usually so careful to keep hidden. That's one reason I loved them so.

That side of you must still exist, George, but where is it? Did the Air Force make you bury it so deeply that you can't *feel* anymore?

Dear George, I'm not mad at you and I'm *not* finding fault or placing blame. Please don't get all defensive. (I can feel you getting all defensive when you read this, and I haven't even mailed it yet!) I am not saying anything is your fault. I am only saying I miss my poet.

Your last letter shows me (perhaps more clearly than you intended!) that my seeing David really bothers you. I know he irritates you, George, but really he is very [Here she had crossed out and blotted over a word. By looking closely at the opposite side of the sheet, holding it obliquely to the light, I had been able to make out the impression the pen had made first. It was the word "sweet."] nice. He doesn't have your mind, George (but my God, who does?) and really I don't think he's serious enough about life. He has always had his father's money to fall back on, and so he has never had to work hard. But he is talking now about writing a novel, and I think maybe he really will. I have told him it is high time he got down to business and *did* something with his life. Sometimes I wish I could give him some of your seriousness and give you some of his—.

No, you don't need anything from David, George. You just need to remember *all* of who you are. Sometimes I get so angry when I think what the Air Force has done to you I start shaking. It makes me wonder if they affect *everybody* that way.

No, no, I know that isn't fair. Getting into flight and doing well in it was a terrific accomplishment, and I'm as proud of it as you are. But George, as much as you love flying, *you paid a price for it.* Was it—*is* it—all necessary? Can't you have both? Can't you be a hot-shot pilot, which I'm sure you are, and still be a poet? Still *feel* things? Still be *alive* inside? My father spent 26 years in the Navy, you know, without being ashamed of painting. And nobody ever thought less of him for it, I'm certain.

God, now we're to the point where I can't even write you a letter without it turning into an argument. Probably I should rip this up and try again, but it's late and I'm too tired to do that. I want to get this off to you so you won't have to wait too long between letters. Probably if it weren't so late, this would have turned out more cheerfully. Next letter will be strictly sunshine and optimism, promise.

Love,
Marianne

P.S. I don't know your physical or financial circumstances over there, i.e. whether you have room enough or money enough for more books. If you'd like me to buy you any, or mail you any of the ones you left with me (Yeats?) send me the titles you want.

Much love,
Marianne

* 6 *

I have wondered, sometimes, if she had a letter on its way to me when I disappeared. The timing would have been about right. Did it arrive at Peshawar and get held there for a time, until the Air Force decided I was a lost cause? If so, what then? Back to her? To my parents, with the rest of my things? And if that, *then* back to her?

I wish I'd written her a better reply to the one I brought here. But I hardly understood what she'd written, and what I wrote then was more or less the best I could do at the time, given what I was then. I would write it differently now. Of course, when I wrote her last I thought I'd be seeing her relatively soon, though two years seemed to stretch out ahead of me long enough, God knows. And anyway, there was little I could have said, little I could have known I felt.

I read and re-read her letter many times as November became December, but it was many a year before her message finally got through.

Chapter Three.

Introductions

I had a long winter and spring ahead of me before I could try to get over the mountains to India, and the monastery was not so large a place to roam. I soon used up its spaces.

I'd get up in the morning—after sleeping as late as possible and then lying in bed staring up and out at the blue-black sky beyond my window—and wander down to the kitchen to fix myself some tea. (In those early days I sorely missed my coffee.) Then I'd make my way down to Mr. Barnard's greenhouse, or his workshop, or I'd pace one of the little patios that open off the main buildings. Sooner or later Mr. Barnard and I would come together and we'd have a lunch, usually some thick slices of bread and butter, or perhaps a few pieces of fruit. And while we ate, and later while we sat in the library rooms or went outside for a smoke, he and I would talk.

At first he answered my questions apparently without reserve, but as I learned enough to make my questions more focused, more pointed, I began to notice that on certain topics he wasn't giving me straight answers.

If he wasn't a monk, why did he live in a monastery? He had come to like it.

But what had attracted him to it in the first place? Oh, it had sounded interesting. ("inter-estin'")

Who had first told him about it? Where had he heard of it? How had he gotten here? *When* had he gotten here? The more pointed the question, the hazier the answer.

He'd said about 50 monks lived here. Did the numbers stay more or less constant over the years? More or less.

What was the smallest number he remembered? The largest? About the same.

Did most of the monks live to a ripe old age? They did all right.

How many of the monks were Westerners? Quite a few.

Was everybody here Catholic? Was he a Catholic? Did the monks, at least, have to be Catholic? No, no, no.

Well, surely they were all Christian? No again.

Well (meant humorously) at least they all believed in God? Long pause. "I don't know that *belief* has got a whole lot to do with it."

Okay, forget all that. How did the monks spend their time? How did *he* spend *his* time? A quizzical look: "You're looking at it."

"But we aren't *doing* anything in particular!"

"I've known worse ways to pass the time."

Of course I didn't badger him with questions one after another, nor did he always meet me with evasions. We had plenty to talk about, and there were always chores to be done: wood to be carried, fires to be laid, pots to scrub, floors to sweep. Fortunately for my peace of mind (and due at least partly to a farm background), I didn't regard chores as beneath me: I was happy to feel that I could pay my way, at least in part.

Nor did I spend all my time with Mr. Barnard, even before I began to meet the others. The second night, he introduced me to the library, and I spent many a dark winter evening reading by the light of lamps burning some kind of vegetable oil.

At first I browsed, for the library was a time-and-space capsule ranging extensively among languages, cultures and subjects. Oddly, although some of the books were very old, none was very new. I never came across one printed after 1937. There were extensive files, too, of English newspapers and magazines—but none after March, 1937. It reminded me (incongruously, I thought) of Winston Churchill's phrase. An Iron Curtain had fallen here, 25 years earlier. Why? How?

I asked Mr. Barnard, and was not surprised that he put me off.

I don't want to give the impression that Mr. Barnard and I spent those long days and evenings with no one else around. Before many days had passed, I had been introduced to the other monks, and had begun routinely to join them at their common meal in the evening. Slowly — or rather, leisurely, for here no one hurries — the various monks revealed themselves to me, and each drew out new aspects of myself; often enough, aspects of my life and thought that I myself had never been aware of. Yet these aspects emerged spontaneously and as if by chance. This alone should have made me suspicious, but in those days I still believed in chance. Also, I underestimated my importance to them. It's easy enough, now, to see what they were up to:

1) Dividing my attention among many individuals helped relieve the pressure on Mr Barnard.

2) Calling forth various unsuspected facets of my being helped prepare me to begin work on myself.

3) The presence of a new personality after so long a voyage without new shipmates was a lure irresistible even to the most reclusive.

But in 1962 I knew nothing of this. I had enough to do to deal with the impressions I was receiving.

The first time I joined in the evening common meal, only a few days after I arrived, I was struck by the sight of them all. Five dozen robes: saffron, lemon, red, orange, various blues and violets. An entire spectrum of color suddenly filling the refectory. They did not shout, but neither did they whisper. The sound of their voices was another novelty.

Disproportionately — two-thirds, perhaps — they were Westerners: whites. Why so many, in so isolated a corner of Asia? Disproportionately, too, the men (and the sprinkling of women) were apparently of middle age. None of the Westerners was so young as I (though three of those I took to be Tibetans were) and only four looked extremely old. Nearly all the others looked to be somewhere between their 40s and 70s. Why should that be?

Mr. Barnard very sensibly did not try to make specific introductions: He announced, briefly, that he supposed that everyone there had heard by now that the lamasery had been favored with a new guest, and he was sure they were all as pleased as he was to have a new face and new mannerisms to get accustomed to, and someone new to hear everyone's old tired stories. Conceivably, he said, Mr. George Chiari had brought some new jokes, although that might be asking too much. Anyhow, he knew that everybody would get to meet me in due time, and he hoped I knew I was welcome to stay for as long as I liked.

He told me much later it was a standard Rotary Club effort; it got me the expected welcoming applause, and that was the last time anybody treated me as a newcomer. From that evening, I was treated, apparently, the same as everyone else. (Apparently. But there were still questions I couldn't get answered.)

Meanwhile I had taken the opportunity to look at the room more thoroughly than I had during the tour. The tables and benches were of a finely polished hard, dark wood. The bowls and spoons stacked at one end of the table were of polished wood, as well. The floor and walls were of stone: large wooden beams supported the ceiling 12 or 13 feet above. Along the north and east and west walls, huge exquisite tapestries were hung at intervals. The south wall was given over to windows and draperies. The net effect was one of airy cheerfulness balanced by easy dignity. It seemed — and undoubtedly had been — designed to provide a relaxed, informal atmosphere conducive to digestion.

Mr. Barnard passed me a bowl. "Eat up," he said. "Tsampa again."

I started in on it. "How in the world did all these Europeans get here, Mr. Barnard?"

"One way and another. By accident, most of them."

Servants (that is, I took them to be servants) placed trays of small rolls on the table, and I took one. It was even better than the bread: hard, chewy, with much whole grain embedded in it. "This is *delicious!*" I said.

A Chinese monk sitting diagonally across from me met my eye. Speaking slowly and courteously, in flawlessly accented English, he said, "Our bread pleases you?"

"The best I've ever tasted."

"And tsampa?"

I hedged. "That's still new to me."

The monk laughed, and spoke in rapid-fire Chinese — Tibetan? — to those near him. They laughed no less heartily, glancing at me good-naturedly.

"It's all in getting used to it, I'm sure," I said quickly. "I have no doubt it is excellent." By a happy thought, I added, "I know that anyone would enjoy any meal served with such hospitality and kindness to a stranger."

The compliment pleased him. "It is always a privilege to serve a gracious guest. I trust that you will enjoy your stay."

"Thank you," I said—and found that I couldn't think of anything else to say. The Chinese monk turned to others and entered into an animated conversation in some other language, thus politely relieving me for the rest of the meal of the burden of exchanging pleasantries.

For the reasons I've already cited, before I came to know them as individuals, the monks had me thoroughly puzzled. Fortunately, that phase of my stay here lasted only a few days. Viewed in the monastery's time-scale, its secrets were unveiled nearly at once. And this is how it was done: Mr. Barnard invited me to tea with Edith Stockbridge Bolton.

As I earlier refrained from painting landscapes of the scenery I passed over on my way here, so I intend to refrain from painting portraits of my fellow voyagers. But for her, as for Mr. Barnard, I must make an exception. Together (working separately) they got me through my first months and made possible much that otherwise might have been long delayed, or entirely forestalled.

* 2 *

Edith Stockbridge Bolton—I discovered as I sat across from her at a small table in an alcove of one of the main music rooms, having tea and cakes in thoroughly English fashion in the thoroughly un-English presence of Mr. Barnard—had piercingly blue eyes, a milk-white complexion, an air of unshakable, serene self-possession and a remarkably direct manner. She looked to be in her 40s, or perhaps in her extremely well-preserved and youthful early 50s. She was neither fat nor gaunt, and even the corners of her eyes were unlined.

"I should prefer that you call me Sunnie, as everyone else does," she said, putting an elegant teacup onto its saucer. "Then I shall feel free to call you George, rather than Mr. Chiari, without you thinking me patronizing. This community is too small for formality among friends, don't you agree, Henry?"

Mr. Barnard broke off a bit of cake and popped it into his mouth. "Yep," he said, nodding, "nothing's deader'n formality."

Sunnie was looking at me, but her air of affectionate amusement was directed at Mr. Barnard. "Henry really is a dreadful tease," she said, "as you will no doubt discover." (It was fascinating: Mr. Barnard actually looked a bit sheepish, like a very young man who had been caught in a *faux pas* by a maiden aunt.) "However, he does possess redeeming qualities, among them energy and intelligence. Also, little though you might think it, sensitivity. Impassioned denial, Henry?"

Mr. Barnard only shook his head, smiling. "We call her Sunnie because that's her disposition, George." He regarded her with positive fondness. "Never a harsh word for a soul on earth."

"Oh, precisely," she said with a dry chuckle. "That is Henry's way of warning you that I am not famous for making charitable judgments. Not the least of my shortcomings, I am afraid, is a tendency to criticize."

Mr. Barnard shook his head again, vigorously. "Sunnie, I keep telling you, it ain't a fault, and that ain't it anyway. You say what you see. Is it your fault you see what's there to be seen? And George, she really *does* have a sunny disposition. She's the most cheerful person here."

"Henry, you are being especially charming today, for some reason, and you know I'm always delighted with your company, but would you mind terribly if I monopolized your young friend just this once? I'm far too old to compete for his attention."

Mr. Barnard stood up, smiling at the maiden aunt. "Your wish, my command, my dear. Now George, you remember, this is one special lady."

"Mr. Barnard, I can see that much already."

He nodded, a little more seriously than I expected. "Well, all right, then, as long as you got that straight. Sunnie, d'you want me to get 'em to send up some more tea stuff?"

She looked at my empty plate and the two cakes that remained. "Thanks very much, Henry, that's a lovely idea. Wouldn't it be heavenly to be in one's twenties again and be able to eat whatever one wanted and never gain an ounce?"

He laughed. "I wouldn't know. When I was in my twenties I didn't always eat real regular. By the time I got where I could afford to, everything I ate went right to fat. But you're right, it don't look like George has got that problem."

And then he left, and Sunnie and I were alone in the music room on a November afternoon in 1962, with sunlight streaming in through the west-facing windows. She asked, "Have you thought how you might use your time here, George?"

* 3 *

I knew, not knowing *how* I knew, that it wasn't a casual question; yet it didn't seem to have much point. I shrugged. "Haven't given it much thought. There's a lot of books to read, it looks like. And if this place is much like my father's farm, I imagine there's always more to do than time to do it in. I told Mr. Barnard, if anybody'd like some help with any special projects, I'm available."

"That's most thoughtful, George. I know he appreciates the offer. There *is* rather a lot to do to keep up a place, isn't there? The natives down below are most helpful, but of course one always wishes to do more." She sipped her tea, drew out the pause. "However, is there nothing you very much wish to do?"

I told her no, that I didn't see what she was driving at.

She motioned toward the little tea-cakes, encouraging me to finish them. "Has your life been so blessed with leisure, then? I am aware that the world has changed radically since I left it so many years ago, but I rather supposed that it had become more hurried, rather than less. A young officer in my day would have had has days and nights adequately filled, as I recall."

I admitted that my life had speeded up when I left the farm. For four years I'd juggled social life and classes while working my way through college. And the Air Force hadn't left me a lot of free time either, between flight school and the specialized schools they send you to, and then Pakistan. "But I can't say I feel harried, particularly. Just busy."

"Ah, then p'raps your problem will lie in finding what to do when you cease to be so busy. You've four months, safely, till Spring. You might find it difficult to fill all that time with chores. Moreover, to do nothing but chores might be to waste an opportunity, don't you think?"

I said again that I hadn't thought about it.

She smiled at me, an enigmatic smile not without irony. "By the time you reach my age, you will have thought about it a great deal. Only the young think life is long. The older one is, the clearer life's brevity becomes. Cruel brevity, George, for those who have wasted the time they were given." She said she supposed that people my age didn't much read Wordsworth. Did I know his lines about the world being too much with us? I didn't. She recited them:

> The world is too much with us; late and soon,
> Getting and spending, we lay waste our powers:
> Little we see in Nature that is ours;
> We have given our hearts away, a sordid boon!
> The sea that bares her bosom to the moon;
> The winds that will be howling at all hours,
> And are up-gathered now like sleeping flowers;
> For this, for everything, we are out of tune;
> It moves us not.

She gave me an ironic smile. "George. Are you perchance one of the pagans suckled in a creed outworn?"

I didn't get it.

"Wordsworth continues:

> Great God! I'd rather be
> A Pagan suckled in a creed outworn;
> So might I, standing on this pleasant lea,
> Have glimpses of Proteus rising from the sea;
> Or hear old Triton blow his wreathed horn.

"You do take the point?" She waited for me to frame a response.

"I guess it was pretty much the same in Wordsworth's day as it is now," I said. "It's easy to get so caught up in everyday things that you forget to look around you." I miss my poet, Marianne had said.

"Here we have been given the gift of time. For the next few months you will have few responsibilities and comparatively rich resources. It is an opportunity to be used."

I began to smell a fish. "Sunnie, do you have something in particular in mind for me?"

* 4 *

What she had in mind, it turned out, was a little book called *Lost Horizon*, by James Hilton. I asked if it was the same Hilton who had written *Goodbye, Mr. Chips*. The same.

"Great book," I said. "Everybody reads it."

"Do they? How very interesting. Henry showed it me once: We have it as it first appeared, in one of our magazines, I cannot recall which at the moment. But do people not read *Lost Horizon*?"

"The name is familiar, but I don't think I ever read it."

She smiled dryly. "Quite apparently."

"Why? What's so funny?"

"Your surroundings here were quite famous once. This is the lamasery at Shangri-La that Mr. Hilton wrote about."

Whatever reaction Sunnie expected, she didn't get it. My only reaction was puzzlement.

There had been a song in the 50s about Shangri-La, and of course that's what President Franklin Roosevelt had named his mountain retreat in Maryland, the one President Eisenhower renamed Camp David. And I remembered reading somewhere that in 1942, when reporters asked where Jimmy Doolittle's bombers had taken off from, before bombing Tokyo, Roosevelt had said Shangri-La. But I'd never known that the name was connected with a specific place: I'd thought it was just another name for paradise, like Valhalla or the Garden of Eden.

"'*Sic transit gloria mundi*,'" Sunnie said, sighing. "I suppose one shouldn't expect that the story would remain in vogue forever. Yet one cannot but hope that there are those who read it still. Such a lovely book."

Sunnie just happened to have the book with her. Such a coincidence! After our tea, I took the hint—and the volume—and retired to the library. I spent the rest of the afternoon there, lighting a lamp when afternoon shadows became too deep. I forced myself to go to the common meal, looking around me in wonderment, torn between profound inability to believe and dawning acceptance. If I spoke to anyone, I cannot recall it: I doubt I would have been able to speak sense. Sunnie and Mr. Barnard were there: I chose not to sit near them.

When the meal was finished, I withdrew to my room, lit my lamp, lay down on my bed, and went back to the story. As evening's chill arrived and strengthened, I pulled blankets over me and kept on reading. Often I rushed through particular passages, in my hurry to find out what ultimately happened. Every time I did that, I had to go back, re-read, pick up what I'd missed. I still hadn't learned to take my father's advice to make haste slowly. I made haste through the entire book, re-reading certain passages. It was long after midnight before I reached out and put the book on the floor, blew out the lamp, pulled the blankets around me more tightly, and allowed myself to drop off to sleep, deeply stirred.

* 5 *

The book—an attractive book bound in dark blue, printed in New York in 1933—told of four Westerners who, in May of 1931, were passengers in an aircraft that was hijacked while on a flight from the town of Baskul, British India, to Peshawar, which was then also a part of British India. They had fled anti-foreign violence in Baskul, expecting to find refuge in Peshawar. Instead, they wound up in northwestern Tibet, a corner of the world even more remote then than now.

The first of the four was Miss Roberta Brinklow, a missionary "of the Eastern Mission," Hilton said, assuming here, as elsewhere, the reader's familiarity with many minor details that have long since passed from the face of the earth. Or maybe the Eastern Mission still exists. Anyway, she was perhaps in her 40s, unflatteringly described as a "small, rather leathery woman," rather brisk and definite, "neither young nor pretty," and deeply, if conventionally religious. Brave enough. Stoic, even. Not much of a sense of humor, as perhaps is only to be expected in a missionary. (But then, Sunnie, who was a missionary's wife, has humor enough. Perhaps the difference is that in Miss Brinklow as portrayed there was something of the fanatic. Sunnie embodies balance.)

The other three were men:

"Hugh Conway, H.M. Consul," a veteran of World War I, which they called the Great War, or simply "the war." Graduate of Oxford, briefly a teacher there, 37 in 1931, with 10 years' experience in the Consular service. An extraordinary man, as duly appeared.

"Captain Charles Mallinson, H.M. Vice-Consul," then in his

mid-twenties, "pink cheeked, intelligent without being intellectual, beset with public school limitations, but also with their excellences." Apparently excitable, nervous, irritable, and unstable as water: now hero-worshipping Conway (as much for Conway's public-school athletic exploits, I suspect, as for his wartime valor or his more immediately useful virtues), now scorning him for his "slack" attitude. Mallinson—it did not escape me—was engaged to a girl in England at the time when his future was taken out of his hands.

Finally, "Henry D. Barnard, an American," described as "a large, fleshy man, with a hard-bitten face in which good-humored wrinkles were not quite offset by pessimistic pouches," who, it eventually turned out, was a man on the run, a financier called "the world's hugest swindler," who had run off with a considerable sum of other people's money just before he could be arrested. He had fled from country to country, finally leaving a revolt-torn town in an airplane that wound up going to Tibet. ("You don't know it, but you're taking to somebody that was famous in his day.")

Lost Horizon's first few pages told how the four passengers gradually realized that they were being hijacked from British India to an unknown destination. I didn't have to guess where the hijacked airplane was going.

I skipped rapidly through the chapters describing their arrival and their questioning of the Chinese monk Chang. But Chapter Five I read in cold concentration, for there more of Mr. Barnard was described, and (except that "my" Mr. Barnard didn't call Chinese "Chinks") the literary figure seemed to match the man in the flesh. This had interesting implications, for—although Mr. Barnard's age was never clearly stated—I got the impression that he was older than Conway, and Conway (paging back to the first chapter) was 37 in 1931. So Mr. Barnard would have to be nearly 80 now if he was near 50 then. But he looked 30 years younger than that. I deferred judgment and read on.

I knew enough to recognize the atmosphere of the inter-war years. The movers and shakers of the 1930s were the men who had grown to maturity in a world that 1914 had destroyed. Their experiences had contradicted the dogma of inevitable progress that had shaped their youth. These were men—particularly the Europeans among them—who had watched (and were watching still) as their world grew continually less stable, less comfortable, less hopeful. Europe had entered economic hard times before the United States, but by May, 1931, America's stock market crash (the crash that had brought Mr. Barnard to flee the wreckage of his financial empire) was already a year and a half in the past, and the Great Depression was well underway.

The stranded travellers soon enough found satisfactions in that cloistered life. Three of them, anyway.

Miss Brinklow concluded that God had brought her here to convert the natives who lived in the valley below. She promptly began to study Tibetan, to prepare herself for the task.

Mr. Barnard didn't put it in terms of divine providence, but he thought himself awfully lucky not to be in jail in Peshawar. Besides, he soon learned that the lamasery was at one end of a carefully concealed supply route stretching hundreds of miles through China to the outside world, along which caravans travelled, bearing books and other samples of the fine and useful arts. He smelled money, and found the source in the gold vein running through the valley, "as rich as the Rand, and ten times easier to get at." He began to think of working the mine more scientifically, with an eye toward a warmer welcome home from the same (gold-hungry) authorities who were at that moment thinking of him only in terms of imprisonment.

As for Conway—

He didn't know why he had been brought here, but here—after an exile's lifetime of pointless danger, random motion, and disagreeable convention—he found peace. Nevertheless he threw it away, that peace. Mallinson was the trigger.

Mallinson, unlike the others, could find no consolation whatever at Shangri-La. Unlike Miss Brinklow, he didn't believe in providence. He wasn't on the run from the law. And he hadn't lived long enough to feel his life a burden. All he could think about was what he had lost in leaving the world: his home, his career, his family, his fiancee. The mountain walls around him seemed a cage. (Certainly I could understand that.) When he learned that a caravan of porters had arrived at their semi-annual rendezvous, a day's journey from the monastery, he persuaded Conway to go with him, without even saying good-bye to Miss Brinklow and Mr. Barnard. But their long return trip ended in disaster, with Mallinson dead and Conway nearly so. Conway was recovering, in a remote hospital in China, when a friend of his, and of novelist Hilton's, encountered him ("by chance") and started to return him to "civilization." But Conway had realized, by then, his error in leaving. At the first opportunity, he slipped away to attempt the long journey back to the place where he had found peace. The book ended with the narrator wondering if Conway ever made it home.

I had been introduced to a monk named Conway. Even as I lay in my bed, reading by the flickering lamplight, I knew that he was the same person. He'd made it back.

But why — if he felt the way he did — had he left in the first place? He'd been told, by the high lama himself, of the monastery's startling, world-changing secrets. How then, I wondered (watching the shadows flickering on my ceiling) could he have left, knowing what he knew, feeling as he felt?

For I knew that his reason, as given by Hilton, couldn't be true.

* **6** *

I came out of sleep in the early morning light (because I'd forgotten to draw the curtain the night before) and lay, half-awake, reluctant to move. Our rooms are always cold in the mornings; we cannot afford to burn enough wood to heat all the buildings and certainly can't afford to do so at night. Our central heating is reserved for the rooms of the old and the ill, and for a few common rooms. I tell myself (and it is true enough) that we are no worse off than Thomas Jefferson's generation, and they got along just fine. But the thought doesn't make it much easier to get up in the morning. Particularly if you have other reasons to hesitate to start the day.

I wanted answers, and I knew I could get them, and I thought I could believe the answers I'd get. But a part of me *didn't* want answers. Part of me suspected that the answers I'd get might lead me farther in a direction that I (or part of me, anyway) might not want to go.

Chapter Four.

Realities

"It's me, all right. The name Bryant that he says is my right name ain't the right one, but if you knew where to look, you'd find the old news stories about me quick enough. Not that it matters: The statutes of limitations don't run any 30 years, and anyway it wouldn't be so easy, extraditing me out of here."

"But except for the names, the rest of the story is true?"

"Oh, more or less. Like Huck Finn says, he stretched it here and there, but mostly he told the truth."

Mr. Barnard and I were standing, in parkas, by the frost-covered windows of his greenhouse room, which the morning sun had turned into a splendid wilderness of illuminated traceries. Mr. Barnard had said he thought I'd like seeing the designs. I was a little surprised that he'd notice such things. I think, now, that he wanted to get my first impression of the book in surroundings as unfamiliar to me as possible in our limited world.

He turned to face me. "I take it you found stuff you think don't jibe. Like what?"

"Well, specifically," I said, forcing myself to bluntness, "the hijacking. Hilton lays out a sequence that just couldn't be real."

"Why not?"

"Hilton says your hijacker landed the maharajah's plane somewhere in the middle of nowhere, and a bunch of tribesmen came out and held everybody inside, refueled the plane with gasoline and then you took off again."

"You don't believe it?"

"Of course not. Think what it would mean. Even if the hijacker knew in advance exactly the day he was going to be able to steal a plane, he'd have had to let these tribesmen know he was coming. Now how was he supposed to do that? And if he didn't, are we supposed to believe that he had that tribe just sitting there — for years, I suppose? — carrying cans of gasoline, waiting for him to drop down on them? It's too complicated. I don't believe it."

"And there ain't any reason you should," Mr. Barnard said calmly. "That's one of the things Hilton made up. He got the story from a friend, you know, who got it from Conway, just like it says in the book. I expect when Hilton came to write it all out, he found pieces here and there that he hadn't thought to ask about, and he filled them in the best he could. My guess is, he didn't know how that machine could fly so far, so he put in the bit about refueling to make the story sound more likely. And, the fact is, all the time we were cooped up in that crate, we were wondering how the devil he kept it up so long. We didn't find out right after we came down, because we were a lot more interested in getting warm and getting fed, let me tell you! But a couple months after Conway broke out of here, I took a little jaunt out to the plateau to do some salvaging and look things over. In those days, it wasn't so important to cover up the traces of our visitors, you can imagine. Anyway, I got a big surprise: It turns out we had near another hundred gallons in the tanks.

"You know, Hilton gives the impression we ran out of gas just at about the time we got to that ledge. On a thousand-mile ride, that would be cutting it pretty close. But that's what we thought then, because we kept waiting for the motor to stop and we couldn't see any other reason for the pilot to be landing us in the middle of the mountains."

"You were lucky it didn't blow when you hit."

"That's what I thought, too. It gave me a funny feeling. But it looks like the guy turned off the gas lines before we got down."

"Sure, that's s.o.p. When I brought mine in, I did the same. But you were still lucky. And I was too."

"Well, you can call it luck, I suppose. Anyway, it turned out the thing was fixed with extra gas tanks, something like Lindbergh's plane, I reckon. The maharajah liked doing things first-class, and he didn't like stopping unless he *wanted* to stop. What else is on your mind?"

"The girl, of course."

* 2 *

"What girl?" He knew, of course. Had to. But asked me anyway. Interesting.

"Lo-tsen. The Chinese girl Mallinson fell in love with."

Mr. Barnard looked hard at me. "What about her?"

"Hilton says Conway fell in love with her first (platonically, I gather) and was told she was a Manchu princess, born in the 1860s — which put her at least in her 60s even though she looked like she was in her 20s."

Mr. Barnard said nothing, waiting.

"Then he said *Mallinson* fell in love with her, and *not* in a platonic way."

"Yes?"

"And that the girl . . . ."

Again he waited for me.

"He says the girl fell in love with Mallinson, too and — demonstrated it. Let him make love to her." Obviously I was going to get no help with this. I was talking to a wall, a suddenly granite presence conceding nothing, offering nothing. "He says that Lo-tsen made it possible for Mallinson to contact the porters, and that she got over the pass to join them, and that Mallinson then tried to join her but couldn't get across by himself. He says Mallinson wanted Conway to come with him— needed him, if only for his mountain-climbing skills—and finally persuaded him only by admitting that he'd made love to Lo-tsen and knew, for sure, that she wasn't any 60 years old. Just a girl, he said. And if you believe Hilton, Conway was sort of balanced between believing and disbelieving what the high lama had told him. When he found out from Mallinson that Lo-tsen was young, he jumped to the conclusion that the lama's story was a fabrication. So he helped Mallinson to escape."

"And broke out with him."

"Right. And realized, somewhere along the way, that Lo-tsen really *was* in her 60s. She started getting old as soon as they'd been out of range of the valley's atmosphere for a couple of weeks—just as the lama had told him would happen. So then he realized he was fleeing from the truth."

"That's a good way of putting it."

"Is it? Well, it doesn't make sense."

"No? Why not?"

"This delicate little Chinese girl got over the pass that a man in his vigorous 20s couldn't? And she—knowing she was in her 60s—agreed to go with him, knowing she was going toward instant aging and sure death? Come on! And these are just the obvious things. It just doesn't ring true. Which makes me wonder about the rest of the story. Not that I wouldn't anyway."

Mr. Barnard's face relaxed into approval—even, I thought, into admiration. "You got your thinking cap on, George, I'll give you that. But it happened, all the same."

"Mallinson making love to her, thinking she was in her 20s?"

"That's what he's supposed to have told Conway, but I don't know, I never asked. Hilton could have made that up for his own purposes."

"Do you think he'd do that?"

Mr. Barnard shrugged, a little cynically. "You know how it is: If you're going to sell to Hollywood, you got to have sex appeal. I'm surprised he didn't turn Miss Brinklow into a chorus girl."

"So she's real, too?"

"She's real. You're liable to run into her sometime, if you're interested."

"Sure I'm interested. Have I seen her at supper?"

"Uh-uh. She don't spend all that much time up here. She's down in the valley, telling people what to believe and how to live, like always. You'll get your chance to be reformed by here, I assure you."

"I see." But I didn't, and I was still thinking about the little Chinese princess. It would be easier to believe that Lo-tsen herself was an invention of novelist Hilton. "Mr. Barnard, tell me this. You're saying that the stuff about aging wasn't made up?"

"Unreasonable, ain't it?"

"It sure is."

He grinned his surprisingly youthful grin. "I agree with you. But how old would you say I am?"

"Well, you look about 50."

"Work it out yourself. You don't entirely have to take my word for it. I been here 31 years, you got to admit. And you know how old Conway is, and you know I'm older. As a matter of fact, I was born August second, 1882—which made me 80 years old three months ago."

"You realize," I said, "that you're talking science-fiction stuff."

(A conversational detour, that. He'd never *heard* of science fiction. He'd never heard of Hugo Gernsback. He had, at least, heard of H. G. Wells and Jules Verne, but he'd never connected the two.)

"Anyway," I said, "immortality is an old science-fiction staple."

Mr. Barnard held up a cautionary hand. "Now, don't get carried away, here. I never said immortality. All I said was that we have got some drug that grows in the valley. *Only* in the valley, far as we know. Between that and some yoga exercises that Father Perrault developed, it'll stretch out your life."

"And it can only be done here."

"As far as we know. There's something about this area, we don't know what. The drug don't have the same effect somewhere else. Nobody's ever figured out why not, not even Father Perrault."

"And you say he lived 250 years."

"That's what the book says, and that's what the monks say. I know it's a lot to swallow, but looking at my own experience, I don't see that you got a whole lot of choice. Of course 250 years is still a far piece from immortality."

Did I believe him? Well, no, not at first. Or perhaps I should say that I fell into the state of mind we use when we're told something so strange, so unbelievable, that it is beyond the bounds of what could reasonably be expected of even a very audacious liar. I treated it like a good sci-fi tale, pursuing the implications even while withholding intellectual consent. After all, how reasonable was it that Mr. Barnard should be 30 years older than he looked? How was I to prove it one way or another?

On the other hand, if the monks *did* have the secret of holding the aging process at bay (as Mr. Barnard put it), it would make it a whole lot easier to explain how so many Westerners could have come to the monastery before World War II. They'd have had lots of time to do so. It was in 1809 that the Austrian soldier, Henschell, set up the monastery's carefully concealed links with the outside world. Lot of years between 1809 and 1962.

Yet how could it be true? For one thing—

"Mr. Barnard, tell me this. Conway was told the same story, and found the idea very attractive. But as soon as Mallinson told him the girl was truly young, rather than miraculously well-preserved, he jumped to the conclusion that the high lama's story was a pack of lies. Why would he do something that drastic just on Mallinson's say-so?"

"C'mon," Mr. Barnard said. "It's cold in here."

"Aren't you going to answer my question?"

"Not me. Come ask him yourself."

* 3 *

The question didn't cause Mr. Conway to retreat into mere civility, or lose himself in reminiscence, or politely inform me that it was none of my business. Instead, quite simply and directly, he answered.

"I had been balanced on a pin-point, with Mallinson and the world I had known pulling me one way and the lama and Shangri-la and my own inclinations pulling the other. When Mallinson suddenly upset the balance I'd thought I'd achieved, I left. My leaving was as surprising to me as to anyone."

"But—"

He took pity on my perplexity. "James Hilton's estimate of my mental state in 1931 is too generous. To him—or to my friend Kallen, whom he called Rutherford—my 'passionless' state seemed a philosophical attitude. The acquisition of wisdom, if you will. But the truth is simply that I was emotionally exhausted. At the critical moment, I couldn't quite bring myself to believe that what I longed for might be true. I suppose one might say I left because of the war."

We were seated in the refectory, the large room where we eat our common meals, deserted at this time of day. He and I and Mr. Barnard were seated at one of the long tables. The table had nothing on it but our hands and forearms and the book I had carried with me. The dark polished wood beneath my hands felt waxed. The mid-morning sun glowed against the wood of the high walls and lighted the purple wall-hangings. The emptiness of the room (which I usually saw only when it was filled with dozens of monks at table) emphasized the height of the ceiling.

Mr. Conway looked to be in his early 40s. His skin (like Sunnie's, I thought, absurdly) was unlined. His eyes were clear and youthful. His movements were direct, economical and vigorous, and unlike Mr. Barnard's did not betray any of the instinctive caution of a man past his prime. If Mr. Barnard was comfortably ensconced in those long middle years between youth and age, Mr. Conway was still in his vigorous early manhood. On a tennis court, I thought, Mr. Barnard (if he bothered to play at all) would have to restrict himself to playing those more or less his own age. Mr. Conway would hold his own even against youngsters, countering their stamina with experience and craft. He was nearly 70 years old when I summed him up with this initial impression.

Mr. Conway said, "My friends tell me you were something of a student of history."

"Well, I majored in history. Mostly modern history — Europe and America since Waterloo."

"Then perhaps you will be able to grasp the effect of the war on my generation. Henry and I were raised in a world of certainties, most particularly including the certainty of inevitable progress. We English, in particular, believed in our imperial destiny, our civilizing task. The war put paid to all that."

"Maybe for you English. Not for everybody."

Mr. Conway turned his gaze on Mr. Barnard. "Not for America. But you didn't get the full benefit of the experience. You received a taste, no more."

Mr. Barnard grunted. "A taste was plenty."

"Yes. But we'd had *our* taste by Christmas, 1914. Summer of 1915 — the Dardanelles — to be generous. And after that taste, we went on killing and being killed, living constantly with fear and misery, for years. Ypres, Verdun, Paeschendaele, the Somme—" He turned back to me. "Your doughboys fought splendidly, and they did get their taste of trench warfare, but only a taste. In 1918, you know, the war on the Western Front reverted to open-field maneuvering, for the first time since the winter of 1914. So you were spared the long agony of four years' stalemate." He paused. "I wonder if you can see even a shadow of it. Henry, I don't think you yourself see it, even with your advantage of having lived through the aftermath."

"Probably I can't. Nothing touches experience."

"No. And sometimes vicarious experience is quite enough, as you said just now." Mr. Conway's tone of voice was suddenly, unexpectedly, sardonic. It could have been Mr. Barnard speaking.

* 4 *

Now as it happened, I knew something about the pre-World War I world that got destroyed. I'd read about it in texts, and, better, in novels, an underrated way to get to understand the thought and emotion of an age. And once I'd heard my father and my Uncle Warren (my mother's brother) talk of their experience in that war. This was when I was very young, in the period between World War II and Korea, when nobody much wanted to hear stories from an earlier crusade to save democracy. On that night, sitting in the dark on our front porch on a long summer evening while their children and nephews and nieces were playing elsewhere, not knowing I was nearby, listening intently, they retold their stories to each other. Some they wouldn't have knowingly told in my presence. Some I absorbed but didn't understand until reading and life provided context.

Not that they'd seen combat. Uncle Warren spent 14 months working at keeping the French railroads functioning between our sector of the front and the docks of the city of La Pallice. Dad, a kid of 18, didn't even disembark in France until three weeks before the Armistice. But in their service in France and during occupation duty on the Rhine in 1919, they had accumulated second-hand tales of combat and first-hand tales of demoralization.

So, when Mr. Conway spoke to us of the everyday horrors of his 38 months of trench warfare, I could fill in some of the blanks he left. He spoke of the mud and filth and insects—and I could mentally supply the rats that proliferated and fattened on human corpses buried and unburied. When he spoke of horse cavalry charging machine-gun nests, or described line after line of unprotected infantry going over the top in the wake of an artillery barrage, I could fill in the details he thought to spare me. The coils of barbed wire to be cut through. The interlocking fields of machine-gun fire. The yellow clouds of poison gas drifting across fields. The long snake-tongue of the flame-throwers. . . . And I could supply the hellish uproar, the acrid stink of exploded nitroglycerine, the frantic leaps from shell-hole to shell-hole, the laying down of box barrages to isolate sectors of enemy trenches long enough for raiding parties to go across after prisoners. . . .

And I knew of the endless offensives, planned in meticulous detail by headquarters-bound officers, expending millions of artillery shells and hundreds of thousands of young lives in order to accomplish precisely nothing. Not "nothing much," but nothing. A few hundred yards of enemy line that became an indefensible salient that had to be evacuated in a few days' time. Failure after failure after unbelievably costly failure, year after year, while a generation of Germans, Frenchmen and Britons, and their imperial subjects, broke their youth on each other's fortifications and armaments, until even the lucky ones who survived were prematurely aged.

"Can you imagine, George, what life was like for us?"

I could, I thought.

"We lived like that from 1915 to the Spring of 1918 — and 1918 we endured in the shadow of what seemed certain defeat, almost to the end. By then we were almost beyond caring. And once we had absorbed the fact that we had lived through the end, we seemed to have no emotion left. We were apathetic. Spent. Sullen, the civilians called us, some of them. Those who had kept themselves farthest from harm, generally. None of us was sane after that. None of us was whole. Some appeared undamaged, and many of us carried on, if only for appearance's sake. Out of inertia, one might say, functioning because we were expected to function. Expected it ourselves. But nothing seemed capable of rousing us. Then without warning some trivial occasion—a chance remark, perhaps—might send someone into a tearing rage. We were neither sane nor whole, and how we would act under renewed stress was utterly beyond predicting—least of all by ourselves. As I learned on Mallinson's last night here."

"Is that what they meant when they said in the book that you were 'blown up in the war'? Were you shell-shocked?"

"I did spend time in hospital once after a shell landed rather too close, but that was nothing unusual. We couldn't be replaced and couldn't be relieved. So we would be wounded and patched up and sent back, and then often enough wounded again and patched up yet again. England was straining every nerve merely to hold the line. My friends later used my having been in hospital as an excuse to see me as a war casualty; not as a slacker."

"I don't understand."

"I was among the class that had been reared and educated and trained to govern the empire. As a decorated veteran, I was expected to seek my place. But after the war, I found myself unable to believe in that life. I could force myself to act the expected part, but could not force myself to *feel* it. My friends charitably chose to ascribe the difference in me to my having been 'blown up.'" He made a gesture like emptying a handful of sand. "Not that I cared, particularly."

For a long moment none of us said anything. The mid-morning winter sunlight was pouring in through the windows high on the refectory walls, but images of the war lay between us like a shadow on the table.

"I guess your experience made Father Perrault's vision that much more real to you," I said, feeling the remark's inanity even as I uttered it. But Mr. Conway did not make the sharp or ironic retort it warranted. He merely said mildly that it is easier to believe in the end of the world when once you've seen it happen.

From that remark to talk of the bomb was a very short step: hardly a step at all.

* 5 *

Hardly a step at all, for of course the final war is the entire point of Father Perrault's institution. Lying on what he thought was his deathbed, long ago in 1789, the old man had entered a trance. Like so many who have been brought to close to the door of no return—like Carl Jung in 1944, for instance—he returned with a message. Like Jung's, his was a vision of great man-made destruction. In that year of the French revolution, he saw in his mind's eye (to use that greatly oversimplified metaphor) men raging "exultant in the art of homicide," trampling civilizations like rare flowers, laying waste all but the most remote and unsuspected pockets. It was just such a remote and unsuspected pocket that he and his friends and co-workers set out to make of Shangri-La. "We may not hope for mercy," he told Mr. Conway in 1931, "but we may faintly hope for neglect."

How much the old man's original vision encompassed, we cannot know. Perhaps, with time, he embellished. But it was clear to him by 1931, a full decade and more before the invention of the atomic bomb began to make his vision technically feasible.

"Inevitable?" Mr. Conway echoed my question. "I don't know that anything on earth is inevitable. I prefer to talk of possibilities, and of a balancing of tendencies. I am not the sort of fatalist who believe we follow a pre-written script."

"'Accidents happen,'" I said, quoting my father.

"Do they?" His smile was warm, perhaps slightly self-mocking. "I'd not care to place that bet, either. I'd say, rather, that the script is written as we act our roles. Not the same thing, quite, is it?"

"But he wants to know, do you think it's going to happen."

Mr. Conway's smile at Mr. Barnard's typically blunt statement was entirely different from the one I'd received. Yet precisely how, I couldn't tell. His words, actions, expressions, contained more fine nuances that those of anyone I'd ever met. This smile combined compassion, irony and something almost beyond humanity: It had a quality of the laughter of the gods, laughing that they might not cry at the folly of mankind.

"You know the record, Henry. How would *you* judge?"

"That's all you're going to say about it?"

"Henry, we have time."

Neither man was looking at me. It suddenly struck me that this was not by chance, and not without significance.

* 6 *

Meanwhile, my life continued to flow, apparently unchanged, in the channels it had found since November. I continued to have pleasant conversations, sometimes surprising, sometimes disturbing, with various people. I worked with Mr. Barnard in his shop. I read in the library. I did my share of the chores that all but the ill and elderly monks shared in: cooking, doing dishes, laundry, tending fires. Sunnie worked at teaching me to draw. Others taught me other things. Mr. Conway and and I spent long pleasant hours discussing — savoring — English and Irish poetry. In all these activities, I kept an eye out for what I could learn about the monastery. I was looking for clues, and of course had no way to know in advance where they might be found. I knew they were hiding something. If possible, I wanted to find out what it was, before I came to leave. It might make a difference.

* 7 *

Mr. Barnard and I were sitting on a bench on one of the patios, wrapped in parkas, companionably smoking cigars from some kind of pseudo-tobacco grown in the valley below and wrapped by him, sometimes with my assistance. There was no moon that night—or rather, it was the night of the new moon. Even after several months, the brilliance of the nighttime sky here was still new enough to me that I reveled in it. I'd never seen the Milky Way as a luminous white band across the sky. I'd never seen so many stars, nor seen them in their different colors and intensities. For the first time, I seemed to see that some were farther from us than others.

After a few minutes I realized, with some surprise, that neither the piercing cold nor the silence left me uncomfortable. It was as though hidden depths of muscle within were beginning to untense. I realized that I'd miss this place. No other place (no place I'd ever been, anyway) offered this kind of conversation or company. I realized that, if not for Marianne, I could get used to living this way. But then, I wasn't living as a monk, and hadn't any very clear idea of what their day comprised. Which raised an interesting point.

"You know," I said (and, looking back on it, it seems that every time I was hesitant to bring up something, I started off with the words "You know") "Mr. Conway didn't make the place sound much like a monastery. Or Hilton didn't, anyway. The place came out sounding more like a cross between a hotel and a library."

"Yeah, it did, but don't forget, when Conway talked to his friend, he'd only seen the inside of the place for a few months. He didn't know that much about what the place is all about. All he knew is what Chang and the high lama told him. And they were careful not to tell him too much, you'll notice. Just as well they didn't, seeing how Conway took off with Mallinson. I suppose that old man knew something about Conway that Conway didn't know about himself."

Did he? I couldn't help wondering how. I pursued what I thought was a different thread. "From what you say, it's obvious that the lama didn't tell Mr. Conway as much as he might have. That says to me that there's something about what you're doing here that you'd just as soon not see in print in the outside world. I wonder what it is."

I had the clear impression (though I'd be hard-pressed to say how it was conveyed) of a man trying hard not to show that he was startled. Trying *almost* successfully.

* 8 *

"The other day, when I asked you how this place had survived all these years, you said it was timing," I said, trying to come at him out of the blue. "What did you mean by that?"

Mr. Barnard said nothing for so long that I wondered if he was going to ignore the question. But after a few minutes, he took his cigar out of his mouth, looked away up at the stars overhead, and began, in some detail, to tell me only a carefully selected part of the story.

"As far as I'm concerned, what you call World War II began when the Japs and China had their first armed incident and the Japs got away with it, just about the time I got here. One thing led to another, and it didn't take us long to see what was happening."

"'Us'?"

"Herrick and me. He was their big man on world affairs." (Herrick was Lawrence Herrick, a British school teacher who arrived in the '80s, I don't know how.) "I hadn't been here long before Herrick and me started meeting pretty regular, talking about world news and what it meant. Don't forget, I was the guy with the latest first-hand experience. Say what you want, there's a difference between just hearing about things and actually being there. Herrick's never *seen* a car, for instance. So even if I hadn't known a thing about what made the world go 'round, they would have needed my point of view. But as it happened, I'd always kept up with things. When you're playing the commodities exchange, you like to keep an eye peeled for what things are going to look like a few months down the pike.

"But Herrick taught me a thing or two about following things. Where I would try to figure out which way things would jump five, six months from now, he looks at six months as being so close we might as well count it as part of right now. He looks for how things are going to turn 10, 15 years from now, and you'd be surprised how much you can see, once you get the hang of it. It's a little like checking the weather, only you look wider and deeper."

All true enough, and all carefully phrased to allow for different interpretations on different levels. But at the time I didn't pick up on that: I was on a different scent. "You're going to tell me that he foresaw World War II in 1931."

Mr. Barnard grunted and puffed on his cigar. "Hell, that wouldn't have been any trick. Herrick tells me somebody predicted the next war as soon as he heard the terms of the Versailles Treaty. And I remember some French officer getting in trouble in the mid-'20s because he gave some lecture and instead of calling it the Great War, he called it World War I. He nearly got drummed out of the army, as I remember it. Seems to me they ought to have made him a general. Anyway, every few months we'd get a shipment by way of the porters, and part of every load was always books and some newspapers and magazines. That's how Herrick and me kept up."

"Hilton didn't say much about how that worked, either, I notice."

Mr. Barnard shrugged. "The details were beside the point, weren't they? And anyway, he didn't know all that much about it."

"But you do."

Another shrug, as he accepted the prompting. "The system was that booksellers all over the world were keeping an eye out for certain kinds of books, and would send them to a certain mailing address in Hong Kong, where they'd be packed up and sent to Shanghai, and then to Peking, and then Chunking and out here. Middlemen all through the process, of course, which jacked up the price, but also made sure that nobody knew too much about the whole operation."

He waved the subject away. "Like I say, the pattern was clear before very long. Herrick had me read stuff and we'd talk about what it meant, and he'd give me the background he knew and I'd throw in whatever I knew, and that way we each one learned something. I guess I was getting my college diploma a little late in life." Suddenly he grinned at me. "And I sure had to teach that man everything in the world about trust companies and stocks and options and business in general. He had the theory, some of it, but lord would he have got eat up alive in the real thing! Anyhow, between us we could see what things were leading to. We didn't see it all, of course, not by a darn sight. You never can, it's too big. Maybe that's how the lord keeps surprises in store for us, so we don't get bored. But anyhow, when we saw Japan fixing to carve up China, we knew."

"Knew it had to wind up as a world war?"

"It was darned logical, if you started from the right place—and the right place was Japan. Once you looked at their history, it was plenty clear. You got to understand, Japan had spent the 1800s watching Europe gobble up everything that couldn't defend itself, which was near everything. So the Japs learned the rules and made themselves into a military power, and beat the living daylights out of the Chinese in 1895 and the Russians in 1905. Plus they got in on the winning side in the World War, and got the Shantung peninsula—that's in China, you know—from Germany in the peace treaty. As far as they're concerned, this was just for openers. They were feeling their oats. But then they hear that the English and the Americans are changing the rules, and from now on all boundaries are permanent and anybody that starts a war is the bad guy."

"Sure," I said. "Everybody was sick of war by 1918."

Mr. Barnard chewed on his cigar, smiling sardonically. "Yeah, and they'd also picked up pretty near everything lying around loose—the winners had—so what'd they need any more wars for? Anyway, the Japs see that Europe's through, and so they think there ain't any reason they can't play the game themselves a little. In fact, without England and France and Germany to worry about, they figure to have the game practically to themselves. Well, they have this big earthquake in I think '23 that flattens Tokyo and that slows 'em down quite a bit, but in '31 they come back stronger than ever. The world depression is on by then, and it's taking all our attention, so when the Japs take a couple of nibbles and nobody's got the ambition to stop 'em, and they take a little more and nobody does anything, they start moving faster, and in half a dozen years, you got China and Japan in a full-scale war, and China getting just clobbered. And by then you got Hitler in Germany and it's clear enough that he's doing the same as Japan: He's pushing as hard as he can and he's not finding anybody pushing back."

He took a long drag on his cigar and blew the smoke out

vigorously into the night air. "To make a long story short, Herrick and me saw that things were going from worse to terrible, as the fellow said, and so we decided to close down the supply pipeline. It was just too risky, leaving a clue that big. Japan was keeping China plenty busy at the moment, but we didn't want somebody putting two and two together in ten, fifteen years and suddenly showing up knocking on our door."

I said I didn't see how they could shut down the carrier network without leaving a trace.

"Like I said, timing. If we'd waited till '49, or '45, or even '41, there would have been loose ends, no question about it. You take a backward country like China was then, fighting for its life and getting pasted regular, losing its seaboard cities and railroads and all: How are you going to bring in stuff from overseas, and get it together in one place, and ship it all the way across China, and pay for it—in gold!—and not have everybody in the army and the government taking their cut along the way, figuring you had *got* to be smuggling something? That's a lot of loose ends, and it only takes one wide-awake guy to put it all together. Sooner or later he gets to your porters and you're finished."

"So you closed it down."

"So we closed it down, is right. We ain't had a shipment in here since October, I think it was, 1937." He finished his cigar and threw the butt away into the surrounding darkness over the wall. "Those last shipments, we went in heavy for tools and things, since we were going to be on our own. That's when I put that shop together. Let me tell you, packing to *go* someplace is nothing compared to packing to *stay* someplace and trying to be sure you got everything you are ever going to need."

"I can imagine," I said. I thought I was in hot pursuit, not knowing I'd missed the trail. "But if your last shipment here was 1937, how have you kept up with the things that have happened since then? It's obvious that you do."

Mr. Barnard shrugged. "The radio. That's all we have. We've been hearing about television for near 20 years, now, but of course we don't have any way to make one, or get one."

"Radio? It seems to me the book said—"

"Yeah, I know, Chang told me they couldn't get radio up here. That's how much he knew about radio. There ain't a shortwave station in the world we don't get at one time or another. Of course, he was just passing on what somebody else had told him. Or maybe that was their way of weaning us from the outside world, I never thought about that. Remind me to show you the crystal set we started with: 40 years old and as good as new."

I didn't have the wit or the background to see through his radio diversion. (Of course, we *do* have radios, three of them, ordered, along with wood-fired electric generators, in the half-dozen years between Mr. Barnard's arrival and their final shipment. If you want to throw somebody off the scent, be sure the decoy looks realistic. Mixed metaphor, but the point comes through, I hope.) Still, something about his explanation didn't sit right, and I couldn't tell what.

"Somehow," I said, coming to the end of my own cigar, "hearing about you having radio makes the place seen even smaller to me. Doesn't it ever give you claustrophobia, being stuck here?"

"Not particularly. They got me quoted in the book as saying, 30 years ago, that it's all a matter of whether you'd rather be in here or out there, and I haven't changed my mind one bit. Oh, sometimes it gets a little irritating, hearing about things on the radio and not being able to figure out what they're talking about, but mostly the news ain't been good enough, these last years, to make me want to go anywhere. And besides, I been here long enough that it would be sure death to go outside, even let alone the Chinese."

Chapter Five.

Preparation

Sure death outside, for them. But not for me. And I had the strongest reason of all to risk it, a reason they could no longer understand except abstractly, intellectually. None of them had a ceaseless longing gnawing at them, for the simple reason that anyone they'd left behind was long dead, or much aged. Their very longevity separated them from the rest of the world, even more effectively than the surrounding mountains. I didn't want to be separated that way from Marianne. It wasn't heroism that made me determined to return: Death or capture seemed easier than living on without her.

As I read these words I have just written, they seem to me impossibly romantic and naive. They seem to idealize her (and me, of course) just like the "little reading" romances Thoreau mocks so devastatingly: "the nine thousandth tale about Zebulon and Sophronia, and how they loved as none had ever loved before, and neither did the course of their true love run smooth. . . ." But I'm not setting myself up as Romeo, nor her as Juliet, and I don't have much experience in love. I can't compare intensities. All I know is that I was one person before meeting her, and another afterward. She said it was the same for her. By our third date, which was two days after the first, it was as if a dentist had suddenly stopped drilling. Or perhaps I should say it was as if I'd been born with a radio blaring ceaseless static into my ear, and suddenly it had been turned off. In her presence I found peace, and completion. Someone had removed the filters from my eyes, and I was seeing the world in vivid color for the first time

* **2** *

It was early in February, 1963, before I decided I needed to know for sure.

By this time, Mr. Barnard and I had fallen into a routine of meeting early in the morning, in the kitchen, for a little breakfast and conversation. Because of the monks' routine, which he and I did not keep, we had the place to ourselves, and could sit for an hour or so over tea and bread and butter and fruit, bringing to life the memories within us as we gave each other glimpses of the different worlds we'd come from.

What my life had been like; what he'd been doing at the same age. What it was like to be born in Southern New Jersey in the 1930s, as opposed to southwestern Ohio in the 1880s.

From me, the feel of a single-engine jet at takeoff: the sudden kick in the pants, the sense of hanging on for the ride rather than coaxing it off the ground, the short, sharp transition to a 45-degree climb. From him, a ride in a Ford Tri-motor: the drone of the engines, the vibration, the slow, dogged climb, the sense of endless time passing.

From me, television and radar and earth satellites like Telstar, and the interstate highway system and nuclear submarines cruising entirely around the world while submerged. From him, crystal sets and long-distance electrical transmission and the Stanley Steamer and Eddie Rickenbacker and Barney Oldfield.

From me, the Cold War; the Cuban Missile Crisis; the Hungarian revolution; Hiroshima; D-Day; Pearl Harbor; the TVA. (Sitting in Shangri-La, he had missed the entire Roosevelt administration.) From him, Winston Churchill's views, delivered in 1929 at a luncheon on the West Coast, on the successful conclusion of the world crisis; tales of Charles Insull's electric-utility holding companies; sharp practices on Wall Street in 1925; lingering effects of mustard gas on a friend he'd visited at a soldier's home after the war; the impact of World War I shipping needs on the Hampton Roads, Virginia, area.

From him, from me, many words on politics and technology and the effects of the passage of time. And from that volume of words—a volume that came not in a torrent but in a long, comfortable meander according to our moods—came an understanding between us. Partly, I suppose, it was that even in this different world we were countrymen, with a sense of shared experience that had, perhaps, all the greater impact because we were otherwise so different. (Or were we? I sometimes wondered.) At any rate, when it came time to put uncertainty to an end, I went naturally to him, rather than to Mr. Conway or to Sunnie. And he confirmed what I knew.

"You got it figured right, George," he said slowly, chewing meditatively on a fig. "Winter and Spring don't have all that much to do with your staying. It just seemed easier to break it to you gently that way. If you figure I lied to you, I can understand it, though I didn't, exactly. But we did set out to mislead you, so it comes to about the same thing."

I'd only asked Mr. Barnard for confirmation of what I already knew. So why, on hearing the truth, did I feel numb, dazed?

Mr. Barnard was apparently giving great attention to pouring us more tea. I could practically *see* him measuring the atmospheric pressure. "George," he said slowly, handing me my cup, "I know it's rough on you. But think what our situation is. As long as the Chinese don't have any idea we're sitting here behind the lines, probably we are safe enough. Right this minute they are plenty busy in Chamdo, east of Lhasa, and I doubt they got attention to spare over here. But if they ever get wind that there's folks hiding out from them here, they're bound to start looking, and sooner or later they got to find us. We got 50 old men and six old women and a few hundred more, all ages, down in the valley. You know we can't go anywhere. The only chance we got is to lay low and hope for the best. We can't be dropping 'em clues like some American flyer caught trying to sneak out to freedom. Hell, we might as well have left your airplane lying out where they could stumble on it."

I was visualizing the empty landscape I'd come down in a few weeks earlier. "Mr. Barnard, what makes you think they'd ever spot me? If they didn't see me fly in, and didn't see me come down, and didn't see the plane on the ground between the time I crashed it and your people got it buried, what makes you so sure they'll see one man on foot?"

He grunted. "Maybe they won't. But maybe they will. There's only so many places to cross the mountains, and it's easier to guard the borders than you maybe think. Particularly in winter. I wasn't telling you the whole truth, but I wasn't flat lying, either. It's a whole lot more risky than you know, and you'd be pretty liable to bring 'em in on us."

I sat there in the kitchen and closed my eyes, slowly massaging my face with one hand, trying to convey a sudden weariness, a disorientation. "It's a hard concept to get used to," I muttered, "being stuck here forever." I hoped my voice was right. Almost before my thought had fully formed, I instinctively hid my eyes from him in the most natural way I could think up.

"Sure it is," he said, "but you can see how things are."

I sighed, opened my eyes, reached for my tea. Mr. Barnard was still watching me intently. I knew I'd have to watch my step. I wanted to express weariness and frustration, which were real enough, and also resignation, which wasn't there at all.

* 3 *

It occurred to me I wouldn't likely give up so soon. I said, "But if I was real careful, how do we know I couldn't get through safely?"

"We *don't* know," he said shortly. "But we feel like we don't care to find out."

What would be a likely response? I waited a few seconds. "If you'd all help me, I'd have a better chance." I waited for him to shake his head. "As it is, it makes me feel a little like I'm in jail."

"Well, I reckon that's natural enough. But that ain't the way it is. You're safe enough here; this place is the only thing that's keeping you *out* of jail. If you can remember that, it'll maybe be some easier to take."

Probably I'd say something about what I was losing. "It's funny to think that my family will never know what happened to me."

He was nodding sympathetically, making the right gestures and sounds, but I had the feeling that he was still watching me so closely that he was practically looking right through me. "It's a hard thing, George, no two ways about it, and I'm as sorry as I can be. If there was any choice, we'd help you on your way. And if we thought you had a half-decent chance to get clean away, maybe we'd let you risk it. But we just plain can't."

I thought it safe to continue to argue. "What if I promised not to mention Shangri-La? You saved my life. I'd protect you."

"George, I believe you. I know you'd try. But you couldn't do it. No doubt you'd hold out a good while, but you couldn't do it forever. Nobody could. And once they made you tell, everybody here would be dead."

I couldn't fault his logic. Certainly the record of GI prisoners of war in Korea wasn't encouraging. But I wasn't about to get caught.

"I do know how you feel, you know. Happened to me, remember? One day you have got your life stretching out ahead of you, and the next day, it's all knocked into a cocked hat. Course, my situation was a little different. It wouldn't surprise me if you were thinking that if you're stuck here for the rest of your life, maybe a short life would be better than a long one."

I certainly wasn't about to respond to that. When I didn't, he said, "Now, when I came here, they strung us along for quite a while about how we would get out in a few months, then always something would come up and it would be another few months, and so on. It was near two years before they'd tell me I wasn't going anywhere, though I'd about figured it out by then anyway. The idea didn't bother me any by that time. But I expect it's a different thing to know right off for sure. It don't give you time to get your balance. Maybe if it wasn't so obvious you can't go anywhere, I'd have tried to string you along the same way they did me."

"I'm glad you didn't. I'd rather have the truth."

"Well, that's what I figured. You had to know on your own that you aren't going anywhere any time soon. But like I say, if the place makes you feel cooped up, maybe you won't like the idea of spending a couple hundred more years here."

I shrugged. "I can't absorb it yet. It's too new."

"Sure. Well, take your time." He laughed. "You've got plenty of it."

* **4** *

So I was stuck here? Not unless I agreed to be. Much as I liked the company, I couldn't see staying for the rest of my life. Granted, there'd be some risk, but I was pretty sure I'd make it. I'd *have* to make it. Half the world away, Marianne was working as a children's librarian and going to Sunday concerts with David Feulner, who she thought was [sweet] nice. How long was I supposed to let *that* go on?

But I'd have to get back without help. And the first step on the road back was to conceal my intentions. The second step I took one afternoon at tea with Mr. Barnard and Sunnie.

"Yeah, sure. In fact, that's maybe one of the best ways you could spend your time. I'm no scholar myself, but plenty of folks here are."

"I think it a very sensible idea. You did tell us, did you not, that you were at university before entering military service?"

I nodded, reaching for another of the little tea-cakes I had become so fond of.

"How fortunate. You possess the intellectual ability, it is obvious. You have obtained the necessary scholastic training. And here you will find resources unmatched the world over."

"I'm sure I will," I said politely. I was thinking of the un-measured miles of shelving in the world's libraries, wedged solid with books, manuscripts, private papers, documents. . . .

As usual, Sunnie listened not to my words but to my feelings. Or rather, to put it more precisely, she read my words and facial expressions and tone of voice (and other things, as I eventually learned) and responded to *me* rather than to the smoke-screen I hid behind. She said, "To be sure, the books in our library are but a tiny sample of the world's total. But the same may be said of the people living here. What are we, one might ask, against such numbers?"

"It's quality that counts, is what she means. Nine times out of ten, quality beats numbers. Any good businessman knows that. You can't read every book in the world, no more than you can meet every person in the world. The only thing you do get time to do, when you get right down to it, is deal with some of the ones closest to you."

"Precisely. That is why it is so awfully important to surround oneself with the best available."

"And George," Mr. Barnard said chuckling, "don't go asking how we can tell what's best. It's a good question, but save it for another time, okay?" (I had to smile as well. Like Sunnie, Mr. Barnard seemed to know what I was thinking almost before I did, so well had they come to know me in a few short weeks.) "What is it you were thinking of studying?"

I leaned back in my chair, shrugged, and reached to pour myself some more tea. "I really haven't given it that much thought, it just occurred to me that maybe . . ." I paused, fearing to seem ungrateful.

"If you made yourself something to do, the time wouldn't pass so slow."

"Well, yes. I did all right in languages in school: I wonder if it would be too ambitious for me to try to learn Tibetan."

I was afraid they'd immediately see what I had in mind, but apparently they didn't. Their delight didn't change to suspicion—at least, not obviously—and they didn't drop casual suggestions that I try something easier. And so I acquired a tutor and a daily hour-and-a-half morning routine, and felt like I had moved slightly closer to getting away.

Evenings I spent reading, burning the midnight oil waiting for the end of winter (for I did accept Mr. Barnard's statements about the dangers of snow) to clear the way.

What did I read? Whatever held my interest. I used books as some might have used drink, to dull the pain. Unacknowledged pain. Unacknowledged even though I would find myself in a sitting position—a book in my lap, the lamp on a table beside me flickering quietly—and realize that I had been far away. Daydreaming, I thought then. I'd describe it differently now.

Other times I would find myself staring through the page, or looking off to the far end of the library room, and my mind, or rather my heart, would be too full for words.

In those earlier days, I had constantly in mind the thought of Marianne, living half the world away from me, undoubtedly thinking me dead. The passage of every day seemed interminable, and the end of each day seemed to bring Spring no closer.

* 5 *

Those days, fortunately, included more than books and brooding thoughts. There were mildly interesting chores to be done, and Tibetan to study, and quiet, inconspicuous reconnaissance to be made as I took inventory of the resources available for my escape. And there were my fellow passengers on this extended stationary cruise: Mr. Barnard and Sunnie most particularly, though not exclusively. They offered me long, unhurried conversations such as I had never known, even with Marianne. Not prolonged into tedium. Not compressed and distorted by the pressure of time. Like Shangri-La itself, in the midst of ice and rock, the conversations, the relationships, were comfortable and even, in a way, luxurious.

The only flaw was self-inflicted. Rather than let the conversation take its own course, I often tried (carefully, indirectly) to steer it into directions that might be profitable. In this way I sometimes half-ruined what I already realized I could never recapture once I left Shangri-La's tranquil space. But, with half my mind always on the requirements of escape, I tried to use what I could find.

Thus one day I asked Mr. Barnard what he and Miss Brinklow had thought, back in '31, when they'd awakened to find Mr. Conway and Mallinson gone. I had waited for what seemed an appropriate moment, trying hard not to seem to be steering the conversation with any particular end in mind.

"I didn't spend any time missing Mallinson, that's for sure. You can imagine that him and me didn't get along any too good. Of course, he was just a kid, but he reminded me of a bull terrier I had once: always yapping at any little thing, just to stay in practice. And he didn't have any use for me. As far as he was concerned, I was a crook and it was a darned shame somebody hadn't locked me up."

"And Mr. Conway?"

"Conway was a different story. Conway and me hit it off right away. He did his job and didn't make a fuss about how good he was at it. And he followed the rules when they made sense, and when they didn't—which was about half the time, it seemed to me—he sort of looked the other way instead of going by the book and doing something stupid just because it was the official thing to do. You take when Mallinson told him who I was. Conway told him, 'so what?' Scotland Yard probably would have told him to clap the bracelets on me right there and then, and bring me in like they say the mounties always do, and Mallinson would have been official enough and self-righteous enough to try it. Conway had more sense."

"And besides, he liked you."

"Yeah, he did, but the point is, even if Mallinson liked me he would have wanted to arrest me, and even if Conway didn't like me, he would have seen that it wasn't practical to do anything just then. When you come right down to it, that was the difference between those two. Conway was practical. Still is. He knew what the world was like. Mallinson was just a kid, and everything was black and white to him."

Mallinson in 1931 was no older than I was in 1962. I wondered if Mr. Barnard was forgetting that. "He sounds like quite an idealist," I said.

He laughed. "Oh yeah. Now, I don't knock idealism. It gives youngsters a solid place to stand until they learn the difference between the way things are and the way they ought to be. But it can get on your nerves after a while, especially when the idealist has you pegged as the devil himself. I missed Conway when he left, sure enough. But I could do without Mallinson without any trouble." He added, "Of course, you got to remember, he was just a kid, with his girlfriend in England and his big ideas about the future he was going to make for himself. And now he has been dead 30 years and more."

This time, for sure, he could not have forgotten. Yet I was sure it was not malicious cruelty, so what was he up to?

He appeared to stir restlessly. "God, how talking brings it all back! You're the first person to come in from outside in all that time, and there ain't much reason for the rest of us to rehash all that."

"So what happened? How did you find out?"

"That was some stir, believe me. Probably nobody had ever busted out of this place before."

"Did they go after him?"

"I don't know. They weren't telling me anything then, and later I never thought to ask. I doubt it, against that many people, porters and all. All I know is that Miss Brinklow and me came down to breakfast and the other two weren't there. We figured Conway had been up late again, talking to the head man, and I didn't worry much about Mallinson. The longer he slept, the better, as far as I was concerned. After breakfast, we fiddled around doing this and that and still we didn't see them, but I never thought much about it until they didn't show up for lunch either. Back then, while we were still new here, they fed us the way we were used to, three meals a day starting about eight, so there was still supper to look forward to. But they didn't show up then either."

"And neither of you suspected that anything was wrong?"

"We didn't have any reason to. These people around here don't exactly go around yelling and screaming. You can't always tell if anybody's around. And people here mind their own business more'n any place I ever saw. You don't go barging around seeing who's up and doing, like at some Chicago convention."

"So how did you finally find out?"

Mr. Barnard appeared to retreat into the past, for the first time since I'd met him. "Chang came in to have supper with us, and as soon as I saw his face, I knew something had happened. Usually, when you're looking for clues from that old boy, you can learn about as much by looking at the wall, but not tonight. He's upset. He's making little movements with his hands, and his mouth is drawn up all tight. I figure this is one night I could play poker with Chang. He don't even give us more'n a couple lines of his usual social talk before he suddenly says he supposes we have missed Conway and Mallinson, and we say we have, and he says, 'It appears that they have departed.'

"Miss Brinklow says, 'Departed!' like it was a personal insult. Me, I'm surprised how bad it makes me feel. I guess that's the first time I realize how much I liked Conway. I say, 'They must have left in a big hurry, not even saying goodbye,' and Chang looks over at me and says 'Yes, in a big hurry, Mr. Barnard.' And by the way he says it, I can see he's holding himself on a tight rein.

"'I would have liked to see them off,' I say. 'It ain't every day you get carried off a thousand miles with somebody. I wish somebody had said something.' Chang, he looks at me and says he does too, and I say, 'You mean you didn't know either?'

"He says nobody did. 'One other may have been told,' he says, and later I figure out he's talking about the head lama, because Conway had been up late talking to him, and for all Chang knew, Conway's departure had something to do with their last conversation. But at the time, I was on a different trail. I think it over a minute and I put the question to him. 'Chang,' I say, 'let me get this straight. They went off with those porters you were talking about?' He nods his head, not a big nod, just a little one. 'They came a thousand miles to get here? All the way from China?' 'Far more than a thousand miles,' he says. 'And they got to go back the same way?' He nods his head again, maybe an inch. I say, 'Now, Chang, tell me this. A guy travels a month or two on the road and finally gets someplace, he isn't going to turn right around and go back, without any rest, I don't care how much food he needs or how little shelter he has. Chang, *how long were those porters here?*'"

Mr. Barnard's eyes were piercing through me. Absorbed in his memories, he had become every bit the steely man of business. I figured that I was seeing the look Chang had seen that night.

"Chang, he fiddles with his sleeve, and then he looks me in the eye and says they had been there for three days. I say, 'You never told us that. Not four days ago, not three days ago, not two days ago. You never intended to tell us at all, did you?' He don't admit it, but he don't say anything different, either. Miss Brinklow says, in her best schoolmarm voice, 'Really sir, I find your conduct reprehensible. I am quite disposed to remain here, and I believe that Mr. Barnard is of the same mind, at least for the moment, but you cannot have been unaware that Mr. Mallinson, in particular, was anxious to rejoin his family and colleagues.'"

Mr. Barnard's face relaxed. He grinned, glancing at me. "Chang gives a tired smile and says that indeed he was aware of it. Mallinson never gave him a rest, you know, all the time he was here. 'And yet you intended,' she says, all indignant, 'to detain him here against his will?' Chang don't answer.

"The bit about Conway still bothers me. I say, 'Listen, Chang, I don't get the feeling that Conway was all that hot on leaving. Mallinson couldn't wait, sure, but I thought Conway was happy enough.' And that's when I get my next surprise. Chang has tears in his eyes! It takes him two tries to say he had thought so too. And then he says we have got to excuse him, the day has been a strain for everybody, the high lama has died. Later I figure that Chang is blaming himself for the lama dying, thinking maybe Conway and him had disagreed or something and the lama'd had a stroke. At least I suppose that's it: I never felt just like asking him. But it was Chang's idea in the first place that Conway should see the lama, and you can see he might feel responsible.

"Of course, we don't know any of that right then, so we just tell Chang we're sorry to hear it, and Chang says the lama died peacefully at an advanced age, and he leaves and that's the last time we hear about it for a long time. It was quite a night."

He paused, and I was afraid he would stop. He hadn't told me anything useful, but I didn't feel like I could safely prompt him in a particular direction. Besides, I was curious. "So what happened? Who took over? Had the lama told anybody about his plans for Conway?"

Mr. Barnard put up a hand, a traffic cop holding up a line of cars. "Back then, you understand, I didn't know a thing that had gone on between the lama and Conway. All I knew was that they talked together a lot. Mallinson used to pester him about it every so often, as you can imagine, but Conway wouldn't say much about it. It was only later that I found out what had happened."

He paused. I said, "And?"

"It turns out the high lama *had* talked to others about his plans, but what he had in mind wasn't exactly putting Conway in charge of the whole place. He figured to make Conway more like an Executive Director, running the day-to-day affairs, but answering to a chairman of the board, one of the monks who would become the new high lama."

"That makes sense," I said. (And so it did, although as it turned out it wasn't true, or wasn't exactly true, or was true only if you looked at it in a peculiar way.) "I *thought* it was strange that Conway was going to become the man in charge when he had only been there a couple of months."

"Sure. Who's going to give a stranger control of the whole works, just on the strength of a good first impression? The guy that told the story to Hilton just didn't get it right."

What I wanted was something about the track to the outside, or about the guards. But Mr. Barnard never came close, and I was afraid to pump him about it.

* 6 *

Where I had formed the habit of lunch with Mr. Barnard, followed by long leisurely conversation, I now developed an equally pleasant habit of afternoon teas with Sunnie, sometimes alone, sometimes with others. Some days we would talk, and I would find myself able to say something—though not all, of course—of what I felt. Other days, we would page through books of prints, and she would talk to me of art and artists, about which she was quite knowledgeable. Still other days, she would bring out her charcoals, and I would sit and watch her draw, or she would attempt to teach me the rudiments.

Evenings I spent alone. That is, I spent them with Marianne, and occasionally with friends or family. And so the winter days slowly passed.

* 7 *

Mr. Conway and I were sitting outside one brilliant starlit Spring night, and our conversation turned philosophic.

"Self-development has been out of style for a good while," he said in response to something I'd said. "Modern man puts his faith in other things."

"Things like?"

"Politics. Ideology. Technology, science. You know the things as well as I. And the more apparent the symptoms of rot, the stronger grows the cry for more of the same. Change political leaders. Change ideologies. Invest more in new technologies. Make greater effort to amass wealth. Work harder to redistribute wealth fairly."

"Work harder at diplomacy," I said, referring to his past.

He nodded, acknowledging it. "Try this, try that. All aimed outward, when the remedy lies within. . . . The result isn't far to seek. As Henry said long ago, the whole game is coming to pieces."

"That was in *Lost Horizon*," I said. "I well remember it. It made me stop, right in the middle of the book, and had me pacing up and down my room."

[The passage:

. . . a single phrase of his — "the whole game's going to pieces." Conway found himself remembering and echoing it with a wider significance than the American had probably intended; he felt it to be true of more than American banking and trust company management. It fitted Baskul and Delhi and London, war making and empire building, consulates and trade concessions and dinner parties at Government House; there was a reek of dissolution over all that recollected world, and

Barnard's cropper had only, perhaps, been better dramatized than his own. The whole game *was* doubtless going to pieces. . . .]

"Rang true, did it?"

"Did it ever! And I couldn't get over the fact that you'd seen it in the '30s. Even now, 30 years later, it wasn't obvious to me until I read what you'd said. I'd never put the pieces together, but all my life I'd been watching Western civilization losing control of the world's future."

"The process was underway well before you were born."

"Well, suddenly that's what I realized. I started to wonder where it was all going to end."

"And what did you conclude?"

I grinned at him. "I concluded that I ought to put those kinds of thoughts on the shelf and finish the book."

In the starlight I could see Mr. Conway's smile answer mine. "It is tempting, always, to conclude that the world is going to hell," he said, "but Henry would observe that it seems never to get there."

"Maybe not, but you grew up in a world at peace, which is more than I ever did." An old memory stirred. "When I was in college, I sometimes used to go to the library and look at microfilms of old newspapers, just to see what old events looked like when they were news. One day, I looked up The New York Times for August something, 1914. The fourth or fifth, I suppose. The headline said: 'Great War of Eight Nations.' Somehow that headline stuck with me. It snapped me back to a mentality that expected wars to be fought between only two states, not between huge alliances. It took an effort of imagination, Mr. Conway: I'd grown up being *used* to the idea of wars involving dozens of countries and hundreds of millions of people. The headline reminded me that it hadn't always been that way."

"I do see," Mr. Conway said.

"Living through the change was what was so terrible for your generation, wasn't it? And why you couldn't believe in much afterwards?"

"After the 1914-18 war," Mr. Conway said slowly, "the only ones with something to believe in were the fascists and the communists, each with their panaceas. Not much to choose from, I'm afraid. As the poet said, 'The best lack all conviction, while the worst are full of passionate intensity.'"

"Yeats," I said.

"Yeats. He isn't still alive, I suppose?"

"Oh, no, he died a long time ago. Before the war."

"Before the—? Oh, yes, of course, the second war. I suppose 'the war' will always mean 1914-18 to my generation. A matter of perspective, is it not? Now I think of it, I believe Yeats would have to be well over the century mark to be alive today. That would be asking a great deal."

"Unless he had made it here."

"Yes. What a stimulating addition to the company he would have made!"

Mr. Barnard came out into the night, saw us, and seated himself with us, sure of his welcome. He lit up a cigar and silently passed me another.

"Were your ears burning, Henry? We were only now discussing your prophecy."

"What prophecy was that?"

"That the world was going to pieces."

Mr. Barnard grunted. "Well, it don't rightly count as prophecy. More like journalism. It was all there for anybody to see. And besides, as I remember it, I was mainly talking about the market."

"Still, it's the breaking up of old forms."

"With the difference," I said, "that when the two of you talked about it, people couldn't destroy the world, and now we can. And it looks like we might."

Mr. Conway nodded. "What a civilization wants, it ultimately gets."

"I know where *this* lecture's going," Mr. Barnard said quietly. "I've sat in on this one before. Conway says people get war because they hate the way they live."

Mutually contradictory desires didn't cancel each other out, Mr. Conway said; they destroyed each other. And he used, as evidence, the outbreak of World War I. "I know *how* it happened," he said. "The question is: *Why* did it happen? For every external reason, there exists an internal reason. When you know the one, you know something about the other."

I remembered the description of Mr. Conway's final interview with the high lama, in which the old man had predicted a civilization-destroying world war. "There will be no safety by arms," he had told Mr. Conway, "no help from authority, no answer in science. It will rage till every flower of culture is trampled, and all human things are trampled in a vast chaos. Such was my vision when Napoleon was still a name unknown; and I see it now, more clearly with each hour." I quoted them the lama's words.

"I tell you," Mr. Barnard said decisively, "if he'd said that to me back then, I'd have said we were going through hard times, but there's *always* hard times somewhere, and things would finally straighten out like they always do. I'd have said the world would settle down again as soon as—oh, as soon as we got rid of the bears in the market, or the labor organizers, or prohibition, or something. But I'd have been dead wrong. I could see that the financial game was going to pieces, but I couldn't see that *everything* was cracking up, like he said. Like *you* said, Conway."

"What amazed me," I said, "was that the book was so modern. The lama saw so much so soon. Before Hitler, before the A-bomb, before guided missiles and all."

"It's the best proof the story's true. George. You could go through poking holes in it, like about refuelling the plane and Miss Brinklow translating Mallinson's propositions to Lo-tsen, but you couldn't argue with that old man's vision. It hit too close to home."

So it did. When Mr. Conway first heard of that vision, he could look back at the bombings and dogfights of World War I. But they were just nothing, as the book remarked, next to what the Japanese did to Chinese cities. And mankind progressed rapidly after that from Guernica and London and Coventry to Dresden and Tokyo and Hiroshima. By the time I read the account, shortly after the world had narrowly avoided going to war over Cuba, there could be no way of missing his point.

* 8 *

The old lama had envisioned Shangri-La as a lifeboat, preserving some of the world's knowledge and culture from the global destruction to come:

"We may expect no mercy, but we may faintly hope for neglect. Here we shall stay with our books and our music and our meditations, conserving the frail elegances of a dying age, and seeking such wisdom as men will need when their passions are all spent. . . ."

"And then?" [Mr. Conway had asked]

"Then, my son, when the strong have devoured each other, the Christian ethic may at last be fulfilled, and the meek shall inherit the earth."

May inherit the earth. What's left of it. On the night I first read that passage, I lay for a long time looking up at the shadows flickering on my ceiling. If they were truly counting on obscurity and the enemy's neglect to keep them safe, we were doomed, however many years it took to destroy us. The lama's words to Mr. Conway were meant to convey hope. But how reliable is concealment by geographical remoteness in an age of reconnaissance aircraft like my poor U-2? And when they succeeded in putting up the network of spy satellites they were talking about, where could anybody hide?

"Well now," Mr. Barnard said when I put it to them, "it ain't like we got a whole lot of choice in the matter. They find us or they don't. They have their war or they don't. All we can do is our best, and that's it. I think you will find, by the time you get to be my age, that there's darn few things that can be helped by worrying about 'em. All you'll do is poison your time, and there ain't any sense to it."

I thought: Easier for you to say than me; your life is mostly behind you—but then I reflected that, in Shangri-La's time-scale, we were both comparative youngsters. And then I was reminded of the lama's speech on how brief and breathless a man's life-span was. I had read his words that same night, lying on my bed, wrapped in a blanket against the night cold. I had let the book drop onto my chest, and I lay there for a while staring into space, watching the oil lamp throw wildly flickering patterns on the walls and smoke-stained ceiling. "How true," I'd thought. "And how intolerable."

Even as a teenager, I'd been appalled at how short and frantic our lives are. Everything I did was set against the background of a ticking clock saying: "Run, run, run, before it is too late." Lying there with the book on my chest, I fully realized for the first time how very much hurrying had filled my life to date. "I miss my poet," Marianne had said.

"Mr. Barnard," I asked, "did you ever have any regrets about not going back to the world?"

He shook his head decisively. "You know my story. There wasn't any way out for me, those first few years. And then later, after the second war, I figured the world was way too different for me to figure out all over again, and anyway, out there I'd be too old." For a moment he was silent, meditative, smoking his cigar. Then he let out a long puff. "I remember what stuck with me, when they told me about us living so long here. I reckon it sounds silly. I thought: Now maybe I'll get a chance to see how it all comes out."

He glanced at Mr. Conway and at me. "You know, I was just past 50 when I came here, and you might say I got to 50 the hard way, thinking that a man's years are threescore and ten, like the good book says, and I'd already used up most of them. And where was I? No money left, my name was mud, police all over the world looking for me: I tell you, it gives you a different view of things. Makes you stop and wonder where you got off the track. There was your whole life ahead of you and you were going to make it come to something—and then there you are, 50, your work ruined and nothing to look forward to but hiding out or going to jail. And the grave in 20 years or so regardless.

"The years I'd lived through hadn't been all gravy, by a long shot, but still, think of the things we'd seen happen. Electricity was still pretty new when I was a kid, and then there was the gramophone, and the telephone, and the radio, and airplanes—. It looked like old mankind had finally figured itself out, and we had a golden age coming. Sure, there had been the war, but those things happen. By 1930 we were pretty sure—most of us, anyway—that it wouldn't happen again. We figured we got through that, we could get through anything. And besides, the war didn't really touch America, all it did was gear us up. Things were really beginning to happen, and it just seemed a darn shame to have to die and miss it all. That's the first thing hooked me on the old man's dream: I wanted to see how things came out.

"When Conway told me the high lama had found a way to keep us all alive, I felt like I had discovered a million dollars. Better than that, in fact, because I already *had* discovered a million dollars. The gold reef, you know. And having to stay here didn't make me lose any sleep. I'd already decided I liked it here. And all of a sudden, I wasn't looking at 20 years, or 30, but 200, if the old man was telling the truth. It made me feel like a kid again."

Mr. Conway's smile was in his voice. "Tastes differ. When *I* was told, I recall telling the old lama that I'd often thought life pointless, and I wondered if a long life would be any less so."

"I remember that," I said. "That's when he told you of his vision of a final war, and Shangri-La's mission as cultural lifeboat. That wasn't enough to make you stay."

"No, I went off with Mallinson. But I'm afraid I wasn't thinking very clearly at that point."

"I guess the vision looked more compelling after you found yourself outside?"

Mr. Conway paused, reflecting. "To be honest, George, I don't believe I thought much about it. I had strong reasons to return, but they had little to do with the fate of the world. I was never very ambitious in that way. I was more accustomed to taking my life as it came."

The lama, I remembered, had asked Mr. Conway how it was that despite his gifts he had so little ambition. Mr. Conway had replied that success in his field hadn't seemed worth the effort. The lama had said Mr. Conway's soul was not in his work.

"Neither my soul nor heart nor more than half my energies," Mr. Conway had replied. "I'm naturally rather lazy."

And the lama had smiled. "Laziness in doing stupid things can be a great virtue," he had told Mr. Conway.

Which summed up Shangri-La very nicely. Mr. Barnard would call it the motto of the firm.

Chapter Six.

Escape

By the end of April I'd spent about three months learning a few Tibetan phrases that might or might not prove useful in the event—long enough to realize that to go beyond these phrases to fluency could require not months but years.

I'd carefully adopted the wearing of a monk's robe, not merely for the sake of fitting in visually but also to save wear on my flight suit.

Oxygen was going to be a problem, obviously, since I had no way to refill my mask. The monastery puts some sort of drug into newcomers' food, to lessen the effect of high altitude on bodies born in lower places. My careful, inconspicuous searches never turned up the drug's storage place. Not so surprising, perhaps, since I didn't really know what I was looking for. I'd have to do without it, and hope the residual effect of whatever was still in my system when I left would carry me past the worst.

I had abstracted two canteens I'd found in the tiny, chock-full storage room. They were old. The canvas around the metal canteens had rotted. I improvised a sling out of some rope. I made another sling to support the food I'd carry in one of the bags woven and brought up from the valley. The food itself, like the water, I wouldn't be able to stock until almost the last moment.

About fire, I debated for some time. On the one hand, I didn't intend sending smoke signals for the benefit of either the communists or the monastery. The barren mountainside provided nothing to burn anyway, and before I'd walked very far, I would certainly begrudge every ounce of extra weight. On the other hand, merely getting across the border wouldn't automatically mean safety. Conceivably I might at some point need to light a fire to signal rescuers, or to save myself from freezing, or even to cook a meal. And the little spark-making mechanism weighed only a few ounces. I decided to take it.

Food, water, shelter. Should I carry something to use as a tent or poncho? I had long since given the monastery my parachute, figuring they'd be glad to use the silk for something. What could I replace it with? This boiled down strictly to a question of weight. I'd be uncomfortable in only my flight suit, but could I survive? If so, I'd be better off suffering cold than carrying extra weight. I decided to carry a blanket (hand-woven, like most fabrics in the monastery, by the people in the valley below) and abandon it when its weight got to be too much. I figured that it would probably be worth its weight the first two or three nights, and that if I felt strong enough after that I could keep carrying it, and otherwise I could drop it and try to get across to safety before I ran out of energy.

What I really needed was a stimulant, and after several days spent wishing that coffee grew in the valley, I realized that the obvious solution was to carry super-concentrated tea in my canteen instead of water. I'd just have to find a time when I could brew it unsuspected.

What else would I need? My first-aid stuff? Reluctantly I weeded it down to my pocket knife and a single roll of gauze and part of a roll of adhesive tape. I left the unguents and iodine. Taking my chances with infection seemed preferable to carrying the extra weight. If I could just get across the border (constant refrain, that!) I could get any medical treatment I might need. For exposure and exhaustion, probably, and maybe frostbite. Not for gunshot wounds, I hoped.

I needed a map, however crude. Hours of poring over the maps in the library convinced me that I knew where we were. Shangri-La was nowhere marked on any of them, but I knew more or less where to start looking. I traced out a route over the mountains that looked at least possible, if hardly easy.

I exercised daily, trying to stay in shape. That was about all I could do.

But how was I going to get out of the building, down to the valley, back up the other trail from the valley to the altiplano outside, and past the guards? I'd figured out the supplies; now I had to figure out the operation.

* 2 *

First came reconnaissance, of course. Since I'd read the book, for me to ask to see Miss Brinklow was perfectly natural. At least, I hoped it would seem so. And to see her was to go to the valley.

Mr. Conway not only raised no objections, he offered to accompany me and introduce me. So, one morning in May, he and I and two natives roped ourselves together and hiked down the trail I'd climbed half a year before. It was as narrow as I'd remembered, and as steep. I'd need a moonlit night and a lot of very careful stepping. Even at that, there was one spot I couldn't quite see trying alone. But—I'd just have to. When we got to the bottom, Mr. Conway asked me what I thought of the ride.

"I felt like a fly on the wall, but the scenery was almost worth it," I said. A moonlit night and no ice on the trail.

He nodded, and said a few words of appreciation to the natives, who broke into wide smiles and chattered back before disappearing off behind some huts. The difference in climate was amazing. Up at the lamasery, it had been warm with the midday sun, but down here, perhaps two miles lower than that exposed shelf, it was unbelievably hot and humid.

Mr. Conway looked around, and I did too, for a different reason. We stood among circular huts made from thatching, but no one was in evidence.

"Maybe she has not yet left the fields," Mr. Conway said. "This yurt is her schoolhouse, where she teaches English and Tibetan writing to some of the children."

"What did you call it?"

"A yurt. It's Mongolian in origin, I believe, but it has been so long employed in Tibet that we might nearly call it indigenous. There she is."

I don't know quite what I'd expected. A shrill, skinny harridan, maybe. Someone looking to be in her eighties, with a prim, stern mouth of constant disapproval. Ice-blue eyes, probably.

Not at all. The woman who came striding up to us might have been in her early sixties; she was neither skinny nor shrill, but robust with what I can only call a solid British earthiness. Her face was tanned and lined and she seemed the type of woman who spends much time gardening and running households. Her eyes—brown eyes—were warm in the way you sometimes see in sentimental retired schoolteachers. Instantly I summed her up in one word: self-sufficient.

She greeted Mr. Conway warmly, and he made the introductions.

"And whatever brought you here, Mr. Chiari?"

"Actually, ma'am, it wasn't my idea," I said. "My airplane fell out of the sky and I sort of came down with it."

Not a hilarious opening line, but I caught a twinkle in her eye. "A very good idea, to be sure, considering the alternatives. But what brought you over Shangri-La?"

Well, she was about as direct as advertised, if not quite so humorless. "I was sort of scouting, ma'am." (What was this "ma'am" stuff? But she made me feel entirely like a schoolboy.)

For a few minutes we talked of the chance—I thought it chance, then—that had brought me here, while in the back of my mind I rehearsed the long climb down.

* 3 *

The inside of the small round building Mr. Conway called a yurt was surprisingly comfortable and well-lighted. The open doorway seemed to diffuse the light against the walls somehow, resulting in an indirect and subdued illumination I found soothing. I said, by way of breaking the silence, "Where are the children?"

"They are in the fields, working beside their parents," she said. "They come for instructions only for about an hour in midday and again in the early evening. You will excuse me if I make my preparations while we talk."

"Miss Brinklow puts in a full day with the others," Mr. Conway said, "and teaches the children as well."

"I taught their parents and their grandparents before them," she said. "And if I did not, no one would." Parents and grandparents before them. I recalled that *Lost Horizon* had said that for some reason the drug and the exercises did not prolong the lives of the natives as it did for outsiders.

She moved not rapidly but decisively and efficiently, bringing out chalks and slates and a few books from a box on the floor. She also brought out mats for the children to sit on. "I am able to teach them but little, I fear, Mr. Chiari," she said as she arranged things. "I haven't proper facilities and haven't the proper support from the parents. I consider myself fortunate if I can impart the rudiments of reading and writing in their own language. And religious instruction, of course."

"She's far too modest, George. Four of her pupils—four pupils of a previous generation, that is,—live in the lamasery. One is the master of four languages."

She did not look particularly pleased. "You know I count none of the four as successes, Hugh," she said.

"I know," he said gently, "but still they *are* religious, and they *did* profit greatly from their instruction at your hands."

"Profit?" Her voice was suddenly harsh. I noticed for the first time something of sadness in those steadfast, kindly eyes. "I should hardly say profit. And you know the apposite scriptural passage."

Mr. Conway saw that I was at a loss. In a neutral tone of voice he said, "What does it profit a man if he gains the whole world and loses his own soul?"

Miss Brinklow looked directly at me and said, "I am quite aware that my activities here are something of a jest at the lamasery, but of course I cannot allow that knowledge to interfere with God's work."

Mr. Conway's eyebrows rose slightly. I wondered why she would tell me something she had not told him in all these years. Or was he merely surprised that she would come out with it before a stranger?

I couldn't decide on an appropriate response. I stumbled in with, "Oh, ma'am, I'm sure they appreciate the things you do here." I received a look that was the distilled essence of a lifetime of persistence in the face of realism.

"Mr. Chiari, plainly you have never been a missionary. You would have learned, quite early on, that missionaries customarily meet tolerance slightly tinged with concealed contempt. At best, we are regarded as idealistic but impractical; at worst, as hypocrites, acting as conscious agents of whatever force the observer fears or dislikes. Chiefly we are considered harmless nuisances, slightly mad but able to circulate in society without restraint or supervision." She said it all in the impersonally

casual voice of a professor of sociology or anthropology. I heard
no trace of bitterness or resentment.

She finished arranging her materials. "I have little doubt that
the members of the lamasery will be surprised to know that I am
as aware as they of the apparent fruitlessness of my efforts these
last years." Thirty years! "I may be stupid, but I am able to
count, and I should need to be considerably more stupid than
they think me, not to realize that I have made exactly 14 converts
in all this time, of whom not one has turned *totally* to Christ
rather than remain half-pagan. I am fully aware of the meager-
ness of the harvest for the effort expended. Like Father Perrault
long ago, I have succeeded in producing only semi-Christians,
converts retaining their Buddhism beneath a new veneer of
Christianity." She viewed the two of us steadily, without anger
or defiance, merely stating the facts.

"But think of the obstacles you have had to overcome," Mr.
Conway said. "One person attempting to convert an entire
society. It would be a little much to expect to single-handedly
overcome all that inertia, surely?"

She looked at him levelly. "I would remind you that the
apostles went singly from place to place with this same message,
which went against the basic beliefs of those societies. Yet they
did totally overcome that inertia, as you term it. They did transform those societies. As yet I see but little success, but, praise
God, success and failure are not in my hands. I am but an agent,
and when God's good time has come, success will come through
His efforts, not mine. My part is but to persevere. We are told to
be patient in tribulation, as well as to rejoice in hope. I pray that
I shall be given the strength to do both until I see victory. The
one thing that saddens me is that the lamasery on the hill,
half-filled with men like yourself, Christians in name, will not
support my efforts. Instead, you pursue some pantheistic dream
which compromises Christ's message in a vain attempt to win
favor with all."

As she spoke, about 15 children came respectfully into the
hut, bowed to us, took up chalk and slate and mat, and seated
themselves quietly. Mr. Conway acknowledged their bows with
a nod of his head, and I followed suit, though far from sure that
their bows had been addressed also to me.

"Hugh," she said, "I love you and your associates as brothers, but I sometimes find it difficult to understand or forgive your hostility to God's work."

More children came in and made their bows, and again we responded to them. To Miss Brinklow, Mr. Conway made no response. Perhaps he would have if I hadn't been there.

"You are both welcome to stay to watch for as long as you wish. I shall not be offended when you leave." With that, she turned her full attention to the children, speaking to them in their own language. We stayed for a few minutes to watch her teach. She ran a tight ship, but the kids seemed happy to be there and eager to work. I saw neither fear nor boredom on their faces, and neither impatience nor boredom on hers. After a while, Mr. Conway and I left, as quietly as possible.

Outside, he suggested that we visit one of the fields, and we walked there in silence. No one was in sight, and for a while we stood feasting on the sight of the green fields, leaning against the side of a boulder.

"The customs here are essentially those of any tropical country," he told me. "For the hours of the sun's greatest heat, the people stay inside, eating and napping. The children in Miss Brinklow's class are an exception."

"They grow a lot down here, don't they?"

"And a good thing for us they do, or we'd be on short commons."

"I can't believe it's so hot," I said. We sat a moment in silence. "She's never said any of that before, has she?"

"No."

After a moment more, I said, half to myself, "She's really something."

Mr. Conway caught the note of self-protection, and said immediately, "People like Miss Brinklow are the easiest in the world to mock. All the single-minded absorption in a cause, and that total unconcern for appearance. But I trust you will see something admirable there, as well."

"Oh, sure. But her cause is a little too narrow for me, I'm afraid."

"No doubt, but the fact that she does have a definite cause is something to respect. Or rather, the fact that she has given to that cause not merely words, or money, but her life, and has done so quite cheerfully."

"She put her money where her mouth is."

"Precisely."

"But I still can't buy it. It's too narrow. Did you notice her calling them 'pagans' instead of Buddhists?"

"I noticed."

More silence. Trying to be facetious, I said, "And are you and your friends hostile to God's work?" He made no answer. After a moment, he pushed himself away from the rock and suggested that we go to the village, where I could meet some of his friends among the natives. He said they'd be glad of a diversion during their midday break, and when it was time for them to return to their fields, we could gather up our guides and return to the lamasery.

After a few steps, he said, "I am not hostile to Miss Brinklow's efforts. I *am*, perhaps, a bit hostile to her intent. It would be different if she intended to bring religion to an unreligious people, but she intends to convert people who are already quite religious — people steeped in religion — and merely change the form and other externals."

"I'll bet she wouldn't see it that way."

"Indeed not. She would think the difference between Christianity and other religions the difference between the genuine and the counterfeit. But I cannot see the good in converting Buddhists into Christians, particularly as it tends to isolate the converts, to some extent, from the rest of their society."

"Is that why you wanted me to meet her? To see that kind of attitude first-hand?"

"I merely thought you should meet her for yourself. She is remarkable: sincere, hard-working, intelligent. She does much good. Those qualities forgive much."

I listened with half my mind, the other half still imagining a long solitary climb down a shelf lit only by the moon, using a trail we'd just traversed safely only by roping four men together.

I didn't like that one place on the trail. I looked it over carefully as we made our way back up to the monastery, trying to devise a way to get by it. I thought of anchoring a rope on the uphill side: If I slipped and fell, perhaps the rope would hold, giving me a chance to climb back up and try again. But it looked like a pretty desperate chance. And I couldn't see anything obvious to anchor the rope to. But I didn't have much choice.

Well, then, suppose I got down to the valley in one piece. How would I get up and over onto the altiplano beyond? Mr. Conway would know the way, he'd done it. But obviously I couldn't ask him. And Lo-tsen wasn't there to ask, either.

* 4 *

There came the night of June 5, 1963. Two days before full moon. Enough light, I hoped, to get me safely down the trail. Enough to help me to find the trail up to the altiplano. Enough to get me (with luck) past the guards and up higher into the wilderness of rock where I hoped to hide out, resting, until the following night. I was counting on their vigilance being directed outward rather than inward, but I'd decided that if it came to confrontation I'd try to duck and run rather than let myself be retaken, for certainly after a failed escape attempt I'd never again be given so little supervision. So I reasoned.

I spent the day—and most of the day before—resting, doing as little as possible, sleeping late and going to bed early and napping in between, trying to store up energy the way a battery takes a charge. I shared a last common meal with the others and helped clean up afterward. I surprised myself with the strength of my regrets and my longing to at least say goodbye. And I sat on my bed in my little room—so familiar, where once so strange—and wondered if I could leave a note apologizing for my ingratitude. Finally did, burying it inside a book of Yeats' poetry. Sooner or later they'd find it, and then they'd know. Here, if anywhere, how long it took them to find it would not matter.

Then I changed into my flight suit and boots and lay down for what seemed endless hours for the building to subside into silence.

* 5 *

Finally I made my move. Gathering up my bedroll and canteens and food sack, I went through the doorway into the darkened hall. I knew that there was never an hour when it was safe to assume that everyone was asleep, so I went straight to the nearest outside door. My timing was good: The moon had just risen and I could see the ground, milky and ill-defined but visible. In less than a minute I was making my way along the trail leading down to the valley, placing my feet carefully as much to minimize the sound of my boots on gravel—which sounded appallingly loud in the still night—as to prevent the stumble and sprained ankle that would bring my escape to a sudden end.

No point in making too big a thing of my escape. I made it safely down to the valley, after a hair-raising passage across the one place I'd worried about. Well before I got to the valley floor, I took my arms out of my flight suit, letting its top half hang down from my waist. I wanted to be very careful not to let the valley's heat start a sweat that would freeze when I got up to the altiplano. Traversing the space between the two trails took about fifteen minutes of stealthy reconnaissance, looking both for the trail and for any possible hidden guards. But I saw nobody, and it wasn't too long before I had climbed high enough to need to zip up my flight suit again.

When I got to the top of the trail, I figured the danger of detection was greatest, and for the first and last time in my life I wished that I had had infantry training. I moved literally by inches, in short, quick, well-spaced movements, remembering that motion, more than any combination of color or shape, will attract attention.

I succeeded. I climbed well beyond the level where I knew the guards were posted, and—still carefully—continued for several hours, moving toward the west. When the sun came up and I knew it was safe to sleep (I wasn't likely to freeze in mid-day) I took off my canteen and food bag, wrapped myself in my blanket, and burrowed into unconsciousness.

* 6 *

And awoke, at about midday, to find Mr. Conway sitting not ten feet away, calmly watching as I came to.

Embarrassing situation!

I nodded, and he returned the nod. I sat up, to even the playing field somewhat.

He held up the canteen from which he had been drinking.

One of mine. Perhaps the noise is what woke me up. "I've had a bit of a wait, so I helped myself to some of your tea. A bit strong, but you'd find it bracing, perhaps, if cold."

Well, why not? I picked up the other canteen and took a long drink, my first.

Mr. Conway wouldn't have come alone, and the fact that he'd gotten here so soon told me that I'd been missed, spotted and followed much sooner than I'd expected. In any case if he could track me so could others. Which is what he was silently demonstrating. I knew I was at the end of my rope.

I'd been willing to *risk* exposing Shangri-La, callous though that may seem, but now I could escape only by preventing Mr. Conway from stopping me. Even if he was alone, what was I supposed to do? Knock him down?

A voice deep within cried out that to give in and go back was to betray Marianne—to betray myself. But there were things I could not do even to win my freedom, and knocking Mr. Conway down was one of them. I resigned myself to going back. Mr. Conway and I talked, on our way back down and up, and I have always valued that long day's talk, for of all those who live at Shangri-La, he was the one who had done more or less exactly what I had done.

Because I returned with him that day, I am now 43 years old chronologically, but physically I look and feel 26. I am still not even quite into my prime of life. And Marianne, at 41 (assuming she is still in the world) is a middle-aged woman, probably a mother. Perhaps a grandmother. And I lost her irretrievably, 17 years ago. Already half her best years—maybe more—are lost to me, lived without me. If I left here this very moment, it would be too late. Life kept us from each other, and there was never a thing we could do about it.

* 7 *

Mr. Barnard took his cigar from his lips, blew out a mouthful of smoke, and looked over at me. "You maybe can't believe it," he said casually, "but I know how it feels. Happens to everybody, just about, one way or another. The thing is to get through the worst of it."

I didn't move my eyes from the mountain across the valley,

its snow incandescent-white in the noon sun. When he said no more, I nodded, equally casually. After a moment I tapped the ash from my cigar onto the courtyard ground.

Finally I had to return his glance. I nodded again, still casual.

"Trouble is, you think I'm too old to remember what it feels like, being young. But it ain't something you ever forget."

"I suppose."

"How long did you say you been going together?"

I shifted position in my chair. "A while. I met her just before Christmas, 1957."

Casually, very casually. "Met her in college, did you say?"

"Yeah. My senior year."

"Long time, for you. A fifth of your life."

I said nothing. We sat and smoked our cigars and looked out at the mountain.

* 8 *

When God closes the door, he opens a window. That's what my mother used to say. Substitute Mr. Conway for God (or consider him to be acting for God, *in loco parentis*), and that's about what happened. Mr. Conway didn't threaten, or reproach, or warn, or request, or advise—then or since. Instead, he opened another door and stepped aside, so that I might enter or not, as I was able.

PART TWO

Another World

August, 1979

Chapter Seven.

Experience

My room — my cell — has one window, facing south. In daytime I see the mountain, but at night the mountain is only a finger pointing to the moon. And it is the moon that I see in my imagination, by day as well as night: The moon, full silver, giving itself a halo of deep blue against the black sky, sailing clear and calm, unmoved by the tragedy and farce below.

At this great height, air is thin. Nights obscured by snowstorms are rare; cloud cover so thick as to block out the moon is scarcely less so. In the many years I have been here, I cannot recall a night whose moon was lost to cloud cover. At most, I have seen layers of cloud illumined from behind, great uneven porous blankets of grey, shining into one halo of light. But mostly the nights are clear with the light of the moon in its phases.

Our discipline requires monks to rise at 2 a.m., but I long ago accustomed myself to rise before that—at about 12:30 or so, I suppose, though I have no clock by which to measure—so that I could meditate without stealing time from prayer. I could take time from daylight hours, but the buildings are never so silent— so death-still—as just before the beginnings of our day.

Mr. Conway knows, of course. He explicitly gave permission years ago, saying he thought it a very good practice. "But what impulse brings you to ask my permission for an action performed entirely within your own room?"

"I just thought it would be better."

The Conway smile, wry and affectionate. "But why today? You've done this 17 months at least."

And so I had, though I'd told no one. How had he known? Well, how did he know anything? Had he not known everything important since I'd dropped in on them?

If he had objected to my midnight meditations, I would have had to give them up, even if he never said another word. Voluntary obedience is given freely or not at all. But I would have missed them sorely. Even on nights of the new moon, my awareness of the moon's presence overcame my inability to see it.

Nobody can look the sun in the eye, and the stars are (seemingly) too remote to call forth from me a sense of personal relation. But the moon, which is so much closer, so obviously a silent, solitary traveller, I know like a friend. This same moon, passing beyond the mountain that lies opposite the mountain on which I and the rest of the monastery perch, looks down also on those other parts of the Earth that I can see no more. My mother, if she is still alive, looks up at the moon, perhaps. My father and brothers and cousins—whoever are still alive—they may see it hanging over the fields as they make their way home from a long afternoon's hunting; or they may see it shining pale in the early morning, before fuller daylight fades it away. Except for the sun (which nobody can gaze at) and the stars (so seemingly remote), the moon is the last bit of human life my family and I still share, a last reminder that we still live on the same planet. At least, that's one way of seeing it.

But even this link, frail as it is through distance and muteness, is but a one-way link. I look up at the silent silver circle, or oval, or semi-circle, or sickle, and know that others of my family half a world away may perhaps have looked up at it a few hours before. Or maybe not. It is a matter of probabilities. But they, looking up at the moon, almost certainly do not think of me. Even a mother, whose love never allows her to forget a child however long after its death, has no particular reason to associate that child with the moon when she has no reason to suspect that the child is still alive to see it.

But then—and it is sometimes hard to remember—neither my family nor most folks back "in civilization" spend much time looking at the moon. Too many alternatives competing for attention. I was—how old?—20 at least, before I fully realized that the moon rises and sets, that it regularly changes course across the sky, that its very size alters with time, now seemingly nearer, now farther away. As a boy I thought of the moon, when I did think of it, as I saw it on the calendar: full moon, quarter-moon, new moon. That a new moon couldn't be seen, that there were other clear-cut phases such as crescent or gibbous, that the moon appears in daylight not seldom but often, I was never told and never observed. My father's farm was on the outskirts of a city of 35,000, and so we lived (not knowing the difference) with the constant nighttime phenomenon of skyglow: background light reflecting from streetlights and electric signs and the lights of houses. We never saw the stars clearly, though we did not realize it. But the moon was there. Why did we pay so little attention to the moon?

Useless rhetorical question, that: Why not ask why we paid so little attention to so *much* of the world around us?

My father, for instance, had grown up closer to the natural world than I did. He had fed farm animals; as a child had plowed with horses; as a boy had had to keep the family firebox filled with firewood as one of his chores. His own father all of his life planted according to the light and dark of the moon. You'd think my father would have been instinctively aware of his ties to the land, which means close to the weather, which means close to the elements, which means, as well, close to the sun and moon.

But he wanted to be modern, as his father was not modern, and so he put his faith in fertilizers and handbooks. Tractors and television and modern life in general took him—took all of us—a long way from the rhythms underlying the world. And it was only God's grace, certainly no will of mine, that brought me here and relieved me of everything I knew.

* 2 *

What drove me to begin writing this was the sudden, disruptive presence of our new guest. Mr. Conway and Mr. Barnard have delegated me to deal with him, for the very good reason that I am (a) the youngest here, and (b) like Mr. Dennis Corbin, an American and a pilot. I am, therefore, presumed to be the person who will seem least strange and threatening to Corbin (and also, I suspect, I am presumed to be the person least likely to be disturbed by his company). I cannot fault the logic, and certainly they have a lot more experience than I in such matters, but already the negatives are considerable.

For one thing, the mere presence of an outsider—someone who, just a few weeks ago, was in the world beyond the altiplano—has kicked up memories, and with them feelings and hungers, long dormant. He mentions that he'd once been stationed in Dover, Delaware—sending my mind caroming from thought to thought. Delaware, across the river from New Jersey and Vineland. . .the farm. . .canoeing on the Maurice and Cohansey Rivers with my friend Ed. . .or riding around the back roads in his pickup, looking for deer. . .making our way in a skiff, looking for eagles' nests in the swamp country south of Dividing Creek. . .tramping through the woods with my younger brother Tommy one brilliant fall day. . .Thanksgiving dinners at Grandmom Napoli's house, back in the years before she got sick and died. . .her children and their husbands and wives. . .13 young cousins around the long holiday tables joined end to end and extended through the dining room into the front hall. . .Fourth-of-July get-togethers on outdoor grills. . .one particular fourth when it rained and we moved the cookout inside Grandmom's garage. . .the almost forgotten taste of hamburgers and hot dogs and marshmallows. . .joining the crowds at the football stadium when the time came for the fireworks. . .birthday parties with cousins from both sides. . .Grandmom Chiari's farmhouse kitchen and the cookie jar in her pantry, always full. . .anise cookies. . .knot cookies. . .Grandmom pressing cookies on you as though they were something that was good for you but you didn't eat enough of. . . .

And as I sit here mentioning the memories that came back, others press in on me, like the day (it must have been in the spring of 1947, because I was already 10 but not yet 11) when I first got to drive the tractor for real. Dad and my older brother Angelo sat on the planter behind the tractor, putting in tomato transplants, and I guided the tractor at a constant slow speed down the row, feeling very responsible and very grown up. At the end of every row, I'd put in the clutch and take it out of gear and Angelo would climb up, raise the planter, turn the tractor into the next row, lower the planter, take the tractor out of gear again, re-seat himself on the planter next to dad, and pick up another clump of transplants. Dad would give the word and off we'd go down another row. Without me Angelo would have had to drive and dad would have had to put in both rows at once. It would have been a lot slower. So I knew I'd been a genuine help, and went home feeling like I'd passed an initiation of sorts, not that I knew anything of such concepts at the time.

Well, there you are: One memory leads to another, and they flood in stronger than the life around me. They are all alive within me—clearer, in some ways, than when I lived among them, but, as Yeats said in another context, all changed, changed utterly. The passage of years is water flowing over stone, eroding all feelings, whether good, bad, sharp, sweet, until finally only memories survive. Some we alter deliberately, others unconsciously. The most painful are remembered only as memories of memories, toned down, muted, until tolerable.

And everything Dennis Corbin says triggers another cascade of memories and associations. Not his fault, but his doing. I wouldn't say I'd been repressing all these memories, but certainly they weren't an active part of my present life.

They are active now.

Portions of my life I'd mostly forgotten; connections I'd never made; details I'd never consciously noted. It throws me off-balance.

And then too, although Dennis Corbin is 16 years younger than I am, and comes from Southern California—which you'd think would give us about as much in common as if he'd arrived straight from Mars—he and I seem to instinctively understand each other.

Well, no, that's not even close to being right. He doesn't begin to understand me, any more than he could understand anyone here. For one thing, he thinks I'm near his age, because, since I was 26 when I came here in 1962, that's how old I look now. (How am I supposed to explain *that* to him? With time, I suppose.)

Still, we do have surprising amounts in common. We're countrymen (*paisans*, my father would say) and that's the same common bond I have with Mr. Barnard, even though his America was of another era. Somehow countrymen come out of a shared experience that leads them to see the world a little differently. Mr. Conway and Mr. Herrick, as Englishmen, sense the same thing between themselves, I'm sure.

Being ex-flyers (though Corbin probably doesn't yet realize that he's "ex-") is another bond, as is military service, which is something I share with Mr. Conway and not with Mr. Barnard, even though Mr. Conway's service was in wartime and mine wasn't.

But of course the most profound experience—this time and place, inner and outer—I cannot even hint at, now or for some time to come.

* 3 *

God opened a door, and I, after some hesitation, walked through. And as I sit here on the other side of that door, writing—a brilliant serene quarter-moon outside lighting the sky and the face of Karakal—I realize how difficult it will be to describe this new place I've come to.

Even to recreate the sequence of events that led me here is difficult enough. As my attention was redirected inward, external events came to mean less and less, and I kept no record. I suppose I could talk to Mr. Conway, and to Sunnie, and to certain others, to refresh my memory, but I find myself reluctant to do that. The facts that will prove most relevant will be those that call attention to themselves—else others would.

And now I suppose my constant arguments with Corbin— here five weeks now, though it seems like more—are beginning to spill onto these pages. For I am very much aware, from dealing with that stubborn and unresponsive person, how very little sympathy my present way of understanding life would receive in the world outside. Although I too once believed in "luck" and "chance" and "accident"—to an extent I'd nearly forgotten until Mr. Conway set me to writing this long memoir—still there was a difference between the way I saw the world then and the way Dennis Corbin, and presumably his generation, sees it now.

In practice I saw the world through materialist eyes, it's true, but still, my Catholic childhood had left me a watertight mental compartment in which I retained an idea of God, and prayer, and a hidden dimension to life. I believed in science and technology and Progress—yet I retained an innate skepticism inherited from generations of Italian peasants in general, and from my spectacularly skeptical father in particular. I assumed that America was the model on which would be constructed the civilization of the future—yet I did not totally dismiss the cautions of history. (In youth I had come to identify with English history, via Winston Churchill, and where were the English now?)

In short, my mental constitution had its own checks and balances, and I cannot believe that I presented the monks of Shangri-La with quite the challenge presented by Mr. Dennis Corbin, who apparently suffers no doubts, is open to no argument, and recognizes no beliefs, expertise or achievements other than his own.

A sore point, Mr. Dennis Corbin. He's my baby, but he and I were instinctively at odds from the moment he opened his eyes in our infirmary. I can understand why he might blame us for the crash that brought him here, but, after all, insofar as we were to blame, it was only because we were what we were. And we—*I* particularly—*did* save his life. You'd think he would bear it in mind. But apparently our existence, and what it implies to him, is too threatening. Has the world changed so much since 1962? Or is he a very unrepresentative sample? The latter, I hope.

In fact, I suppose the gap between us is mostly explained by three specific differences: He is many years younger; he hasn't spent 17 years among companions and knowledge and a reality to be found nowhere else on earth; and he hasn't received special training.

Particularly the last.

* **4** *

By August, 1964, enough time had passed since my escape for me to know beyond doubt that the inhabitants of what must become my world did not hold it against me that I had been willing to jeopardize their world to try to regain mine.

Mr. Conway's sole comment, delivered on the altiplano, had been that I should consider my escape as an experiment demonstrating how difficult it is to elude unnoticed surveillance. The Chinese, he had said, were known to be at least equally vigilant, although their surveillance relied on different methods; I should consider my life saved. His logic was unassailable. (Only later did I notice everything his brief statement implied.) And in any case, I had instantly given up any idea of regaining the outside world when I had opened my eyes to find him watching me.

The others never referred to my little hike directly or indirectly, unless I mentioned it first, which I soon felt no need to do. Only with Sunnie, sometimes, would I talk of Marianne, allowing myself to feel something of the loneliness and the sense of the irretrievable passage of time. And often Mr. Barnard and I, after listening to the BBC news, would find ourselves going back again to life in rural and urban America as one or the other of us had experienced it. Otherwise, I let thoughts of the outside world sink below my horizon, and kept busier than I would have had to, deliberately doing more than my share of the innumerable chores that go into maintaining a place. (Just hauling up the wood we need is an undertaking that leads us to live to a rhythm somewhat like that of the animals: particularly busy storing up in summer, then very slack in winter. This rhythm I'd seen close enough, growing up on my father's farm. It fit very comfortably.)

I thought to take this life one day at a time, following my father's advice on getting through any apparently endless chore. "Just work one row at a time, George," he'd say. "Don't do the other rows till we get there." One day early in the winter of 1964, I thought of us following the sweet-potato digger, working bent over, picking up the sweets from the sifted ground and packing them into bushel baskets. I had to smile: Getting through one day at a time in Shangri-La might have its difficulties—its pain, even—but at least it couldn't get much worse than some of the truly numbing aspects of farmwork.

* 5 *

I stood at the window of Mr. Conway's cell, watching the sun withdraw its light from the valley in the fleet sunset that is all we see in our low latitude. (Lhasa, for comparison, is at about the latitude of Cairo, Egypt.) It created a striking contrast: Below, the ink-black valley; at our own level, fast-gathering darkness, with the glittering white reflection retreating up the mountain wall far to the east; above us, the lightest part of the sky, as yet undimmed. When the last bit of light was gone, Mr. Conway lit a lamp, and suddenly, quietly, on that August day in 1964, he was asking me what was wrong. I had been here then 21 months, living the routine I have tried to sketch. I said nothing was wrong, and he continued to sit quietly watching me until I realized that maybe there *was* something.

"It isn't much, really. Something about that sunset. It's beautiful, I wish they lasted longer, but something about it disturbs me. I don't know what."

"How do you feel about the dark, George?"

I shrugged, I remember. "Not much, one way or the other. When it gets dark, you turn on a light."

Mr. Conway smiled. "Do I hear your father speaking?"

I gave out a short sharp bark of surprised, delighted laughter. "Yes! You do! That's dad speaking, exactly!" I laughed again, a vision of my matter-of-fact, one-thing-then-the-next father suddenly fresh before my mind's eye.

"So when it gets dark, you turn on a light. And is that all that darkness means to you, George? An opportunity to dispel it?"

Some shooting-star of a thought flashed by, too fast for me to make it out. Whatever it was, it left me uneasy. "I don't know," I said, hoping to dismiss the subject. Mr. Conway had called me into his cell for a reason. What was it?

"Do you see? That sunset stirred deeper feelings than you realized. The mere mention of the significance of sunset, of the coming of darkness, leaves you restless. And there behind you is the nighttime sky. Does that mean nothing to you but a backdrop for a lantern, or a campfire?"

Still leaning against the wall, I shrugged. "I guess I'm not much of a poet."

"We are all poets, George, only few of us write verse. We all have the ability to respond to the movements of the world. Some are inspired to write verse, some to sing, some merely to expand silently like a flower."

I smiled skeptically. "Mr. Barnard?"

"Do you think he did not respond to the world? How could he have become a successful man of business but by some deep attunement to the world's cycles? And he *was* successful, you know, quite successful, until the world changed more quickly than he could adjust to."

"Mr. Conway, I'm very fond of Mr. Barnard, and I can see

that he has a lot of fine qualities, but I can't quite see him writing poetry and watching sunsets in between pyramiding utility stocks."

The twinkle in his eye showed how my irony had struck him. It was much the sort of comment he might have made. "One might argue that a greater awareness might have enabled him to evade disaster."

"Watching sunsets?"

"Sensing rhythms."

"I don't get what you mean."

"No, but I fancy Henry would. Ask him, some time, about the rhythms of securities exchanges and commodities markets and such. His life in business and finance provided him with graphic experience of the cyclical rhythms underlying our life."

He motioned me to the cell's other chair—obviously another of Mr. Barnard's (really quite polished) productions. "George, I ask you to consider: How did I know that our brief sunset stirred feelings deep within you? You were scarcely aware of it yourself."

I didn't have to think very hard. "You watch people," I said. "You watch movements, and the expressions on faces, and you *listen*. You hear people's tone of voice, and hesitations, and things like that."

"All right. But is that all?"

∗ 6 ∗

My father taught me—silently, by osmosis, as was his way— a deep distrust. Of the complementary errors of naive credulity and naive *in*credulity, he instilled in me a deep wariness of the former, and only a faint echo of the latter. It's better to believe too little than too much. So he believed and so he lived; so, inevitably, he taught his children, while we had little or no defense. Unfortunately, he never realized—or anyway never conveyed—that you can go quite as far wrong by closing yourself to new ideas as by rushing to accept every new idea without reserve. Those who resist new ideas—like me, like most of my family, and even more like Mr. Dennis Corbin—naturally remain captive to *old* ideas, including a lot of unexamined baggage that came with the territory: the things that were generally accepted when they were growing up. And if you have been raised to react with instinctive hostility to any new way of viewing the world, it's pretty hard to escape from the prison-bars of your assumptions. In fact, it can be nearly impossible for you even to believe that the bars exist.

Now, by the time Mr. Conway called me into his monk's cell and used my reaction to the sunset as his excuse to offer me their training, I had been there long enough to have some of my assumptions shaken. So when he asked me if close observation entirely explained how he'd known what was going through my mind, I knew what he was getting at, if I didn't really know how to answer.

Actually, I suppose I was a little bit afraid to answer. I didn't know how much I wanted to know, or how much I wanted to admit to knowing. "I suppose you want me to say that sometimes it seems like the people around here read minds," I said reluctantly. [Even putting it in a way that set the greatest distance between the idea and any sense that I *believed* in the idea, I felt like a grown man admitting that he believed in ghosts, or was afraid of the dark.]

Mr. Conway didn't let me slide by. "*Is* that how it seems to you?"

"Well— [even more reluctantly] the thought has crossed my mind from time to time. Mr. Barnard comes awfully close sometimes to answering things I haven't said. And Sunnie, in particular, seems to know an awful lot about what I'm feeling, even when I work pretty hard to cover it up. [And am I surprised to hear myself come out with *that* sentence!] But I guess I don't *really* believe it; they just pay close attention, I guess. Like you."

Mr. Conway nodded, listening, considering. "Anything in the nature of 'mind over matter' is as alien to you as it once was to me, I take it. Speculative at best, absurd at worst?"

"That's about it," I said, relieved. "It's something it would be nice to believe in, but I don't see any reason to think it really exists."

"Particularly," he said dryly, "in light of your extensive research into the subject."

Which brought me up short. Unexamined assumptions.

"No point in arguing possibilities, George. But you might, sometime, find it diverting to consider the subject of telepathy in

121

connection with such phenomena as mass hysteria and fads and [a small, wry smile] political gatherings. And you might think of it not as conscious, directed action but as unconscious reception. Not reading, but receiving hunches. Intuition. Dreams. Interesting connections may suggest themselves."

* 7 *

However, as Mr. Conway pointed out, in such matters belief meant little; experience, everything. He offered me the experience.

"Your life had some purpose in bringing you to this place at this time. Your life's circumstances are a unique opportunity. Everyone's are. Your life is the puzzle that has been set for you, and your life's challenge is to decipher the puzzle's meaning by living it, by growing into it, until you *become* the pattern."

I said I didn't understand what he meant, and in any case didn't even *see* a pattern. He assured me that no one ever did, except in retrospect. "Do you think God would set you so easy a challenge that it could be understood in advance? He has greater respect for you than that." He stated quite flatly that the pattern was there to be found, and that no one's life was ever meaningless, however it might look from within or without.

"In your own case, you have been afforded an opportunity you would never have sought out. Your life outside these walls has ended; you have accepted that. You have no one for whom you are responsible. You have no cares that cannot be accepted by others. Duties and responsibilities and distractions have been lifted from your shoulders. You are free to do as much as your courage and honesty and stamina allow you to do. Not many people have been offered so favorable an opportunity."

But—I asked him—what was the point? No, I didn't know what my purpose in life was, but so what? If it had a purpose, wouldn't I find it in the living of it? If not, what was the use searching for it? I wasn't all that interested in the question of mental telepathy and such things anyway. What was in it for me?

He made a tent of his hands. "I don't want to mislead you. Powers are not my focus, yet the path I would start you on leads to insights and abilities that many would call magical. You know already that I can read your mind more easily than you yourself can. You will find yourself suggesting thoughts to others, and knowing their thoughts before they do. You may learn to say the words to others that touch their deepest well-springs of emotion. As you become more whole, more all-of-a-piece, you will acquire a personal weight, a gravity, that exacts respect and even deference from others. You will learn, among other things, the totally unsatisfactory nature of words. [And if I hadn't learned that lesson long ago, this long exercise of writing would have brought the lesson home!] You may go well beyond these gifts, to more important things: mental recall, emotional stability, compassion. The working of miracles."

I had been watching him all the time he spoke, but my attention redoubled when he said that. "You really mean that," I said.

"Yes, I really mean it. You'll find it one of your chief obstacles, perhaps."

I didn't understand.

"This is where many fail. Miracles are a great distraction. The point of your training would be, not to give you these gifts of the spirit, however desirable they may be, but to help you tame the drunken monkey, and sober it, and put it to better use."

"I guess I still don't know what you're talking about."

"I'm sure you don't. You've never noticed the monkey's existence. But soon you will, and then you will understand."

"Well, I'm glad, because right now I sure don't. Am I being particularly dense, or haven't you gotten to the punch line yet?"

He smiled. "The punch line is that I would like to show you how to save yourself and others."

"From the fires of hell?"

"From the fires of self-involvement and isolation from the world, which are perhaps hotter flames, more continuously stoked and assiduously tended."

Again I didn't understand. What could be farther removed from the world than a monastery on a mountain in remotest Tibet?

"We each have a unique point of view of the world, George. That is what we have been given to work with. As we develop that gift, we make our contribution."

"To . . ."

"To the human race. To life. Each of us is given something unique, to enrich the whole."

Thinking about some of my fellow airmen—not to mention some of my college fraternity brothers!—I smiled. "Do you really think *everybody* has something to contribute?"

"I don't think it, I know it."

"Even if they did, how would they do it? You don't want everybody writing autobiographies, I imagine."

"Your Thoreau said truly, somewhere in *Walden*, that more is published than is ever printed. We publish our lives to everyone we touch, George, whether we would or not."

"We do?"

"Who could live out his life without affecting those around him? And, less obviously, we are all part of mankind, and our experiences and sensations cannot fail to be recorded upon the memory of the human organism."

"Ah, the racial unconscious," I said. "I always thought that was only a metaphor."

Mr. Conway looked pleased. "You are familiar with the work of Dr. Jung?"

"Only superficially. I've read his book *Modern Man in Search of a Soul*."

"A pleasure we have not had. Someday, after your training has progressed beyond its initial stages, you would place us in your debt by reconstructing it for us."

"Oh, I couldn't! It was a couple years ago that I read it."

A smile. "Everything you have ever experienced is within you. You could retrieve it all now, if you knew how. When the time comes, you will be able to do it with far less trouble than you can imagine."

"Tell me how, and I'll do it right this minute."

That statement delighted him. "If it could be *told*, George, don't you think the instructions would have been written down long ago? I can guide you along the way, but I cannot simply tell you. Like so much else, it is beyond words."

[I thought at the time that perhaps Mr. Conway was exaggerating the promise, but sure enough, in 1975 I was able to give the monastery, as a sort of general Christmas present, a substantially accurate transcript of *Modern Man in Search of a Soul*. Mr. Herrick, in particular, expressed great gratitude.]

Mr. Conway repeated himself (as he did only rarely) as a form of underlining. "Beyond words. But I intend to escort you as other escorted me, and as you no doubt will later escort others."

"Here? Doesn't everybody here already know everything I'm supposed to learn?"

"By no means. Different people have different gifts, different tasks. Also, they progress at different rates. I judge that you would progress quite rapidly. If you are willing. . ."

A pause, which Mr. Conway showed no disposition to fill. "Well," I said at length, "I suppose it'll help pass the time. I'm not making any promises about how good a student I'm going to be, but if you're willing to take me on, I'll give it the old college try."

* 8 *

I had committed myself to a strenuous routine. I would awaken at 2 a.m.; would engage in silent meditation until a 6 a.m. meal; would receive instruction from Mr. Conway for two hours; would read passages in works he would provide and would think about what I had read. I would meditate some more until the noon meal. After noon I would meditate, spend two hours in intense physical exercise, and then would be in bed and asleep by 6 p.m., ready to be awakened again eight hours later. Mr. Conway assured me that the regimen would be neither so easy as to be boring nor so difficult as to be beyond my strength. In any case he would be there observing—or rather, participating—and could adjust the routine as necessary. He told me that the routine he had outlined was far more taxing than that followed by the monks of Shangri-La—and assured me that I would find the results worth the effort. I asked when we should start. He smiled, and I knew he was asking: Why wait? Now is the time.

* 9 *

I was in bed by 6 p.m., keyed up as I had not been since the night before my induction into the Air Force. As then, I told myself that I could handle anything they could throw at me. As then, I wished I had a better idea of what I was letting myself in for. He had told me I was to bring no food or drink to my room.

125

"Were you to bring even a glass of water, you would find that your thoughts soon tended more toward the glass than toward your true objective. Right now, when you are at the very beginning, you must eliminate every indulgence, as the only way to eliminate distractions. Later, different rules will apply." I wondered what the different rules would be.

I lay awake a long time, staring at the blackness above. I knew I should sleep, but my body just laughed at me and said it was far too early. I said we'd have to get up early, and it said, in return, that we could worry about that when the time came. I knew better than to argue: I've never been able to force myself to sleep. So I made myself lie quietly, concentrating on not wearing myself out tossing and turning. I knew a few tricks for luring sleep, but tonight they wouldn't work, so there I was. After a while I let the thoughts flow freely, and followed where they led.

For a while, they moved back and forth, retracing my time here. Meeting various people. Mr. Barnard's story of the monastery since 1931. The differences from the story that was told in *Lost Horizon*. Sunnie's story of her introduction to the place. Mr. Conway's experiences in the trenches of northern France.

Something sent me back to happy days in the U-2, soaring high above everything, monitoring instruments with half my mind and day-dreaming with the other half. Not so long ago, but already seeming like scenes from somebody else's life.

I thought about Marianne. I had resigned myself long ago to the fact that every so often, be it at intervals of weeks or months or days, my thoughts would return to her. I found it amazing that certain types of pain seemed absolutely unblunted by the passage of any amount of time.

Some college memories came back, including one which presented itself with great insistence: two of my friends, David and Lou, trying to persuade me to join them in playing with hypnosis. David had learned, somewhere, how to do what he called hypnotic regressions, supposedly bringing back people's memories of past lives. I'd wanted no part of it, considering it occult foolishness. [Was that what I was getting involved with now? I brushed the uneasiness aside. If I got in too deep, I could always quit.]

I hadn't thought about David and Lou for some time. David had whole-heartedly believed in reincarnation. Well, by now he'd had years to find out if he'd been right. He'd been killed in a car crash in '58, about a year and a half after we got out of school. It was an odd thought: If he was right about reincarnation, he might already be back in another body somewhere.

I wondered, lying there, what Lou had done with his life. Married, probably, and raising a family.

Which, of course, brought me right back to thoughts of Marianne, as usual.

Chapter Eight.

The Monkey

Mr. Conway's hand on my shoulder brought me awake, and I got out of bed, shivering in the mid-night cold. One advantage to wearing robes: it wasn't hard to get dressed. Seeing his face by the flickering oil lamp, I got a sense of the experience—not to use the embarrassing word "wisdom"—concealed behind that youthful face. Our silence reinforced the impression.

He worked with me to find a comfortable position for the meditation exercise, telling me (to my surprise) that I would not have to torture myself into the cross-legged lotus position favored by yogis. "Without years of preparation, you would be unable to sit for long with legs crossed. The pain would be intolerable."

"When I did a little yoga in college, they seemed to think the lotus position was essential," I said.

"I don't believe in doing things the hard way," he said briefly. "How long did you study yoga?"

I admitted that the yoga, to me, was only a secondary aspect of a jiu-jitsu course I took.

"A pity you did not continue with yoga."

"How do you know I didn't?"

Again, that smile. "You wouldn't move as you do, and you wouldn't jump around mentally quite the way you do. Come, now, let's get to work. I've brought this bench Henry made long ago. It should serve."

The bench was about ten inches wide and six inches high. He had me sit on the bench with legs crossed on the floor in front of me, and satisfied himself that I could do so without pain.

"You may experience some difficulty in keeping your spine straight over time," he said. "If you do, merely relax for a moment and then resume position."

"It's all right to break position like that?"

"Better that, and back to work, than hours spent trying to ignore back pain, accomplishing nothing." A smile. "But don't start spending your time deciding whether you need to relax for a moment. Concentrate."

He then proceeded easily and naturally to sit on the floor and cross his legs, tucking each foot upon the opposite thigh. Almost before I could absorb what he was doing, he was sitting with his back bolt-upright, his hands folded one inside the other, placed on his lap. His eyes were almost, but not entirely closed. And there we sat. It was time to try following the instructions Mr. Conway had given me.

The instructions were simplicity itself. Experience immediately demonstrated that not everything that is simple is easy. All I had to do—to try to do—was to keep my mind entirely blank, rejecting any efforts of my mind to pump in thoughts, reveries, daydreams, speculations, fantasies. . . .

All I had to do. Try it. Try sitting quietly, without external distractions, holding your mind still. Try maintaining consciousness while denying it the right to manufacture images to be conscious *of.* Try it for five minutes, and then imagine keeping up the effort for four hours—only 240 minutes, after all. I think you'll be surprised to learn what I was up against.

It sounds like such an easy trick, and it proves to be so frustrating. If there's a more graphic illustration of how little in control of our minds we are, I haven't heard of it. I started off thinking it would be fairly simple. Within the first ten minutes I lost the stillness probably 30 times, and I began to realize that I was in for a harder struggle than I had expected.

Just for a few seconds, I would clear the decks, and everything would be in precarious equilibrium, with noisy intruders banished below. Then, a second's inattention and I would, in a sense, "wake up" to realize that some fantasy had led me down the garden path. Or, more frustrating, I would attain a moment of quiescence, and suddenly would fully realize it, and would be filled with a burst of elation and self-congratulation—which of course ended and negated the achievement.

"Well," I'd think, "I didn't expect success the first time. I'll just have to work at it." And I would realize that this noble resolve was itself a thought—and so forth.

I suppose you could have much the same kind of fun by

spending your time slipping off a floating log into ice-cold water, and climbing back dripping wet and freezing, to try again, knowing even as you tried to balance that it wouldn't be long before you would be back in the water. And knowing that your expectation of a dunking would help dunk you.

And this is how I spent those long pre-dawn hours of that first day. I would cheat occasionally, stealing looks at Mr. Conway's untroubled face to see if he was still in position, which he always was. I wondered if he could see me through those slitted eyes. I guessed not, but I wouldn't have been surprised if he had suddenly said something to make me aware that he knew I was having trouble keeping my concentration. I wondered if his own concentration was as simple and unbroken as it appeared from outside, or if his level still included struggle.

Long before this first session was over, I had evolved an analogy (which activity in itself was a breach of the concentration I was supposed to be developing and maintaining): I decided that the mind was like a ticker-tape machine, endlessly spouting quotations whether you wanted them or not. My job was to turn off the main switch, or pull the plug.

I wondered if Mr. Conway would approve the analogy—and realized that to mention it would be to tell him that, so far at least, I had failed.

I went back to the beginning. Achieved concentration for a moment or two, lost it in a trickle, then a flood, of random associations. Thinking about *anything* was far easier than thinking about *nothing*. I started to wonder how long it would take me to attain the kind of control over the stock-ticker that Mr. Conway wanted. Caught myself and sought blankness of mind. Certainly Mr. Barnard would approve of the analogy, I thought. And remembered to clear my mind. And reminded myself to mention it to Mr. Barnard. And cleared my mind again. And was distracted. And cleared it again. And was distracted again. For four hours.

At 6 a.m. we heard the gong resounding through the buildings, calling the monks to their morning meal. Mr. Conway opened his eyes, arose without a hint of stiffness in his joints, and lent me an arm to lean on while I got to my feet.

"Oh, my aching back!" I said as I got up. "I don't see why you aren't crippled for life."

He smiled. "One soon gets accustomed to it. The monks schedule a certain amount of yoga daily, if only to improve suppleness and assist circulation."

We moved quickly down the hall to the refectory, I as eager for food as if I were back in basic training. It was only 6 a.m., but I felt like I had already put in a hard day's work moving heavy machinery.

By the time we got there, the room was already half full. We got our food and sat with Mr. Barnard and Mr. Herrick, toward the middle of a long table.

"How's the new recruit?" Mr. Barnard asked. "Achieve enlightenment yet?"

I shook my head silently, a little depressed by the contrast between his cheerful words and my own sorry performance so far. I suppose I expected his irreverence to be met with disapproval, or with strained tolerance, but Mr. Conway and Mr. Herrick chuckled, instead.

"This is not one of your famous American land-grant colleges," Mr Herrick said to him. "I doubt he's ready for his certificate quite yet."

"However," Mr. Conway said, apparently gravely, "being an American, George will no doubt learn in one month what others of us required years to learn."

"And then require three more years to return to the beginning and get it right," Mr. Herrick said, laughing.

"That's all right," Mr. Barnard said complacently. "*Being* an American, in *six* years he'll have the whole darn course of study revised, and it'll turn out you can enlighten the whole blamed valley."

"I see the vision before me," Mr. Herrick said, putting down his spoon and pointing as though reading words on the wall. "In great illuminated signs, cut into the rock walls, I see it: 'Achieve infinite compassion. Also, buy Barnard's cigars.'"

"George Chiari's Spiritual Correspondence School," Mr. Conway suggested. "Enlightenment for all, no waiting."

"Time tested, over three weeks' experience," Mr. Herrick said.

As so often before, I marvelled at the playful high spirits of the monks at table, almost as if in deliberate compensation for any excess of seriousness in their day's routine. I concentrated on my meal, and wondered if I would ever get to the point of *enjoying* tsampa.

"George is pretty quiet this morning," Mr. Barnard said. "Maybe he is farther along than you think, Conway. You don't suppose he's going to achieve Buddha-hood right here at the table, do you?"

"Not on this diet, I guess," I said. Not a side-splitter, but they laughed, and I saw Mr. Conway's nod of approval, and I concluded that for some reason too much seriousness was to be avoided. At any rate it was clear that I was not going to be allowed to discuss the morning's session during the meal as I had hoped. So I decided, sensibly, to save it.

* 2 *

Mr. Conway sat across from me in the little study. "Now you have had your first experience with the drunken monkey," he said, smiling.

"It's unbelievable!" I cried. "I just couldn't hold onto it."

"You will, with persistence. I did. Others did. Success does not come easily, to anyone, but it does come, to those who persist."

"It's going to be a long fight, I can tell."

"Not necessarily. Much depends upon your will and your innate energy level. But you have taken the first step: You have recognized, for the first time, that you, yourself—your essence, if you will, your soul—are not the same as the thoughts and random associations that flow through your mind."

I moved a hand in a gesture deprecating what I had accomplished in the earlier session.

"Before you began, George, you weren't even aware of the existence of that unceasing chattering machinery. Now you have begun to bring it under control. This is the first step."

"And the second?"

"The second is to pass beyond resolve, into accomplishment."

He proceeded to quiz me on the morning's successes and failures, and to offer suggestions—disappointingly few—on how to improve. Then he talked to me for some while on the nature of the mind and the relation between the mind that perceives and the object that is perceived. His objective, he said, was to present the subject in an intellectual way, since my mind was constantly looking for meat to chew. I asked him (having told him my analogy) if feeding my mind more ideas wouldn't just encourage the stock ticker, but he told me not to worry about it. He said my mind would in any case seize any excuse to ratiocinate, and that it was less a matter of adding to the stock-ticker's energy supply than of using that energy to convey and mull useful information. My subconscious mind would work at assimilating the new knowledge even as I worked to keep my conscious mind blank. "Indeed, your subconscious mind will function all the better for the lack of interference from your conscious mind."

He then proceeded to begin the long and interesting process of filling me with the basic material behind a different point of view—a new way of seeing, as he put it. When he paused, I waited for him to continue, but he said that two hours was enough. I was amazed. It had seemed twenty minutes.

After a trip to the facilities, we returned to my room. Mr. Conway handed me a sheet of paper, saying I was to read these Buddhist scriptures and ponder them till he returned. Then he left the room, and I was alone for the first time that day.

* 3 *

The paper contained five neatly written quotations. I read:

Wherein does religion consist? It consists in doing as little harm as possible, in doing good in abundance, in the practice of love, of compassion, of truthfulness and purity, in all the walks of life.

And I read:

Never think or say that your religion is the best. Never denounce the religion of others.

And I read:

Do not decry other sects, do not deprecate others, but rather honor whatever in them is worthy of honor.

I read:

> It is nature's rule that as we sow, we shall reap; she recognizes no good intentions, and pardons no errors.

Finally, I read:

> As a fletcher makes straight his arrow, a wise man makes straight his trembling and unsteady thought, which is difficult to guard, difficult to hold back. As a fish taken from his watery home and thrown on dry land, our thought trembles all over in order to escape the dominion of the tempter. It is good to tame the mind, which is difficult to hold in and flighty, rushing wherever it listeth; a tamed mind brings happiness.

I re-read the quotations, and asked myself "Now what?" If breakfast took 40 minutes and Mr. Conway and I talked two hours and I was to meditate again from 10 to noon, I had about an hour and 20 minutes to spend on this exercise. Was I supposed to read the quotations forty times? When he had told me he would provide passages for meditation, I had assumed that he meant pamphlets or articles of some length, not five short paragraphs.

Well, so I was wrong. Time to figure out what he wanted me to do. I looked again at the first quotation. "Wherein does religion consist? It consists in doing as little harm as possible, in doing good in abundance, in the practice of love, of compassion, of truthfulness and purity, in all the walks of life." I decided to analyze it as if it were an exercise in analysis. Mr. Chiari, what does the message tell you about the person who wrote it? What does he believe? And what point is Mr. Conway attempting to get across to you?

I thought about it.

Well, sir, first off, it's striking, the things he *doesn't* say. Not a word about God, or heaven and hell, or religious ceremonies and duties. He seems to think of religion as the practice of six virtues, without regard to ceremonial or theology. He doesn't say "follow me," and he assumes we know the difference between doing harm and doing good. And he says that virtues can be practiced in all walks of life, which implies that he doesn't believe in any special priesthood.

And how does this impress you, Mr. Chiari?

Offhand, pretty favorably.

Try the next.

"Never think or say that your religion is the best. Never denounce the religion of others."

Comment?

Clear enough. But (uneasy thought for someone who has left the bounds of the religion he was raised in) doesn't it imply that you also shouldn't denounce your own religion or say another is best? Hmm. Bears thinking about. Go on.

"Do not decry other sects, do not deprecate others, but rather honor whatever in them is worthy of honor."

Honor whatever is worthy of honor. I guess that goes for good solid Catholicism. Christianity in general. All religions contain some good: Find it and honor it. I don't know how much more I can get from that one.

"It is nature's rule that as we sow, we shall reap; she recognizes no good intentions, and pardons no errors."

Pardons no errors? That doesn't sound much like a God of mercy. But then, the quotation is talking about nature, not God. In fact, you know what it sounds like? It sounds like mechanics: What you get depends on what you *do,* not on what you *intend* to do. [I was a bit pleased with myself. I understood *this* one, anyway.]

I re-read the longer one about taming the mind. Stuck in by Mr. Conway for the sake of encouragement, presumably.

Well, now what? I'd been through them all twice. How much time had it taken? No way to know, since Mr. Conway had told me not to wear my watch.

Go through them again, I suppose.

I re-read the first. "Wherein does religion consist? It consists in doing as little harm as possible, in doing good in abundance, in the practice of love, of compassion, of truthfulness and purity, in all the walks of life."

As little harm as possible. The old physician's motto: First, do no harm. Try to lead a blameless life. Don't injure others. Do good in abundance. Not only don't do harm, but do good. No harm comes first. Because it's more important? Or does it have to come first before you can do good? Or is it just a meaningless stylistic choice?

Practice love. Well-wishing. No, more urgent than that. Love. But just what is love, really? Unselfish love, I suppose. If that phrase means anything.

Love. Not desire, surely. Not attachment? Maybe just genuinely caring for others and being willing and eager to help when you can? Leave it at that for now. And *don't* go thinking about Marianne. Leave that for later.

Compassion.

Pity? Sorrow? More like empathy, I'd guess. Pity is degrading, and the word "sorrow" seems too limited here. You can feel compassion for somebody when there is really no occasion for sorrow. Like when you see that somebody is really ignorant and doesn't know it, and you can't get to him but you know it's only a matter of time till he finds it out.

Truthfulness. Well, do no harm. But sometimes lies don't hurt anybody. What my mother called manners is mostly polite lies.

Truthfulness. Well, (to quote Pontius Pilate) what *is* truth, anyway? We never know the whole truth. Maybe it's just not pretending? Being yourself and saying only what you believe? Boy, what chaos that would bring!

Would it? Maybe if we got used to it, people wouldn't get their feelings hurt when somebody told them the truth. We'd know more who we are, maybe. But the first person to start telling the truth is going to have an interesting time! [I thought of my awkward friend Lou, always putting his foot in his mouth through a naive willingness to say whatever was in his mind.]

Purity. Sexual purity? Virginity? Well, what else *could* it mean? But: "all walks of life." Couldn't mean virginity.

Purity. Unmixed motives? Transparency? Consistency? Integrity? Funny: I had no idea what the word did mean, even in a sexual context. Continence? Chastity?

But, no point in getting caught in a game of semantics. Purity, if it means anything, must mean preferring what is wholesome and avoiding what is corrupt and corrupting. Defining which was which would be a task—but something inside me knew the difference, as my conscience had proved to me, uncomfortably, many times.

"In all walks of life," it says. You can lead a religious life no matter what your profession or external circumstances, as long as you practice these six virtues. Which means that members of certain professions *can't* lead a religious life, certainly. You couldn't very well be a gangster and still do no harm to yourself or others. You couldn't—

But, as I thought about it, I wondered if anyone could lead a religious life in *any* of the "walks of life." At least, it would be difficult to do and still prosper. I couldn't quite see a businessman or lawyer or politician always telling the truth. I couldn't see an accountant ceaselessly practicing compassion.

Which said something about the professions.

But where *might* it be possible? Housewives could practice the virtues, perhaps. Hospital orderlies. Most anybody who was not in authority over others. An analogy to the rich man and the kingdom of God?

But actually, why *couldn't* an accountant practice compassion? Mostly because of the race for eminence and money, probably. If exercising compassion cost him money in reduced or deferred fees, it would hinder him in the running of the great status race. Still, if it meant enough to him, he *could*—

Mr. Conway re-entered the room, and to my surprise it was time to begin the final two-hour meditation before lunch. And I had hardly begun to explore the ramifications of the thoughts already suggested.

"I think maybe I've learned something about this meditating over texts," I said, smiling up at him.

* **4** *

I wanted to jump right into discussing my morning's work, but Mr. Conway smilingly shook his head and refused to listen. "We'll talk after the noon meal," he said. "Until then, concentrate upon the task at hand. You may find this period before noon the hardest: For this very reason, you can make it the most productive period. Concentrate, George." He added, obviously quoting something, "Righteous persistence brings reward."

We re-entered our meditation positions. Mr. Conway immediately half-closed his eyes and withdrew into his own world. I delayed, watching his face, marvelling at its tranquillity. His boyish face seemed never to have known strain or sorrow. If it were true that his vital forces had been badly depleted in his youth, the wells of life had obviously long since risen again within him. He appeared to overflow with quiet vitality.

After a moment or two, I again turned inward—not without some reluctance—to spend a long 120 minutes wrestling with the ticker-tape machine within my mind. It wasn't a bit easier than the first session had been. If anything, it was harder, because I couldn't help being a bit discouraged by what seemed to be my total lack of progress.

All the rest of that morning I wrestled with the uncontrolled word-producing, image-making, daydream-spawning, escapism-oriented stock-ticker of a mind mechanism. All morning I learned the infinite number of traps the mind could set up to defeat my efforts to turn it off.

If I battled the thoughts to a standstill, the awareness of the battle itself became a distraction. If I gave in to the thoughts, or was caught unaware by them, I found myself waking up at the end of a long series of rapid-fire associations, knowing that I had lost again. If I got angry at having been side-tracked, the anger was a distraction. If I maintained ceaseless vigil and succeeded for an instant in holding back the thoughts, awareness grew that I was holding them back, until it seemed that I was straining to hold closed a door that had, on the other side, a terrific and growing weight of water. When the weight forced the door open even a crack, it burst open immediately and washed me away— and after the water had entirely emptied out, I had to swim and wade wearily back again, to shut the door and know that the same build-up was beginning again.

Sometimes it was memories, and I could fight them pretty well, overcoming (usually) the temptation to linger over the pleasant ones, or rehash the unpleasant. Sometimes my mind filled with bars of music, or—worse—with lines from popular songs. As any ad-man knows, songs are a lot harder to exorcise than words alone. Sometimes the damned phrases, or ad jingles, would get stuck in an endless loop, playing over and over and over and over until I felt ready to scream. And then the anger and frustration became the distraction.

None of the things running through my mind were neatly sorted out, of course. Memories were mixed with daydreams, and fantasies (especially sexual fantasies) mixed with speculations and other busy inventions. And all the while, like the one-armed paperhanger my father used to talk about, or the fireman with a leaky bucket, I was running from thought to thought, putting out sparks here and sparks there, refilling my water bucket and finding that it was filled with kerosene.

"Righteous persistence," Mr. Conway had said. I righteously persisted all that long morning, and made no progress that I could see, and was ready to sleep for three days by the time the noon gong sounded.

Again Mr. Conway helped me to my feet, and again the refectory was half full by the time we had made our way the few dozen yards from my room. It was strange indeed to move from the twilight of my mind into the bright and cheerful sunlit room.

Again we sat by Mr. Barnard and Mr. Herrick, and it was only after the pattern had repeated itself meal by meal and day by day for over a week that I realized that it happened not only by the intention of the three, but also by the active cooperation of everybody else. Which in turn led me to suspect the considerable interest with which my progress was being followed by the rest of the community.

Again the conversation was light, even frivolous; in no way offering opportunity for serious discussion of the difficulties I was experiencing. I made no attempt to join in their talk. It was more relaxing to let my mind free-associate at will, picking its way through the suggestions offered from within and from the overheard conversation around me. This it madly proceeded to do throughout the 40 minutes allowed me for lunch.

* 5 *

We returned to my room. Mr. Conway stressed that I was to try to keep my mind blank, as in the morning, and not let myself give in to the temptation to pursue the newly suggested thoughts of the afternoon. "They will likely appear in the guise of important and fleeting religious insights," he said. "You will be tempted to think them of such intrinsic worth that they merit your immediate concentration. I tell you now that this is but distraction. Your proper course is to assume control of your mind's mechanisms. When you have accomplished *that*, then you may pursue other insights."

So, for the third time since 2 a.m., I began to meditate. It was now about quarter to one, and I was worn out. I learned now another reason for not allowing the eyes to close while meditating: Not only did it hold down the fantasizing while you were alert and full of vigor; it also helped keep you from falling asleep when you were ready to drop. In that urge to sleep I made the acquaintance of another, perhaps the strongest, of the adversaries I was to contend with for so many days.

Weariness changed the nature of the opponents. With my mind reacting more sluggishly, the stock-ticker seemed to become less capable of transmitting (originating?) complicated messages and association-chains. It tended, instead, toward repetition: The drunken monkey became a disc-jockey. But although song fragments, show tunes and commercial jingles are harder to get rid of than word associations, at least they were less likely to seduce me by catching me unaware.

This time, whether or not from wishful thinking, it seemed to me I was doing better. Possibly I was acquiring the knack! [And then I realized that this was but another distracting thought.]

I fought diligently, but now I was all too aware of the aching in my back and the leaden weariness of my mind. Resolution degenerated into a sort of dogged persistence, as increasingly I found myself on the verge of sleep. One of the (unwelcome) thoughts that came to visit was a sour memory of my confidence of the night before. I could handle it, couldn't I? After all, it was all in my mind! I'd gotten through basic training, hadn't I?

With some dismay, I realized that this was the hardest work I'd ever done.

It was a great relief when the two hours were over and it came time for me to exercise. I did breathing exercises, and muscle toners, and sit-ups and push-ups and others. By the end of an hour and a half, I was winded and physically tired, but the sheer relief of movement had helped burn off a lot of the tension that had been accumulating all day.

The last half-hour was reserved for a hot bath in the tub downstairs. I lay soaking, and it was luxury indeed. When I changed into a clean robe, and rejoined Mr. Conway in my room, I felt fresh and vigorous.

This illusion was swiftly dispelled when I began the final two-hour session. My mind was deeply tired, and my effort quickly deteriorated into a confused mass of distractions, aches, wearinesses, and general fuddlement. It went on for a long time, and then I was glad to see Mr. Conway rise and say it was 6 p.m, and time for sleep.

I was tired beyond words. I slept the dreamless sleep of the just (or something) and about six minutes later was awakened by Mr. Conway. It was 2 a.m. again, and time to start the cycle of another day.

✳ 6 ✳

And this routine became my life. I rose at 2 a.m., meditated, or tried to meditate, until 6. I sat through a jovial and increasingly unreal half-hour at breakfast, and returned for another two hours of instruction and meditation on scriptures Mr. Conway picked for me. Another two-hour meditation, and then I would sit bemused through a second meal and would spend the afternoon in meditation, exercise, and meditation again.

I have long since lost all objectivity: I cannot tell if that *sounds* like a difficult schedule. I found it almost a killing pace, and I wondered how Mr. Conway kept it up. With the exception of an hour and a half at midday when I was working with texts, he stayed with me all day. I couldn't imagine where he got the stamina.

I learned how he did it after I made my first breakthrough. The exercises were not draining his energy, but renewing it. This was how he could remain so youthfully energetic amid so strenuous a schedule: He was tapping a source of virtually unlimited energy.

I got a glimpse of that source—just a few seconds, if that—after about two weeks of the routine I have just described. For the briefest moment of time, the stock-ticker turned off.

Beyond it was silence. Beyond the silence was a deep peace, reminding me of the restfulness of sleep and the visions of childhood.

Then the stock-ticker was back in action, excitedly commencing to analyze just what had happened, trying idiotically to make it happen again.

I won't go any farther in attempting to describe the indescribable. Those who have experienced it will recognize the event. Those who have not, will attempt to understand it to death, trying to make it fit what they have experienced, or what they can imagine experiencing. I do not intend to offer additional material for misinterpretation. Also, Mr. Conway has asked me to skip any further description of the process. He assures me that he has his reasons for asking my silence on this point.

So, suffice it to say that, once having caught a glimpse of what I was working for, I redoubled my efforts and did begin to attain results. I began to enjoy a reflux of energy. My mind became clearer, and calmer, than I could ever remember. Certain forms of awareness accompanied that increased clarity and calmness, and in time they led to other insights and abilities.

Of course, at the same time I was penetrating into the calmer areas of my mind, I was narrowing my focus. My interest in outside events dwindled. My ability to make casual conversation practically disappeared. In this sheltered environment this temporary development did not matter and was, in fact, all to the good.

For quite a while, Mr. Conway gave me no Christian or Jewish scriptures, knowing that resonance from my early education would inhibit my response and interfere with my progress. Instead, I was given extracts from the scriptures of Buddhism, Hinduism, and Islam. After a bit, I was given quotations from the Talmud, Mr. Conway assuming (correctly) that these would not have been force-fed to me in my childhood. I quickly developed a fondness for its pithy, matter-of-fact statements. "Without religion there can be no true morality," I would read, or "He who does not add to his learning diminishes it," or, my favorite, "The best preacher is the heart; the best teacher is time; the best book is the world; the best friend is God."

Gradually I felt a hardness within me dissolving, and I became more open to the message of the scriptures. I came to realize that religion did not, at all, consist of external authorities and rules, but was inward, stemming from the possibility of uniting with something—Someone?—that far transcended individuals and circumstances. When I fully realized this, I realized that we do not walk blind and alone, among external accidents. We are part of the whole, as important, and as *intrinsic* (rather than accidental) as any other part. I had heard it before, of course, but had thought it wishful thinking.

* 7 *

Day followed day without alteration or interruption of my new life. Once the difficulty and fatigue of the first few weeks passed, and some progress had become apparent, I threw myself ever more into the work. I felt I was well on the way toward routing the drunken monkey, though Mr. Conway warned that it would not be so easy or so quick. I could *feel* the results of increased control in the new mental resources available to me. My life before this came to seem a feverish dream. My curiosity about what might be happening beyond the valley, or even beyond the walls of my room, lessened day by day until I found even the daily meals a shadowy irrelevance. In this, I see now, I was to some extent deceiving myself, walling myself off from thinking about certain painful subjects. Still, whatever else was going on, I immersed myself in endless work, and as the weeks went by forgot past and future tense.

* 8 *

That long, difficult effort was my first experience of really taking things day by day. If I had known at the beginning how long an effort I was in for—two and a half years, as it turned out—I wonder if I would have had the nerve to begin. But Mr. Conway never spoke of times to come, or what would follow. Instead, he showed me, mostly by example, a new way of experiencing time: not straining ahead toward next month or next week or tomorrow, but living always in the very moment. After a long time, I came to realize that this is all we can do anyway: The time is always "now" and that is always just as much as we can handle. But until Mr. Conway began to work with me, I'd been accustomed (without realizing it) to daydreaming my life away, living on plans and anxieties, memories and regrets. As I began to overcome the drunken monkey, the stray moments of true, full consciousness of the moment became more frequent. They became, for the first time, true consciousness.

Useless to write about this, though: Everybody thinks they're already conscious, until they set out to prove it. Until then, there's hardly any point in trying to tell them the truth. It's odd, when you think of it, how few people live in the here and now.

PART THREE

❄

Messenger

August, 1979

Chapter Nine

Corbin

W e were chanting.

Years ago, chanting used to irritate me. It had seemed a needless relic of the Middle Ages. But I'd long since changed my mind about that, as about so many things. I'd discovered its virtues.

Partly we chant for the joy of the sound; partly, for the spiritual side effects to be had by losing ourselves in a chorus. The Latin chants in particular—which I once would have found highly irritating—I now found soothing, those ancient Latin words, sung of the beauty of God and God's world. And blended in with the sounds were the smell of the incense, the rich colors of the tapestries, and the weight of the hymnal I myself had helped to manufacture the paper for, 11 years earlier.

I joined whole-heartedly in the chant, yet from moment to moment I functioned, as well, as an outside observer, for there was something very pleasing in these faces. They were extremely strong faces, whether masculine or (in five cases) feminine. They were strong from the years of effort expended in overcoming temptation, the temptations that torture even those in monasteries:

Gluttony—even for an extra slice of bread;

Sloth—even for a few minutes' extra rest on a warm cot when the night air was particularly cold;

Lust—for they are, after all, still human, with bodies that make angry demands on the wills that keep desires in check;

Anger—from any of the multitude of reasons provided by fellow voyagers known in every detail, known to a perfection not exceeded by the old whalers on their four-years' unbroken voyages.

And there were other temptations to fight against: envy, pride, etc. They had experienced them all, had battled them all and were battling still, years and decades into their strenuous life here. The effects of that long sustained effort showed on those beautiful childlike faces.

Childlike, not childish. There was something very open and trusting in those eyes that had concentrated so long on their own imperfections (rather than on those of others); eyes whose owners, for year on year, had trusted God to show them the way. Knowledge of sin had sobered them, but had neither defeated nor depressed them. Instead, it had encouraged them to abandon control of their lives to God, trusting God to bring them safely home at last, rather like Emerson:

As the bird trims her to the gale,
I trim myself to the storm of time,
I man the rudder, reef the sail,
Obey the voice at eve obeyed at prime:
"Lowly faithful, banish fear,
right onward drive unharmed;
The port, well worth the cruise, is near,
And every wave is charmed."

Throughout our worship, I was aware of those faces, and of the souls behind them. And besides the observer, there was a part of me that split itself off to quietly taste my deep joy at this my home, the home I never would willingly have come to.

It was August. November would mark 17 years since I had been brought here. Nearly 17 winters on this cold mountainside. Seventeen of the almost unbearably poignant springs and autumns. Seventeen brief hot summers, of which the last was not quite completed. Seventeen years in which my parents had grown older—died, perhaps—knowing nothing of what had happened to me. Seventeen years in which my brothers and sisters had grown up, and Marianne had lived from youth to middle age. But all things had their price, and there had never been a thing I could do about it. On the other hand, it had been 17 years of one deepening relationship, one overwhelming reality. I was content. I was home. I had penetrated to life's deepest joy.

And just about that time—as life would have it—there came the sound and the jarring of a terrific impact, as though some giant had swung a hammer against the side of the mountain.

∗ 2 ∗

The chant stopped instantly, the monks looking at each other wide-eyed. It had not been an earthquake, but an impact, and impacts are made by things hitting other things. Our world is without the machinery which "civilization" takes for granted: railroad trains, highway traffic, airplanes, motors of any kind. They simply don't exist. So what could have caused the noise and the jarring? We had reason to stare. But then the eldest of us calmly resumed the chant, and we joined in with him, though our concentration was not what it had been.

The chant finished, another began. Though the earth broke up or the stars fell down around us, we would continue to stand and chant to the end of the hour, partly out of obedience, partly out of long-ingrained routine, but mostly out of conviction that prayer is more important than the things of the moment, however unusual. But as I entered into the second chant, I felt a light pressure on my elbow, and turned to see Mr. Barnard, who leaned close and said, quietly, "Come quick."

It took but a moment to make our way through the rows of monks, and then we were moving quickly through the hallway, I nearly blinded by the midday sun through the windows, after the incense-laden darkness of the chapel.

"Something up your alley, George," Mr. Barnard said. "Airplane crash."

I glanced at him, my heart an indescribable mixture of incredulity, excitement, and fear. "Whose?" Could it possibly be American, after all this time?

"Didn't get a look at the markings. Didn't even see it until it had dropped down between the mountains. The blamed thing came shooting by practically at window level. One minute it was in front of me, and the next minute it slammed into the side of the mountain a little farther on."

"Good God! Did it burn? What do you think the chances are that anybody's still alive?"

"Didn't burn right off. Couldn't say what the chances are. You're going to tell me, I hope, if we can get there quick enough." We hurried through a door and were out on one of the patios that overlooked the descending slopes. "See it?"

"No." Then, following his outstretched arm down the slope

and off to the left, I did. "Well, it isn't burning yet, that's something. But how are we going to get down to it?"

"I sent a couple chelas off for some rope, if we need it. Let's see how close we can get."

Mr. Barnard had the body of a 55-year-old man, and he had spent 20 years of his adult life in boardrooms and offices, but he had been a mining engineer in his youth, and had somehow retained the muscles his early life had given him. I found myself having to hurry to keep up with him as we picked our way down the steep slope.

We were able to get within about 50 feet of the smashed aircraft before we were stopped by an almost vertical descent, with no way down except by rope. My eyes went not to the cockpit, but immediately to the one undamaged wing. What I saw there chilled me, even in the August midday sun. "Chinese, Mr. Barnard," I said desperately. "We're dead."

His face was a study in dismay. I'm sure mine was too. Even when you've been waiting for it, it takes you by surprise. Year after year of lookouts and vigilance, year after year of reprieves, until you begin to relax, thinking that the old man's prophecy might yet come true—at least, the part about the monastery surviving—and then all of a sudden the end come crashing down out of the sky, and you are compelled by your own values to go to the aid of the men who would wind up destroying you.

But, first things first. We'd have to see if anybody inside was alive. I looked down at the twisted airframe. It had hit at an angle, bellying in. The tail was intact, but most of the nose and much of the left side had smashed themselves into the rock of the mountain. Half the left wing was gone; looking back, I could see at least a twisted portion of the end of it, several hundred feet away. A hundred feet above the fragments I could see the scarred rock that had snagged and broken it. I wondered how securely the wreck was perched. I wondered how much movement would be required to start it sliding, then tumbling. I made a mental note to move cautiously.

Three chelas arrived, carrying a coiled hemp rope.

Mr. Barnard had said nothing since I'd pointed out the markings. "Let's take a look at that rope," he said now. But, hoping to avoid an argument, I'd already taken the end of the rope and tied it around myself. "You three stand by to help me get up if need be," I said. "Let's get that other end secured."

The chelas bent the rope around a boulder (there being nothing else to fasten it to, so far above the tree line) and stood ready to haul against my weight. Mr. Barnard said, "Here, lad, I can see it makes sense for you to go instead of me, you being younger and lighter, but how about one of them instead? They're as sure-footed as cats."

"I'm all set, Mr. Barnard. And what do they know about jet planes?"

"About as much as I do," he said, nodding. "Okay. Keep your eye on the ball, going down."

"Yeah. Let me get down there *fast*, before this thing decides to blow." The expression on his face, as I saw it before lowering myself down, was almost comical in its sudden change from mild worry to active alarm. His experience with airplanes had never been all that extensive, and of course he knew nothing at all about jets.

I walked myself down the 70-degree slope backwards, rapidly, hand over hand, using the rope to balance myself. In half a minute I was at the wreck, standing by the nose. It was a big plane, big enough to hold ten men or more. In fact, I suddenly realized that I recognized it: It was an American airframe, a Buffalo.

When I'm under stress, I talk to myself. Argue, too, sometimes. I asked myself, "What are the Chinese doing riding around in American planes?"

I disengaged myself from the rope and quickly went entirely around the part of the airplane that was not smashed against rock, looking for a way in, finding nothing. "There's the door, but that's not going to open from the outside. Looks like I'd better find something smashed, which sounds like the cockpit windows."

The windows were indeed smashed. "Well, I guess it's this or nothing, and time's a'wastin', as Snuffy Smith used to say. Let's see if I can't get in there." Biting my lip, knowing that the wreck could burst into flames or explode at any time, I got up my nerve, used a stone to smash out the remaining shards of glass around the frame, and climbed inside. There was a smell of kerosene: strong, but not overpowering. "Not great odds, but I suppose they could be worse," I told myself.

To get in, I had to force my way past the bodies, practically stepping on one of them. Pretty grisly. I tried not to look too closely at pilot or co-pilot. Both were obviously Chinese, and both were more than obviously dead. "Never knew what hit them," I said, "which is trite. And true."

I worked the latch of the door to the main compartment, but couldn't get it open. Twisted. I put my foot against it, still holding the latch open, and kicked. Two kicks and the door bounded away from me.

I stepped carefully into the passageway. Dark inside, with the electricity gone and only a little light filtering in from one unblocked window. My first impression was that the area was entirely filled with machinery. My mind was entirely filled with the smell of jet fuel. I decided I wasn't risking my life for papers and machinery. "If this baby happens to still be here in an hour or so, we'll take another look," I said. "But for now, this is more than good enough."

But as I started to turn back, I noticed a single seat, set in among the machinery, with a body sitting slumped forward, held in the seat only by the seatbelt. The man wore a flight suit, but no flying helmet. Instead, he wore headphones attached to the instruments he had apparently been monitoring. There was a gash on the back of the head where some of the coarse black hair had been scraped off in a collision with something hard.

"If you'd had a helmet on, instead of that headset, you wouldn't have gotten that bump on the noggin, buddy," I said. It took only a moment to get to him; between the time I moved and the time I got my hands on his shoulders, I realized that he was alive. I pushed back his head—carefully—and gasped. The man was definitely not Chinese, but Western. American, in fact—though I couldn't have said how I knew that.

"Wonderful," I said. "And alive, too." I put my fingers against his throat, felt a strong pulse. "Okay, Benedict Arnold, let's get you out of here before we both go to glory and I have to explain to Saint Peter why I'm in bad company." Flippant words, to give myself courage. How in the world could I drag an unconscious man, bigger than myself, through that cockpit window? (Besides which, my stomach turned over at the thought of again climbing over the body of that pilot.) "Nothing to be done, though. That's the way in, that's the way out. And let's get a move on." But then I remembered, and looked around in the gloom until I found the door in the side.

"Possible? Well, this part of the fuselage isn't all twisted up. C'mon, baby, don't be jammed." I put my hands on the lever and applied pressure, prepared to put my entire weight into it. Anticlimactically, it moved readily, and daylight streamed into the cabin as the door swung open. Moving as quickly as I could, I unbelted the man and dragged him to the edge of the airframe.

"Hope you don't have any broken bones, boy. I sure can't see leaving you here till the ambulance comes." I jumped down three feet to the ground, then reached up and pulled him out by the armpits. I didn't like letting his legs drop to the ground, but he was far too heavy for me to carry. As a desperate expedient, I put both arms around his chest and backed a little away from the airframe; one leg slid out, and I was able to get my own leg underneath it in time to somewhat ease it down. I did the same for the other leg—not very gracefully, as he was really more than I could handle—and let him slip to the ground. I went around to where I could see Mr. Barnard looking down.

"What do you need, there, George? Anybody alive?"

"Just one live one. I'm going to tie the rope under his arms and have you pull him up. He's injured, and probably we shouldn't be moving him, but it sure isn't safe *here!* Do you think the three of you can get him up there without banging him around too badly?"

"Wait. Let's try to get him up on a stretcher. There's five of us now." Lobsang, one of the chelas, came lowering himself quickly down a rope.

"Look out below!" came Mr. Barnard's voice, and I looked up to see another rope on its way down, with poles and a roll of cloth tied to the end. It got stuck, but a yank on the line from above freed it.

Lobsang and I got to the injured man. He was still breathing. We stretched out the cloth, set the poles out atop it, parallel to each other, and folded the cloth over the poles so that the weight of the man's body would hold the frame together. Then we laid him on it and walked him around the airplane to where we could see the men above. There we found that Thubten had come down, and stood there holding the ends of two more ropes from the ledge above, and another, shorter rope.

"George, if you don't have any better ideas, what do you think about tying him in and tying those other ropes to the ends of the stretcher? Then we can haul in on you two, and help you bear the weight too."

Good old Mr. Barnard: always thinking. "Sure, let's go before the real excitement starts."

Thubten went hurrying back up his line, and made ready to help the others pull. I looked at Lobsang, we checked each other's knots in the lines we had tied around our chests, and he gave the signal for the men above to start pulling.

Leaning far out away from the cliff, using the tension on the ropes maintained from above to help neutralize the man's weight, we were able to keep our footing on the steep slope, and guide the stretcher so that it didn't hit. In almost no time, the thing was done, and the chelas were hurrying the stretcher to the monastery's small infirmary.

I said, "Mr. Barnard, you sure do think fast."

He grinned. "That's from years of watching the tape and working on borrowed money. Good work down there, Tom Mix. Now let's get out of here."

Picking our way, moving as fast as we could, we got back to the buildings. At the door, I halted, looking back at the airplane, and Mr. Barnard stood with me.

"I don't see any sign of fire. I'm beginning to think I was a little hasty in there. If that guy has any internal injuries, I may have really messed him up."

Mr. Barnard shrugged his shoulders. "I suppose so, but it couldn't be helped. That thing could have blown up and he'd be dead, and you with him. I think you did darned well getting him out of there at all." We stood there, unable to stop looking at the wreckage. "Who do you suppose he is?"

"I don't know. I didn't have a lot of time for introductions."

Mr. Barnard grinned. "I mean what country is he from, as you know darned well. I didn't get much of a look at him, but he sure wasn't Chinese. Russian, do you suppose?"

"Could be. I got the feeling he was American, for some reason. I don't know why."

"Well, if he comes to, we'll have some questions for him. If he don't, maybe we'll learn something when we go through his pockets."

We stood looking at the wreckage. "George, you said that thing could still blow up. How long till we can figure it ain't going to?"

"Hard to say. Every minute that goes by, helps. With all those kerosene fumes, and the heat, and the impact, the time for her to go would have been right after she hit. I suppose I'd give it another half hour or so, just to be on the safe side."

"Think you could stand to go back in there?"

"Looking for clues, you mean? Sure. It'll be a lot easier, with the door open. Mr. Barnard, what happened?"

"The only thing I know, I was standing out here, having a smoke, and I heard the lookout call, and I looked over and about swallowed my cigar. This thing came in here—I just can't tell you how fast it came tearing through. One second it wasn't there, and then it was, and then it piled into the side of the mountain there."

"It looks like it scraped a wingtip against that point there, and broke it off."

He closed his eyes with the effort of visualizing. "Yeah, maybe. It looked to me like something pushed them sideways, almost, and they broke off the end of the wing, like you said. We ought to be able to find a considerable scar on the rocks down over about there. You can see that's quite a ways from where it finally hit. The wing hit, but the thing went right on, except its head came up and it faltered, like, and then blam! down she came."

"I get the picture, I think. They were flying down here, where they didn't have any business being in a big tub like that. All it took was a little gust, and they clipped the side. When they tried to recover, the pilot stalled it, or maybe another gust hit them. Or maybe he'd lost too much control surface. But what was he doing flying so low in the first place?"

"Well, my lad, I don't think that's so hard to figure out. I'd say they were way up, and happened to see the green of the valley. Probably they were coming in to look at it when they saw our buildings here. Probably they came in for a closer look, and maybe the pilot did two seconds' sight-seeing too many."

"They came in too close, too fast, and ran out of room," I said. "That sounds about right."

Still we stood looking over at the remains of the intruder.

"We'll have to get the bodies buried," I said. "I didn't tell you, the pilot and co-pilot were Chinese."

He nodded. "Red Chinese markings, it didn't matter all that much if the pilots were Chinese or more hired help like our friend on the stretcher. Big trouble either way. I just hope they didn't have time to get on the radio to their friends back home."

I hadn't thought of that. We stood in silence.

"Mr. Barnard, what are we going to do?"

Mr. Barnard seemed to shake himself awake, like a dog shaking himself dry. (Later, I decided that we'd both been a mild state of shock, like the time I'd crashed my U-2.) "Well, first thing, we're going to get that big 'Kick Me' sign off our front lawn."

"You want us to strip it, I imagine."

"Darned right! We're going to want every piece of machinery, all the papers, everything you can get out of that baby. Then if we have time, we want to take it apart and bring it all inside, or bury it somehow. We've got to get it covered."

"Okay. You know, half an hour is probably more than I need. Let's say a few minutes."

"No, take your half hour. You'll need it getting things organized. I'll ask the boss if we can get everybody in the house, and more from downstairs. We've got to get moving."

* 3 *

People who think monks are unworldly should see them respond to an emergency. Within minutes, Mr. Barnard had detailed two of our young helpers from the valley to be my go-fers, and had sent another down the long path to the valley. While he went to appraise Mr. Conway and others of the situation, I tried to think of everything we might need.

"We will need ropes, Kesang, and winches. You know winches? Good. We will need many hands to lift heavy things. Gompo, we need the cutting machine. You know? Mr. Barnard's machine that uses fire to cut metals?"

"Torch," he said, nodding vigorously. "Many times Mr. Barnard use it. Many sparks."

"Yes." I was glad Gompo knew what I was talking about. My Tibetan doesn't extend to technical terms or machinery. "You get the torch, please. Bring it on a cart. Kesang, we will need work carts. You might as well use the other for the ropes and tools. Bring the big toolbox." The carts were something Mr. Barnard and I had put together a few years before. We'd mounted two heavy wooden wheels, fore and aft, beneath a platform four foot wide by eight foot long. With steady hands at the handles at all corners, the carts could be made to negotiate our rough trails without overturning.

I sent off Gompo and Kesang, and rehearsed the operation in my mind. God, I'd forgotten the very first thing and my go-fers had already been dispatched. But here were the rest of the monks, ready (despite being very senior to me) to do my bidding. They could make up for my lack of foresight. I asked five of them to bring the special hose and every container they could find, and meet me where Mr. Barnard had recently stood above the wreck. I told them to check with him if they couldn't find the hose.

At the same time I got back there, Thubten arrived, carrying the ropes we'd used earlier. He and I usually worked well together, being able to read one another's intentions from the slightest of clues. Without my needing to say a word, he began handing a line around the boulder we'd used before. This time I didn't bother to knot it around my waist, but merely passed it around me and held it.

"As soon as I'm down there, try to find a way to anchor some line, Thubten. Many more coming, much to lift. As three arrive, send down one. Keep the strongest one with you. Send Gompo and Kesang down with the tools they bring." Thubten, bless him, never needed repetition. I could forget my instructions as soon as I gave them.

The Buffalo, looked at with a view toward dismantling it, seemed to have grown monstrously. First things first: Where were the fuel tanks? More important, where were the bleeder valves? The jet-fuel smell had gone away. Good sign. And here was Mr. Barnard, hurrying down the path that ended above my head, leading a procession of workers.

I was the expert on jet planes; he was the expert on efficient organization. I could let him take care of that end of matters, as long as I got my few down here. I went over to where I could call up to him.

"Mr. Barnard!" Even as I called, five chelas were climbing

down the steep slopes at the end of ropes held by their fellows. "I need the containers first. We've got to get the fuel out of here before we do any cutting."

"I've got 'em working on it," he called down. "Got 'em tying hooks to the end of a couple of the ropes. You just hook the cans on and we'll take it from there."

Sometime I'll have to ask him where we'd gotten so many five-gallon gas cans. In the long years of shipments before 1937, I suppose, though they look pretty new for that. Six empty cans tied to the end of a rope came down on us, those above jerking the ropes when the cans caught. Kesang got to the cans and untied them, and we went back to the wreck.

"Gompo, call for some more men down here. Go inside through that door. Get everything out from inside. Don't break things, but don't lose time. Okay?"

"Oh, sure, very much okay," he said placidly. If the world burned down, Gompo would be sure to see it, but he wouldn't hurry to get a better seat. Kesang and Tserang and I got wrenches and started bleeding off the fuel.

When next I looked around, I saw what seemed to be a giant cargo net being hauled up, eight brawny chelas straining at the ropes. I didn't see it, but I imagined Mr. Barnard organizing the men into teams—eight to wheel each cart, a few more to load them (and others on the other end to unload them) and many more to carry or pass material along bucket-brigade style.

We'd sent up perhaps 30 cans when he came down to see how we were doing. "Much more in there, do you suppose?"

I straightened up, resting my back, which was already cramped and sore. "Yeah, I'd think so. This thing's full of fuel. Are we going to have room enough for it?"

"Oh, Lord yes. We can empty out the wine tubs and put it in there, if we have to. You're looking at gold here. I just need to know about how much."

"That, I can't tell you. This isn't my plane. But I can tell you right there"—pointing at the extra fuel tanks— "this thing was designed to go long distances."

"Those tanks'll come in handy. Maybe we can get 'em up full."

"Do you think so? That would sure save a lot of work. Time, too."

"Yeah. But can you get 'em off without having to use the

torch? If you can't we'll just do it the hard way."

I left Kesang and Tserang with the siphon and cans, sent them two reinforcements, and went to look over the tanks. "I guess if you've got the right size wrenches, we ought to be able to do it."

"We got 'em," Mr. Barnard grunted. "Made sure of that 40 years ago."

"We're going to have to put some supports under them while we work. They're going to be heavy."

"You get 'em off the plane and I'll worry about getting 'em home."

And somehow he did. Not only got the awkward, heavy fuel tanks swayed up to the trail above, but got them securely fastened on carts never intended for such loads, then shepherded the carts back to the monastery and got the tanks safely to rest in a hastily cleared basement storeroom.

And, I learned a couple hours later, between organizing and supervising those operations (a good day's work in itself), he had somehow thought of, suggested, and generally made possible another surprise for me. Sunnie and some of the frail or elderly monks, unable to assist in fetching and carrying, had nonetheless made themselves useful. Down to the valley had gone the call for all the cloth available. As it arrived, they'd basted strips together. My parachute, I noticed, reappeared after all these years, along with the three from the Buffalo's crew.

"Camouflage," Mr. Barnard said proudly as the massive bundle arrived at the plane. "I figured that it might take us a while to cut that thing up and haul it away."

"Mr. Barnard, I'm speechless. That's terrific. But we're going to have to paint it."

"Already taken care of," he said a little smugly, enjoying my stupefaction. "Many hands make light work."

I shook my head, lost in admiration. Then Mr. Barnard was directing several people at once, getting the bundle down the slope, getting it unfolded without tangles, getting it draped loosely over the entire superstructure, getting it anchored it all around with stones, except for the areas where an unending line of hose still continued to empty the dead bird's tanks.

"The only thing is," I said to him when next we both had a minute, "radar would see right through this netting. I suppose all this rock will protect us, but I don't know what new gadgets they've invented. We may be just wasting our time here. Especially if they had this thing locked into a homing beam of some kind."

"Any way to know for sure?"

"Not really. It could be in the nose, all smashed up. Or it could be something new that I wouldn't recognize. And you know," I said, struck by the obvious for the first time, "they probably had this baby on their radar screens when she came down." I laughed at the back-breaking, single-minded work we had done. Working before thinking. Most untypical of Shangri-La! "Mr. Barnard, if they had this ship on their radar, they know just where to start looking. And if they start close, they won't have to find the wreck. They won't be able to miss the buildings."

"I already thought of that. It goes in the category of things you don't worry over because you can't do a thing about 'em. Anyway, it ain't a sure thing."

He could see I didn't follow his reasoning. "Look, if we leave this thing here and they come by, they know for sure they're in the right place, and they stop looking. But if they come over here and see us—see the buildings, I mean—maybe they're thinking that ain't what they're supposed to be looking for, and they don't report it. Or maybe they report it and the word comes back to keep looking for what they're *supposed* to be looking for. You stop and think about it. The big boss in Peking or somewhere sends out some airplanes looking for one that's maybe crashed. They don't even know for sure it did crash, you know. Maybe in the back of their minds they're wondering did he take it on the lam. So that's got 'em wondering. Now, if they get a call on the radio says 'we found some old buildings way the hell up the side of a mountain,' how are they going to react? Are they going to say, 'Well, that explains it'? In the first place, they ain't even going to know for sure there's people living here—not unless we get real unlucky and they come over while we're still here swarming like bees. Even if their man on the radio sees us, are they necessarily going to believe him? And if they do, I still say, why should they connect us and the airplane?

"And last," he said before turning away to be pulled back up the slope, "remember this. Even if they get the report and they *believe* the report, who's to know it ain't something everybody else already knows about? You know the communists don't go encouraging a lot of individual thinking. Hell, for all we know, we been discovered a dozen times already, but everybody figured what he just found out, everybody else already knew."

* **4** *

Finally, long after sunset, we finished extracting the last bit of fuel from the main tanks. (With the right tools, the job would have been pretty easy. Working the way we had to, it was a killer.) When the last can was swayed up, I motioned for a rope and followed it up.

"Mr. Barnard, I've been thinking about what you said, and it makes a lot of sense. Tell you what: Get some food sent down and get me a couple of helpers and I can start working on cutting up the frame tonight. The shroud ought to hide the sparks, if I can work without setting it on fire." I accompanied that with a smile, but it wasn't much of a smile. I was tired!

Mr. Barnard's smile was tired too, but he clasped me firmly on the shoulder. "That's a handsome offer, lad, but I already worked it out. You stick around to tell us where not to cut, and I guess Conway and me can pretty near get it. He's fresh, you know. All day long, he's had the easy part, keeping things organized inside. So he can go first while you and me rest, and then I'll do some and little by little we'll get it. Or, say, I'll tell you what. Why don't you scare up some chalk and mark where we ought to cut? Then we won't waste any time later. You understand, we want pieces as big as possible. More useful later, and anyway, bigger pieces means fewer cuts."

As always, I was impressed by his foresight and energy. I turned to go back down. Knowing I was tired, and not wanting to take chances, I was tying myself in, rather than merely holding the rope, when he had to add, "Oh, and George? I didn't forget your grub. First things first with you, I know." I was still grinning about it a few minutes later when he and Mr. Conway were swayed down to begin work.

But then there were two dead pilots to be cut out of their twisted tomb, and a long night's monotonous, wearing work cutting up the tell-tale airframe, converting it into resources for future use. By the time we finished, the summer sunshine was not far behind, and I was ready to sleep on the rocks until Mr. Conway suggested that I would be in the way. So I came in, to fall into exhausted sleep, while others finished removing the traces.

Chapter Ten.

Interrogation

I awoke early that afternoon. That is, Mr. Barnard woke me up, touching my shoulder with one hand while holding a cup of hot tea near my nose with the other. Most unusual. Then I remembered the day before, and our long night. "Did they get the engines up okay?"

"No, they didn't. Too blamed big and heavy. But they piled three feet of rock and dirt on 'em. Think that's enough?"

"These days, God knows, but I suppose it'll have to be. Just so they're out of sight, we ought to be all right." I remembered something from sleep, and sat up abruptly. "Say, Mr. Barnard, you know what we forgot? We ought to comb the rocks near where the wing tip hit first; there were fragments all over the place. Not so big a clue, but all it would take would be for the sun to reflect off just one piece. . . ."

Mr. Barnard put the teacup in my hand (having moved it just barely in time to prevent my sudden motion from spilling it all over my bed) and told me to calm down. "The same idea came to me, and the same way. Seems like you and me do some of our best work while we're asleep." We smiled at this innocuous version of one of his slightly off-color stories. "But I didn't break up your beauty sleep to remind you how brilliant I am. And it wasn't just jealously, either, seeing you sleeping the sleep of the just while your betters stand watch. The fact is, the boss wants to see you pronto."

I rolled my feet out of bed and got up. "I know for sure he was still going when I quit," I said. "Doesn't anybody ever sleep around here besides me?"

"It's age, George. Don't matter how slow it happens, the older you get, the less sleep you need. Ready?"

Somebody had very thoughtfully left water in my jar. I poured some into the bowl, plunged my hands into it, and thoroughly massaged my face. "Ahhh, that's cold," I said, feeling for the towel. "That's one thing I miss about the old life: hot water in the morning without having to hike down the hall and fight over the bathroom. I take it I don't have time to shave?"

"Later. Come on."

Mr. Conway was waiting for us in his room. On his table were some cards and papers which he invited me, with a gesture, to examine.

An American, for sure. One Dennis Corbin. Mr. Dennis Corbin's personal papers, found in his wallet, included among other things a California driver's license, a Social Security card, a San Francisco Public Library borrower's card, three oil-company credit cards, four other credit cards, and two flimsies for gasoline bought with the credit cards. Also $85 in twenties, tens, and ones.

I looked at Mr. Conway.

"What do you make of all this, George? Does it appear authentic?"

I shrugged (which, Mr. Barnard keeps pointing out to me, is my usual response to a request for an opinion.) "Any document can be faked. If these are fakes, they're good enough to fool me."

Mr. Barnard said, "The currency look too small to you?"

"Too small?"

"Yeah." He took a dollar bill out of his pocket. It was the size of an IBM card. "It didn't look right to me, but I wasn't sure, so I fished around and found one I had on me when I came here. You can see they ain't nearly the same size."

I laughed. "A couple of things have changed in the U.S. since 1931, Mr. Barnard. Didn't you ever see the bills I brought here?"

"Guess not. So that looks okay to you? What's it all tell you about him? Assuming the stuff's for real."

"Not much. He's 26 years old, lives in California—San Francisco probably but not definitely—and he was there as recently as June 13th, when he signed for gas at this Exxon station, whatever Exxon may be. In 1962, $85 would have been a fair amount of money to be carrying around, but it may not be that much now, I wouldn't know. And he may have stocked up for a trip."

"Recall whatever you observed yesterday," Mr. Conway said. "What impression comes to mind?"

"Mr. Conway, I don't know that I had any particular impressions, it all happened so fast. He seemed young and pretty normal, that's all. Except he was flying in an American plane with Chinese markings and Chinese pilots."

"This is not idle curiosity. Our new guest is on the verge of waking up, we believe. He sustained a concussion and bruises, nothing serious. But fortunately, he remained unconscious long enough for you to get some sleep."

"Fortunately?"

"He's your boy," Mr. Barnard said in explanation.

"Mine? Why mine?"

"Because you and Henry are the only Americans here, and Henry convinced me that you are the better suited to the job of becoming comfortable with Mr. Corbin—or rather, having him become comfortable with *you*. You and he will appear to him to be of an age, which surely will help."

I smiled uneasily.

"Now George, don't worry," Mr. Barnard said. "It won't be like you won't have us around. We'll be here. But you're the front man."

"Imagine yourself in his place. He will be wondering where he is, who we are, what we intend. Remember your own experience."

"If he's got a guilty conscience, that ought to be clear right away. And don't forget, your walking into his room is going to be a big shock to him."

"Is it? Why?"

"For the same reason *he* shocked *us* yesterday. There ain't supposed to be any other Americans out here."

"Yeah, I guess that *would* throw him, wouldn't it?"

"Do you require a script, George?"

I looked at Mr. Conway blankly, I'm sure.

"You are kindly, but firm. He is trespassing, but we are inclined to be lenient if we are satisfied he is telling the truth. No answers about Shangri-La—don't mention the name, incidentally—until we have learned all we care to know. Can you convey all that?"

"I can try, I guess." I would have shrugged again, but remembered in time Mr. Barnard's persistent ribbing on the subject of shrugging.

The situation had its humorous aspects. I walked in and found Mr. Dennis Corbin staring at the ceiling. I could still remember being on the other end of the same kind of conversation. I determined to try to alter it.

"Good morning, Dennis," I said. "My name is George Chiari. Our doctors tell me you weren't hurt very badly and I'm glad to hear it. How do you feel?"

Corbin took his time answering. For a moment he lay there, looking me over, sorting things out in his mind. When he finally spoke, I was struck both by the soft, pleasant tenor of his voice and by the harsh overtones his mood added to it. A quiet, shy boy trying to act tough? A proud, intolerant personality superimposed on what had been a more pleasant youth? Merely the natural reaction of anyone trying to get firm footing in a bewildering situation?

"You know my name, but I don't remember you. Does that mean I should remember talking to you already, or did you get my name by rifling through my things?"

Not the reaction I'd expected! It was hard not to be put immediately on the defensive. But then I realized the implications of what he'd just said. And I remembered Mr. Conway's instructions. Kindly but firm. No answers first. Trespassing. I sat down on the room's only chair. "Does that mean you don't remember where you are?"

He seemed undecided whether to answer the question at all. Why? Surely he was reluctant to give me so great an advantage.

"For your information, Dennis, I pulled you out of the wreckage of your airplane yesterday. Do you remember the crash?"

This time I waited out his silence. Finally he said, "I thought it had to be something like that. Where the hell am I?"

Trespassing. "You don't remember where you were when you came down?"

Somewhat impatiently: "I don't remember a thing after eating breakfast this m— *yesterday* morning now, I take it."

"And where was that?"

More silence. "Maybe you'd better tell me where I am. Is this Pakistan?"

"No. You are in Tibet. *Still* in Tibet, I might say."

"And why might you say that?"

"It's clear enough that you are trying to work out why you're talking to another American. That tells me either you haven't seen many lately, or at least you didn't expect to see any at the moment." I wondered if this sounded as pretentious to him as it did to me.

Corbin still made no attempt to sit up, which, in his place, is the first thing I would have done, if only to alter the balance somewhat. But looking up at me seemed to bother him not at all. He was very self-contained—or was it self-centered? "I'll accept that," he said after a while.

In his place, in 1962, I'd have been overflowing with questions. Where was I? What happened? Who's in charge? He seemed to have none, or rather seemed to have no interest in getting answers. Suddenly I realized that he was playing interrogation games. Interesting: Why did he regard himself as a prisoner?

"You accept that. Fine. So why not tell me what you remember and I'll tell you what we saw and we'll piece it together. We pulled you out of a big airplane yesterday. I'm pretty rusty, but it looked to me like a Buffalo. Does that bring back any memories?"

He looked at me with new interest. "That's right, a C-8A. Are you a flier?"

"Used to be. It's been a while. Pretty old plane to be flying around in, isn't it?"

"It has its advantages." His tongue loosened, perhaps, by the temptation to talk shop, he added: "If you've seen it, you know what it is. It's your basic STOL utility transport plane. Twin turbo engines, maybe a basic 1200-mile range at these altitudes. It was plenty big enough for three people, even with all the equipment we jammed in there. And that low stall speed helped."

He paused.

"Because—?"

He declined to be led, so I prodded.

"We took a tremendous amount of equipment out of that wreck, Dennis. Any of it worth keeping?"

"Hell yes it's—" He stopped. I waited some more, then asked him if he'd care to explain why he was riding around in an American airplane with Chinese markings and Chinese pilots.

"Nothing to explain," he said off-handedly. "I was working for them. Why did you take the equipment out? What did you do with it?"

"Aren't we talking at cross-purposes here? Why not answer my question?"

"I *did* answer your question. I was working for them, that's why I was riding with them. I was maintaining that equipment you evidently put your hands on. And if we really are still in Tibet, I'd suggest you be careful with whatever you took: It's valuable equipment and the Chinese government is going to want it back. Actually, so is ours: That's all U.S. owned." Slowly, carefully, he sat up. "How about the pilots? Are you giving them the third degree too?"

"They're dead, I'm afraid. We buried them this morning." No perceptible response from him. "Does this feel like the third degree to you?"

Corbin looked around, found his boots on the floor nearby. "I guess I'm allowed to get dressed? To walk around?"

Kindly but firm. "Naturally we have questions, and good reasons for needing those questions answered. But this room is a hospital room, not a cell. You aren't a prisoner, you're a guest. After I get a doctor and he says it's safe for you to move around, you can get dressed and I'll show you around."

He lay back in bed. "Okay," he said. He closed his eyes, waiting for me to call the doctor. I began to find that self-assurance slightly irritating, yet there was something attractive about the boy nonetheless. I didn't like to think of him working with the communists.

"I need a little more information first, Dennis, if you don't mind, before I call the doctor. I still don't have a clear idea of how you got here or what you were doing in the vicinity." My God, I thought: Was that kindly but firm? To myself I sounded bureaucratic and prissy. (Later I decided I could have done worse. Unconsciously, I'd chosen a persona that Corbin knew how to respond to.)

He opened his eyes again and laughed, a short, sardonic laugh worthy of Mr. Barnard. "This isn't the third degree, but I can't get dressed until you call the doctor, and you won't call the doctor until I tell you what you want to know."

Well (I thought), at least he's responding. "Dennis, be

reasonable. Don't make the situation into something it isn't. Are you in a cell, being hit with rubber hoses? Are people shining lights in your eyes and making you sit on the edge of your chair—or stand in one place—for hours on end? It's pretty cold in here, I know, it always is in the morning, but did we put you in here without a warm robe and blankets?"

His eyes narrowed a bit and his lips compressed. "If you think you will intimidate me, you have the wrong boy. Go ahead. Do your worst. But sooner or later somebody else is going to make you answer some awkward questions about all this."

Partly a pose, of course. Bogart and John Wayne and God knows what other tough-guy stuff he watched on TV. But I admired it all the same, even if it also exasperated me. "I wasn't giving you a list of coming attractions," I snapped. "I was telling you that you're making yourself the star of the wrong movie. You aren't the lone tough-guy hero, stuck in a Nazi prison camp. You're the mysterious stranger who rode into town for un-known reasons, and I'm the head of the committee [I almost said 'posse', but shied away from the you're-under-arrest overtones] sent by the townsfolk to find our your intentions."

The shot hit home. He relaxed a bit. Not much, but some. I pressed my advantage. "So forget all that 'you can't make me talk' stuff and tell me what I have the right to know. We *did* pull you out of that wreck, you know, at the risk of our lives. And we *did* give you medical care, and bury your friends. We *do* intend to treat you well. But we have a right to know where we stand."

Then I waited.

He had been watching me attentively during my little speech. Again there was a pause while he decided. A cautious Charlie. "I guess it could look like that," he said, a bit reluctantly. "Okay, ask. But if you ask something I think I should not answer, I will not do it."

"That's fine. I don't have to know all your secrets. Probably the things I'm most concerned about aren't the things you want to keep secret anyway—like what all that machinery of yours did."

Another shot that hit home.

"What I *still* want to know is: Why were you in a Chinese aircraft? Where did you come from and what were you doing here?" Trespassing. Kindly but firm.

"I told you," he said, picking his words through mines I couldn't see, "I was there to maintain the equipment. They flew the search pattern, I maintained instruments to see what we were flying over."

"You were prospecting, then?"

Defiantly: "I am not going to tell you what we were looking for, so you can for—"

"I'm not sure we care, Dennis. Prospecting sounds like you were looking for mineral deposits. That right? Mineral deposits rather than—oh, downed aircraft or troop concentrations or something like that?" What I wanted to say was "man-made objects," but I didn't want him associating our anxiety with the existence of our buildings.

He decided it was smart to admit that he was looking for minerals. He even volunteered information. "That's one advantage of the C-8A—you can fly at pretty slow speeds, even at 22,000 feet. That helps a lot. When you're taking thousands of readings a second, the more time you have over the terrain, the better."

"So you were mapping the whole country? Or were you looking in one specific place?"

Again hesitation. "I suppose there isn't any reason not to tell you. At the very beginning of the project, they marked off certain areas—pretty large areas, though—and told us to concentrate there. But we'd done those, and we had a couple of days left, and we were doing a couple of fringe areas, just on the chance."

"I don't need specifics and you don't have to answer this at all if you think you shouldn't, but whatever you were looking for, did you find any around here?"

He was looking me straight in the eyes. "I don't have the slightest idea. The last thing I can remember is breakfast, as I told you." He shifted restlessly. "Speaking of that—"

I stifled a smile. It seemed to me that Dennis Corbin and I might get along okay.

"Soon, Dennis. Right after the doctor."

"Who is right after more questions," he sighed. But he was far more relaxed than when we had started.

"Maybe you can see what I'm driving at."

"Yeah, I think I do, except it makes no sense. You want to

know if we came looking for you or if we got here by accident. And now you know the answer. Then you want to know if our mission requires mapping this particular territory, because if it does you can hardly expect to remain undiscovered. And I am sure you will want to know if anybody will be coming to find us. They will be, of course. Probably they are already on their way."

"Did you keep in radio contact with your base?"

"I don't know."

"Did they have some sort of electronic beacon that would have given out your position automatically?"

"I don't know that either. I didn't fly the thing, I monitored instruments."

I believed him. "And you don't have any way to guess if the pilots radioed a mayday before they hit."

"I don't even remember the flight; I *sure* don't remember the crash." He paused, and I didn't fill the pause, having run out of questions. "But none of this makes any sense to me," he said. "Why are you worried about being seen? Who are you? What *is* this place?"

I stood up. "Good questions, Dennis," I said.

"Did I say something wrong?"

"No, not at all. I'm going to get the doctor, so you can get your breakfast."

Mr. Meister was going to spend enough time examining Corbin to allow me to check with Mr. Conway and Mr. Barnard on our next move.

Chapter Eleven.

Isolation

"**D**ennis Corbin, I'd like you to meet Mr. Conway, the man in charge here. This is Mrs. Bolton. ["Sunnie," she interjected pleasantly.] Mr. Barnard, our only fellow American."

Procedures at Shangri-La are nothing if not flexible. Mr. Conway, on hearing my fast sketch of Corbin's background, attitude, and mission, had swiftly decided that the five of us should have lunch together—presumably on the theory that no surroundings are quite so disarming as an informal meal. So it was that, within half an hour of our receiving Mr. Meister's seal of approval on Corbin's health, I was escorting him to one of the library alcoves that doubled, according to the occasion, as den, living room tea-room or—as now—dining room. And so he was introduced, with no greater ceremony, to three people who would be at the center of his life for the foreseeable future.

Corbin looked around at the alcove, at the bookshelves lining the walls, the sunlight flowing in through the windows (the thick white draperies pulled back to either side), the dark polished table, the elegantly simple chairs. We watched him glance out the window, watched his gaze be caught by the shining white presence of the mountain called Karakal—Blue Moon—on the far side of the chasm that is the valley. I had spent hours of my life doing that, except that I had done it in isolation, letting the mountain's peace flow into my being.

In short order, Thubten brought what had been asked for: cheese and butter and loaves of bread and the various fruits and a pitcher of valley-brewed beer from the prized kegs in our basement vaults. I could see Corbin conclude that Thubten was a servant. I wondered if this erroneous conclusion raised or lowered his opinion of the four of us. On the surface, four white Westerners being served by the humble native boy. But he'd have plenty of time to amend hasty conclusions.

I set about slicing the loaves while Mr. Barnard poured out the beer and Sunnie set the places. Corbin felt the heavy cloth of the napkins and was impressed despite himself. Or did he see it as more evidence of decadent luxury?

"You must pardon our informality, Mr. Corbin," Mr. Conway said. "We proceed on the assumption that a good appetite is not only the best sauce, but the best place-setting."

"It looks pretty good to me," Corbin said, and I remembered that he hadn't eaten in more than a day.

"Lord, Conway," Mr. Barnard said jocularly, "you don't suppose he could have an appetite like George here? We may have to send out for more."

Corbin, not yet being in on that particular inside joke, assumed a carefully neutral expression.

"Mr. Barnard's jest is at Mr. Chiari's expense," Sunnie said quietly. "Please be assured that we are blessed with plenty."

"Sure. It was just a joke. Those of us that can't eat a thing without it going right to fat envy those that can, that's all. Eat hearty."

Interesting. Mr. Barnard cultivates his reputation as a character, and Sunnie is always very direct, but that little byplay sounded slightly rehearsed. At least, to my ears it did. Their way of putting Corbin at ease by seemingly showing Mr. Barnard as a crude buffoon? And if they had rehearsed that little miniature sketch, what else did they have planned? It was unusual to have beer with a meal: *very* unusual to have it with lunch. Hospitality? Liquid truth-serum? I glanced at Mr. Conway speculatively. He read my mind, and his eyes twinkled. Approvingly, I thought.

As it happened, Mr. Barnard's statement, however calculated, was also correct. Corbin ate and ate and ate. Slice after slice of bread and butter, mounds of figs, great slices of cheese, two melon halves, several glasses of beer—and he ate effortlessly, as only a boy in his twenties (or teens!) can eat. I still look like I'm 25 or so, and I out-eat everyone here, but evidently my metabolism is slowing down a bit, as Corbin proved by providing comparison. I shared a little of Mr. Barnard's frank envy of Corbin's appetite and capacity.

As we ate, we learned something of Corbin's personal history, thanks mostly to Sunnie. She has a way of listening that draws you out, leading you to say more than you intended, often more than you were aware you knew. I could testify to that!

It seems that Mr. Dennis Corbin was a hot-shot combination electrical engineer/computer programmer/systems designer, whatever all that meant. (He did try to explain.) He was working for a certain company on the West Coast (he wouldn't give the name), designing new computer-controlled detection instruments (he wouldn't go into detail, not that we could have understood any of it) that could be used to detect certain valuable resources (no details) from the air.

"Of course," he said, we knew that there were space satellites that could do somewhat the same thing. (Of course we knew no such thing.) But this was a little different. (No details.) Since he was one of the chief designers, and since they needed a "beta test-sight" anyway (whatever that may have been, and he may have said "beta sight test," which still makes no sense), they'd asked him if he wanted to spend six weeks of his life riding around Tibet in an underfurnished airplane staring at dials all day. He'd jumped at the chance.

"The thing you have to understand, you see, is that there are only three of these babies in the world, and they were letting me play with one of them, and no forms to fill out. You know? One for me, two for the whole rest of the world. In-freakin'-credible. Except that now there's only two and I don't have either one."

Mr. Barnard passed him the pitcher and he poured himself some more beer. "I'd kind of like to take a look at it, if you don't mind. I mean, if you really did cut up the whole airplane— which, I still can't believe you *did* that, but if you did, you must have pretty much butchered ARDA, and I'd just like to see how badly."

ARDA, he informed us without much hesitation, stood for Airborne Resources Detection and Analysis, and damned few people even knew the acronym, and even fewer people knew what it stood for. Listening to him brought back my Air Force days. Words like ARDA conjured up Lackland, and Keesler, and the briefing room at Peshawar.

"It won't be any problem, your getting to see it," Mr. Barnard said after glancing at Mr. Conway. "You might even be able to put it all back together if you want to. Easier than putting your airplane back together."

Corbin could smile at that. "Yeah, well, your runways don't much look like they're FAA approved, so I guess that doesn't matter particularly." He shook his head, drank some more beer. "I can't believe you cut up the whole damned thing," he laughed, "and put it in the cellar."

Mr. Conway took that as his cue. "We wouldn't go to all that trouble without reason, Mr. Corbin. I assure you our fears are not irrational. The present rulers of Tibet are our sworn enemies, hostile to everything we are, everything we represent. When they find us, we will die, or worse."

"Worse?" Corbin smiled. "The old fate worse than death?"

Mr. Conway met his smile, but retained his seriousness. "Such fates do exist. Some would prefer an easy death to a long period of mental and physical torture. If it came to a forced choice, I would myself."

"Torture? Who's talking about torture?"

Sunnie entered the lists. "It appears that but few *talk* of it. It proceeds nonetheless. More than a million innocent inhabitants of this country have been murdered since the Chinese occupation began in 1950. Some died in battle, but most died of torture, imprisonment, starvation or general mistreatment. Hundreds of thousands have been punished for supporting their exiled Dalai Lama, or for clinging to their ancient religion, or even for refusing to desecrate shrines and insult monks and lamas. Surely you have heard of all this."

Apparently Corbin had *not* heard of it. Later, comparing notes, we four agreed that his reaction was unfeigned. He smiled. "Come on! It can't be all *that* bad!"

Mr. Barnard said, "Can't it? In the last 10 years, the communists wrecked more than 6,000 Buddhist monasteries. They burned about two-thirds of the country's literature. Two-thirds of everything that's ever been written and still existed. There's a quarter of a million political prisoners in concentration camps right this minute. And like Sunnie said, there's a quarter of the population dead and the whole rest of the country turned into a big penitentiary. If that ain't enough for you, how about the fact the communists been insisting the Tibetans plant rice and wheat instead of barley and millet? Then when the rice and wheat don't come up, Tibet starves. And they been pouring in millions of Chinese colonists. Six million of 'em, the best guess we heard so far. They're turning the Tibetans into a minority in their own country."

Corbin wasn't quite ready to back down, but he looked a little less certain. "Where'd you hear all that?"

Mr. Conway cut in lest Mr. Barnard say too much. "I'm afraid we must decline to tell you that, at the moment. But rest assured, we are not retailing rumors and gossip. These things happened, Mr. Corbin. They are happening yet."

"And they didn't happen in the dark," Mr. Barnard put in. "It's all been printed in the West."

Corbin looked at him curiously. "Now how would you know that?"

"Short-wave. BBC, if nothing else. Like I said, it ain't any secret."

"Which makes me wonder," I said, "why the U.S. government's letting your company play footsie with the communists."

"Man, where have you been? It was seven years ago Nixon went to China. Times have changed."

"Yeah," Mr. Barnard said, a bit sourly. "I remember listening to bits and pieces of that. But that still don't explain matters. Nixon and all had to know what the *Great* Cultural Revolution did to China. They had to know what the communists were doing to Tibet. Why get in bed with them? Or maybe nobody cares?"

Corbin—he made clear—didn't care much about politics, and he wasn't any fan of Presidents Nixon or Ford or Carter. But he supposed that re-establishing relations with China was mostly a balance-of-power ploy, giving both China and the United States leverage against the Soviets. And he hadn't heard about all the things we seemed to think were true. But after all, how much could the U.S. do for Tibet anyway? "Everybody has to look out for himself," he said simply, as if that was the ultimate answer. "And," he added, addressing himself to me, "I don't know how long you've been gone, but if you went home, you'd be surprised how much things have changed, maybe. People aren't that hot and bothered over anti-communist crusades the way they used to be."

Sunnie said, lightly, that we in our situation could not afford to be quite so tolerant.

"Why not?"

"Because we, like other inhabitants oɪ Tibet, know our enemies."

Corbin paused, considering his options. "It takes two to quarrel, I'm told," he said mildly.

I was tempted to snap at this, something on the order of: "That sounds very reasonable, but try telling it to the concentration camp's jailor." But I hesitated—he *was* our guest—and the moment passed. And then Mr. Conway spoke.

* 2 *

He'd been awaiting the proper time, perhaps, and judged that it had arrived. We'd finished our meal, even Corbin, and were at that moment that leads either to a quiet ruminative digestion or to resumption of activity. "I think it is a bit unfair to our guest," he said, glancing around at the three of us, "to allow this particular conversation to continue without first furnishing him its background." Immediately he had Corbin's full attention. Corbin knew he was about to hear something worth hearing, though he couldn't have guessed what.

Mr. Conway warned him he was about to hear some pretty incredible things, and asked him to suspend judgment till the end of the story. He assured Corbin we'd all been told the same story, all had found it at first impossible to believe, and all had been led, with the passage of time, to accept it.

He sketched out Shangri-La's history, beginning not with Father Perrault's arrival here but with his own. He told of how he and Mr. Barnard and two others had been hijacked (he said Shanghaied), had been graciously received here, and had waited for the arrival of porters to escort them home. He told of his conversations with the high lama: the promise of added life; the request that he care for the monastery until the day came when it would be needed to help renew a world exhausted by war.

"He intended us to serve as the Christian missionaries had served the wreck of the Roman Empire," Mr. Conway said. "Civilizations always flow from small, protected pockets of grace, integrity and purpose."

He had caught his audience by now. He told of his own

doubt, his exhausted mental state, his abrupt departure with Mallinson. He passed quickly over his suffering in China and totally omitted (with good reason!) any description of his route of return. He told how he found, on his return, that the high lama, now dead, had left instructions for Conway to be given charge of the lamasery's day-to-day operations. And he told how he and others had labored to make Shangri-La ready for any contingency. Nodding to Mr. Barnard, he gave him credit for shutting down the supply pipeline before it could give away their secret. And he sketched in a few phrases their life of isolation after 1937.

"In those early years we were comparatively safe, and knew it. Yet for the first time we were faced with the threat of aerial surveillance. Flight greatly reduced the protection that geography had always afforded us." He reminded Corbin—what I myself hadn't known—that during the war more than one straying Allied bomber overflew Tibet, one over Lhasa itself. At least one flight crew, he said, had had to bail out in Tibetan territory, and were sent to Lhasa and then courteously forwarded on to India.

The point was that Shangri-La could no longer afford to maintain contact with the outside world except second-hand, through the radio sets Mr. Barnard had ordered, with their wood-fired generating sets. Then, in 1950, the Chinese invasion made matters even more precarious, particularly when they began to built motor roads where roads had never been, in a vast semicircle along the plateau from the east, along the southern border, to the northwest. As early as 1954, a road had been built—uncomfortably close—from Gartok to Sinkiang province.

The communist invaders (he explained to Corbin, though it should have been obvious) were unpopular from the beginning. Their troops came in great numbers and required the native inhabitants to furnish their provisions, which brought first hunger and then actual starvation to the country. Worst of all, the atheist invaders regarded Tibet's Buddhism (lamaism) and reverence for lamas as contemptible superstition. Preserving a facade of respect for the Dalai Lama, they moved to transform Tibet into a mirror of the communized provinces north and east of it.

"The predictable result apparently took them by surprise, not once but repeatedly. In 1959—20 years ago—the people of Lhasa became convinced the Chinese intended to kidnap the Dalai Lama. They rose up in rebellion. The rebellion was crushed, of course, but fortunately it did result in the flight of the Dalai Lama to safety in India."

"Good thing, too," Mr. Barnard said, "or they would have had him in their hands when they started their goddamned cultural revolution. That's when things in this country got a whole lot worse."

"How worse?" These were Corbin's first words in many moments.

Mr. Barnard said, "The 60s is when they got down in earnest to colonizing the place."

"But that was after the revolt of the Khambas had begun," Mr. Conway said, "not so many months before a Captain George Chiari, U.S.A.F., came flying overhead, intending to photograph Chinese troops invading India." He looked at me. "Perhaps you never realized that what halted the Chinese invasion of India was less Indian resistance (not particularly effective, I fear) than Khamba resistance based in the province of Loka. The rebels operated widely in Chamdo, which sits squarely on supply lines to the south. Peking was wise to halt military operations and negotiate."

Corbin was looking at me thoughtfully, and I knew what he was thinking. "I'm 43," I said. "I was 26—just about your age—when I came here in 1962. So you can see the treatment Mr. Conway told you about works." As an afterthought, I said, "Come to my cell later and I'll fish out my ID and you can see for yourself."

An inspired thought, that. I could see Corbin accept my age as already proved.

Mr. Conway saw it too. "Perhaps our interest in avoiding detection is more understandable now, Mr. Corbin. The communists would have three reasons to hate us: We are an institution at once Tibetan, religious, and linked to the West. They would destroy us without compunction."

"You think they'd just murder you?"

Unexpectedly, Sunnie spoke, after a long time spent listening and observing. "Perhaps they would not intend to do, but that would be the inevitable effect. Our situation here offers unique advantages, but it has the defects of its qualities." She smiled.

"Far be it from a lady to tell her own age, but I see no objection to telling tales on others. Mr. Barnard is—how old are you now, Henry? Have you reached the century mark?"

"Not quite, my dear," said this 55-year-old man across the table. "I'm 97 next week. August 12, 1882."

She turned to Mr. Conway. "Hugh?"

Smiling at Corbin, rather than Sunnie, "June 6, 1894, Dennis. Do I look to be 85?" He looked, and acted, about 40, as he well knew.

"And I myself shall never again see 21," Sunnie laughed. "But once outside this valley—"

"And you can count on it, the Reds would certainly move us."

" —aging would be only a matter of a few weeks at best."

"It seems the body wasn't designed to renew itself forever," Mr. Conway said to Corbin. "Even in this favored spot, we cannot halt the aging process, we can only retard it."

"Only! A hundred years! Two hundred years!"

Mr. Conway—all of us—smiled. "Spoken like a youngster," Mr. Barnard said. "I assure you, no matter how many years you get, it's always too few."

"We haven't a desire to make them fewer, certainly," Sunnie said, looking at Corbin quite seriously. "If we are once discovered, we and this establishment are all at an end."

All at once Corbin made the connection. I'd been through it myself, not *so* very long ago. I remembered the mental process. First you're following the discussion, grasping it, but on an abstract level. Then suddenly—it's always suddenly—you realize that there's a reason why these people are telling you these things.

* 3 *

Everybody else sensed it at the same time I did. Corbin stiffened, almost imperceptibly, and his expression hardened. But he didn't say anything. He waited.

Mr. Conway obliged him. "'But what does this have to do with me?'"

Corbin nodded. "Yeah. That's about it."

Mr. Barnard said, "You might not like it much."

"I can't get out of here, can I?"

"Not if Shangri-La is to live," Mr. Conway said.

Corbin looked quite calm. "You don't trust me to keep your secret."

"No, we don't. But not for the reasons you assume."

"Which are—?"

"Oh, that you have worked with the Chinese authorities. That your political sympathies might lie elsewhere. That you might prefer to sacrifice our existence to assure your security." The winning Conway smile, the warmest I've known. "Did I miss anything significant?"

Corbin shook his head silently, a little mollified.

"Unfortunately, honorable men are not invulnerable to pressure. If you were to leave here, those pressures would immediately overwhelm you. I wonder: Do you understand your situation fully?"

"Tell me," Corbin said tightly.

"How would you explain where you had been? For that matter, where would you go?"

"I'd go back to the airbase, if I could get there."

I said, "You really think that's such a great idea?"

"Sure. Why not? I'm on contract to them, and I've lived up to it. I don't have anything to hide. The fact we crashed certainly isn't *my* fault."

"And then they could decide if they wanted to send a bomber to wipe us out, or a company of infantry to take us over."

"What makes you think they'd do either? How do you know they wouldn't just settle for getting their airplane back?"

"Dennis, this is a *religious* community! Whether you believe in religion or not, do I have to remind you what every communist community on the face of the earth has done to every religious community it could get its hands on? In Tibet particularly?"

"All right, let's not get off on a big discussion of communism and religion. Let's say I don't tell them about this place at all. Suppose I just tell them we crashed and I'm the only survivor. That's certainly true enough!"

"How did you stay alive in the meantime? Who fed you, for instance? You sure didn't forage for food all along the way."

"I could make up a story. Maybe some remote village fed me."

"'Fine. Bring us there.'"

Corbin bit his lip. "I see. That would be a problem."

"'And where are the remains of your aircraft with our secret and valuable equipment, Mr. Corbin? Kindly lead us to it, so that we may salvage anything remaining.'"

"Maybe there's nothing left of value? It blew up after I got myself free?"

"'We will judge for ourselves. Perhaps you are engaged in some trick?'"

Corbin's face had lost much of its color. "Well, I got this bump on my head, and I can't remember the crash. The first thing I knew, I was wandering around on the plateau."

Mr. Conway: "And yet you made your way back, from an unknown starting point? Remarkable."

"After a while I started to recognize landmarks."

Mr. Barnard: "You weren't ever here on foot. How'd you recognize anything?"

Mr. Conway: "'In any case, bring us as close as you can to where you were when you regained your memory. We will proceed from there.'"

"Maybe I can't retrace my steps. Maybe I got lucky. Or, say, why do I have to return to the same field? Why can't I wander somewhere else?"

Mr. Barnard: "Anywhere you wander to, they're going to draw a circle and say you pretty near had to be inside that circle, to get here in this many days. What do you do when they don't find the airplane inside the circle?"

Corbin shrugged. "Is it my problem if they can't find it? This is a big country."

I said, "It's your problem when they come back to you for more details. Dennis, it isn't hard. If I'd come back to Peshawar in '62 and said I'd come down in the mountains of Tibet, maybe they'd buy it and maybe they wouldn't, but the most they could do would be send another plane looking for mine. But if your fancy prospecting gear is as special as you say, they're not going to just kiss it off, are they? I'll bet they call in ground troops, helicopters, light planes, jets, everything, until they're convinced it's gone without a trace."

"I can be pretty stubborn," Corbin said, stubbornly enough. "I just don't know *where* we came down."

"Yeah, but suppose they were tracking you when you came down and they know the general area. Then they bring you somewhere nearby and you'd *better* start recognizing things."

I don't think he'd considered this.

"Assume persistence on their part," Mr. Conway said. "Assume diligent search and close questioning, resulting finally in a moment-by-moment chronology of everything you admit to remembering. The moment they notice the slightest evasion . . . ."

"The questions will get a lot rougher," Mr. Barnard said. "'Guard! Escort Mr. Corbin to a cell and let him think about the consequences of lying to the people's representatives.'"

Corbin sat unmoving, except for the fingers of his right hand, wearily massaging his eyes and cheeks. Finally he said, "Do you really think it would have to be like that?"

"Do you really think it could be any other way?"

I give him full credit. He didn't like the logic, but when he couldn't get around it, he didn't pretend it didn't exist. "God," he said, more or less to himself. "It looks like I really did it this time, didn't I?"

"Of course you might be tempted," Sunnie said, "to spare yourself unpleasantness by telling them at once what had happened to you, for which you were in no way to blame." Corbin started to object, but subsided as she continued. "However, I cannot see that this would much improve your situation among them."

We saw it. Corbin didn't, yet.

"Eyewitness," Mr. Barnard said. "You'd know too much."

This startled Corbin even more. "But I'm an American citizen! I know you don't think much of communists, but you have to realize, they need good relations with the United States right now. If they started jailing American citizens—me particularly, considering the mission I was on—they'd be shooting themselves in the foot. My company would be mad, and my bosses would make sure the government got mad. If they had to, they could go to the press and make such a stink the Chinese would wish they'd never heard of me. They *have to* know that."

Mr. Barnard toyed with the unfinished glass of beer in front of him on the table. "You got a lot of faith in a lot of things: your company, your government, the press. I don't say you are definitely wrong, but that's a lot more faith than I got. Course, my memories go back a ways, and maybe things have changed—though I notice people don't change so much." He looked up at Corbin. "Say you're right and they'd all back you to the hilt. Here's what bothers me. Right now, you are among the missing, am I right? And probably your bosses and your government have been told. Am I right? Well," he said, slowly, chillingly, "is there any law says the Reds got to tell anybody the minute they find you? Any law says, if they don't like the answers they get, or they decide it ain't in their interests, they *ever* got to say you turned up?"

I examined the bottom of my empty glass. Mr. Barnard and Mr. Conway glanced at each other, then stared at the table. Only Sunnie kept her eyes on Corbin. "Perhaps you think it very unkind of us to require you to realize these facts so soon after your arrival," she said compassionately. "I confess, it does seem rather a brutal procedure. I'm certain we all would much rather have put this off to another time."

"But we couldn't," Mr. Conway said quietly. "You would have wanted access to a radio transmitter, and we should have had to lie to you or make feeble excuses. It seemed more straightforward to tell you at once."

Corbin, it appeared, bounced back quickly. "Well, probably you're right. I hadn't had time to think about it yet, and maybe I never would have come to the same conclusions, but you've convinced me. I can't go back to China. Make up a story or tell the truth, I'm dead either way. So how do I get back to the States?"

I didn't say anything. I'd been there.

"Dennis, you got a problem there too," Mr. Barnard said, slowly, reluctantly. "Don't it occur to you?"

Corbin looked genuinely puzzled.

"Didn't you tell us this machine of yours was one of only three in the whole world? And didn't you say you were testing it for your company at the same time you were working it on a job here? And didn't you say they were liable to be real upset when it turns up missing?"

"Yeah, they will."

"Well, then?"

A blank look. "Well what?"

"Don't you see we can't send you back home either? You're

going to wind up with the same kind of questions. What happened to the airplane? Where did it come down? How did you get out? Why are you refusing to tell our customers information they got a right to know?"

"This isn't going to do your career with your company any good, either," I said. "They aren't going to be anxious to jeopardize relationships—and future contracts—for the sake of one employee. Ex-employee. And if your coming back alive gets in the way of better relations between the two countries, the government is going to blame you, even though none of it's your fault."

"So you can't go home either," Mr. Barnard said. "And where else can you go? You wouldn't have papers, you couldn't explain yourself, you'd be in trouble in 20 minutes. Sooner or later you'd get turned over to Uncle Sam—you sure couldn't hide being a Yank—and then you'd have to try to talk your way out of why you'd been doing the hiding you'd been doing. I was on the run once, lad, back when I was already a whole lot older than you are, and more experienced. And I had money, too. I'm here to tell you, it gets on your nerves real fast."

Corbin said nothing.

"It's a losing game for you, Dennis, anywhere but here. Here, we know who you are and why you're here and everything is fine. Anywhere else you go, you got to face questions you can't answer, or you got to murder everybody here. It ain't your fault, it ain't anybody's fault, but I can't think of one place in the world outside of right here that's safe for you. You got no other place to hide."

No reply.

"Dennis, look at it this way. If that plane you were riding in had crashed on the other side of the mountain, what shape do you figure you'd be in by now?"

"Dead, I suppose," Corbin said wearily.

Mr. Barnard nodded sharply "Damn well told, you'd be dead. Come down in the middle of the Kunluns somewhere and even if your Chinese friends send people right off, who's going to find you in time? Am I right?"

Listlessly: "Right."

"If you'd died in that plane, your life on the outside'd be over. And if we hadn't been here to drag you out, you'd have died just the same. So maybe it will help you to accept the way things are. Your life outside is over. As far as the world is concerned, you died in a mysterious crash. It's important the world don't stop thinking that way." He looked at him intently. "You see?"

Corbin frowned. I went back to fooling with my glass at the table. Nobody said anything for a long time. When Corbin did speak, it was in a voice so constricted that I looked up in surprise. Up to this point, Corbin had been a cucumber, Mr. Professional, in control.

"Is there somewhere I can take a walk for a few minutes? Would anybody mind that?"

From the sound of his voice—though not from the expressionless look of his face—he was close to tears. Mr. Conway suggested that I take him outdoors and show him the quarter-mile stretch of rock ledge that we whimsically call our promenade, where we walk and walk, back and forth, back and forth till our legs ache, on days when we sicken of life led too much indoors.

Chapter Twelve.

Adjustment

Finally he was ready to talk.

I had brought him outside and showed him the trail and offered to walk with him if he wanted. He had set out, as I'd expected, alone, without a word. I had settled onto one of the stone benches on the patio—which Mr. Barnard always called a veranda—and, after a few minutes, had taken a cigar from my pocket and lit it with a sparker, feeling a little like Mr. Barnard myself.

I had told myself, while I sat there waiting, that we had told Corbin for his own good, that waiting would have meant deceit, that ultimately this was kinder. I had told myself that this was Mr. Conway's decision and that Mr. Conway didn't commonly make mistakes. I had told myself that Corbin seemed to be a bright kid and would undoubtedly have figured out the situation soon enough.

But Corbin's eyes, as I remembered them, outweighed all this logic, and I wondered if for once Mr. Conway had miscalculated.

Also, something about Mr. Barnard's explanation to him bothered me. I couldn't put my finger on it; there wasn't any particular loose end my mind was tugging at; but something—if I could find it—wasn't quite right.

I had sat so long after finishing my cigar that I was considering starting on another, just to pass the time, when Corbin returned. He had obviously walked far enough, vigorously enough, to burn off some nervous energy. Equally obviously, he had stood, or more probably sat, looking out at the vast expanse of emptiness that was the barren mountainside—and at the enigmatic mass of rock and snow that was Karakal. You can't long be surrounded by so much sky and bare rock and silence without being taken from behind with serenity. Comparative serenity, at least. In his case, not serenity, not tranquillity, but a certain stillness. He was visibly calm, visibly more tired, as he picked his way back to where I was and stood facing me.

I held out a cigar. He shook his head. "I don't smoke."

I put it back in my robe's pocket. "How about talking? Want to talk?"

He smiled with half his face. "What's to talk about?"

I motioned him to take a seat and after a moment's hesitation he sat on the other end of the bench, extending his feet far forward and leaning back against the building, his hands interlocked behind his head, gazing up at the blue-black sky.

"Dennis," I said, "I know it's hard for you to believe, but what you're going through now, everybody here has gone through at one time or another. None of us—not one of us—came here of his own free will. God brought us here, if you want to put it that way."

"I don't believe in God," he said shortly, almost contemptuously.

"All right, forget about God. Say it was life that brought us here. It amounts to the same thing. It isn't something that anybody has chosen."

Corbin didn't bother to reply.

I knew that when his feet were firmly planted on the ground, he would be cock-sure, even arrogant. But he'd been knocked off-balance. Perhaps he would open up a little.

"Are you close to your family?"

The question was unexpected, I could see. He stopped looking off at the sky and looked at me instead. "Does that make any difference?"

"It might."

"I don't see what it has to do with anything, but I don't have any brothers or sisters and my mother died when I was still in high school. My father is a jerk."

"Are you married?"

He shook his head.

"Engaged?"

He shook his head again, impatiently. "Knock off the questions, okay? I don't even have a steady girl friend, so I suppose that makes it okay that I'm stuck here now. My career doesn't count for anything, what I want doesn't matter, everything happens for the best. Except, my life isn't here in your little dream world, it's out in the *real* world. I've got friends and responsibilities out there. I don't much feel like giving them all up for a monastery on the side of a mountain."

Quite a vivid portrayal of the pain he was in. I already knew that Mr. Dennis Corbin did not ordinarily display his emotions. He reminded me of somebody I once knew.

"Listen, Dennis, I'm not going to sit here and just tell you to look on the bright side of things. It hurts. And it's going to hurt like hell for a long time. I know."

"Do you?"

I did. But how could I convince him I did? I looked for an approach. "Something tells me you're a reader, Dennis. That true? Read a lot?"

"Sure," he said dismissively, not seeing where I was going.

"Fiction? Not just technical stuff?" There was that public library card. That wouldn't have been for technical stuff, surely.

"Some. When you're trying to keep up in three fields, though, you don't have a lot of time for pleasure reading."

"No, I'm sure you don't, and you've been working particularly hard, it sounds like. Well, how about when you were a teenager, or in college? Much fiction then?"

"Some."

I asked him to tell me some of his all-time favorites, hoping there would be at least one I knew, and there was.

"*The Virginian*," I said, echoing him. So that's still in print. Great. Read it when I was 15. The young cowboy, on his own since he was 14. The young New England schoolteacher, worlds above him socially. The Virginian making his way in the world, tying to make her love him."

[I was using *The Virginian* for my own purposes, but unexpectedly found myself moved by my memories of the pictures it painted. The wide-open Western country, the forested mountains populated by bear and elk, the thousand miles of emptiness in the heart of the fledgling nation. Suddenly those imagined memories fused with real memories of sleepy creeks in the pine barrens and brilliant sunlit days amid the leafy canopy of the forest of the Appalachian Trail in Virginia, and the icy streams of New Hampshire. I had to make an effort to prevent myself from getting lost in those pictures—and smells (pine needles)—and sounds (mourning doves. Mocking birds!).]

"If it's one of your favorite books, something in it must have moved you."

"I guess," he said casually.

I smiled. "Relax. I don't want to know what. I'm just pointing out that Owen Wister wrote that book before our fathers were born, but he touched us, just like he touched millions of others. Sure, everybody's different, but not all *that* different." A little reluctantly, I realized what I would have to do to try to help him. "Let me tell you a little story. True story, about myself. I was just about your age when I came down here, and I had even fewer reasons to like it here than you do."

That aroused a faint flicker of interest. "Were you some kind of hot-shot?"

"Not like you. I was just your ordinary garden-variety flyboy. But I had my ties to the world, naturally." My parents growing old, perhaps dying, without me. My brothers and sisters marrying and having kids I'd never see. Marianne. I was surprised to realize, as I sketched it out to him, that acceptance hadn't removed—only altered—the pain. He heard it in my voice. He heard it as an echo of my own, and for the first time began to really accept the connection. So I found myself telling him about Christmas, 1963, my second Christmas at Shangri-La, but the first after I'd accepted that I'd never again see the world and the people I'd left.

* 2 *

That was before Mr. Conway had begun my training, in the days when I was still merely a guest, filling my time as I pleased with chores, conversation, studies, reading—and radio.

Sometimes—but not too often, for I had left the world too recently to hear its voice without pain—Mr. Barnard and I would listen to the BBC and other broadcasts. It was from the BBC that I heard the inconceivable news that President Kennedy had been murdered. Mr. Barnard had heard the news first, and had summoned me, as he sometimes did, and I had assumed he wanted me to listen so that I could help him interpret some event for the others. No doubt he had that in mind too, but he did it primarily, I think, because he thought I'd want to know.

He'd seen a lot of the world, and he'd lived through many things, but he was about as shocked and incredulous as I was. Yes, there had been three other assassinations, but none since 1901. Now? In 1963? The fact took a while to sink in.

Then came a period of mourning, for I remembered Kennedy as an attractive, intensely alive person. Debating during the 1960 campaign. Decorating John Glenn. Integrating Old Miss. Getting the Soviet missiles out of Cuba. And I remembered sitting in this room, listening to this radio receiver, hearing him announcing the Nuclear Test Ban Treaty, ending nuclear testing in the atmosphere, underseas and in outer space. "A significant accomplishment," Mr. Conway had said. "Perhaps the most significant turning point since Sarajevo, but in the right direction." (I didn't understand quite why he thought so.)

And now he was dead.

I couldn't quite remember what Lyndon Johnson looked like, and couldn't remember a thing about him except that he used to run the Senate. I wondered what my father's reaction would be.

Probably it was Mr. Kennedy's assassination, indirectly, that made that Christmas so hard. In the wake of the tragedy, I lost myself to the radio, listening for longer and longer stretches at a time. For the first few days, I switched from broadcast to broadcast, seeking news, hungering to hear more, as though continuous listening could somehow change what I listened to. But by Thanksgiving day, a few short days later, I was listening to anything. With enough channels and a proper location (and was Chang wrong about radio!) you can hear pretty nearly any kind of thing you want to hear, any time day or night. I spent some lonely December evenings alternating, as my mood changed, from classical to jazz. Naturally, the more I listened, the more I missed the world the sounds were coming from, the world beyond the mountains.

Christmas day, I knew before I got out of bed, was going to be hard. For that reason I stayed later in bed, missing my breakfast with Mr. Barnard entirely. (I half expected he'd come hunt me up, so ingrained was our morning habit, but in this I underestimated his perspicacity. Or maybe they'd been talking about me.)

Christmas, 1962, had been lonely, thinking of my family going about their Christmas routine without me. But in 1962 I'd thought I'd be back in the world by the following summer at the latest, and I'd felt a certain guilt over the shadow that my being reported missing would have cast over the day. Somehow even the guilt helped make the situation less grim.

But I'd only been missing two months then. The determined among them could find solid reason for hope. By Christmas, 1963, they had surely been reduced to hope against hope. And for me there *was* no hope, so I lay late in bed and wondered how I would get through the day.

I'd reached up and opened my curtain, and estimated by the angle of sunlight that it was perhaps 10 a.m. Half a day behind me—halfway around the world—my family would soon be going to Midnight Mass. And when Mass was over, they would each get to open one present from under the tree, and then they'd have a huge 1 a.m. breakfast of eggs and sausages and toast and pastries, and would stay up till three or so, talking, teasing, making bad jokes.

I had wondered, lying there, if maybe there wouldn't be fewer jokes this year. Maybe with the first of the children dead (presumed dead) the holidays wouldn't be quite what they were. Maybe there would be a pall on the holidays. A tear came to my eye, and I brushed it away in impatience and some irritation. What was I doing? Ridiculous to cry for myself. Especially since I wasn't even dead! But they wouldn't know that.

Why should that thought bring a stab of guilt? Not *my* fault, for God's sake! Unless joining the Air Force could be considered to be the decision that brought me here. But by that reasoning, why not blame the fact that I'd read *The Spirit of St. Louis?* Think—I told myself—of something else. Or of nothing at all.

But that proved not so easy. Staring at my blank ceiling, I found myself wondering where Marianne would be spending Christmas. (With her parents, probably, at Virginia Beach.) I wondered if she still had her job in D.C. (Why not?) I wondered if she was still seeing David Feulner. (Think about something else.) I wondered what my family would do when they got up today. If Marianne still missed me. If she had already put me into her past. . . .

I threw off the covers, cupped on a pair of the thick warm socks I'd been given, got into a fresh robe and stuck my feet into my sandals. Maybe the day was going to be hard: I didn't have to take it lying down. . . .

"You understand?"

Corbin nodded.

"It wasn't any easier for me, Dennis."

"So what happened?"

"Christmas Day? Oh, I functioned. Merry Christmas to this one and that one, many happy returns of the day to another one. A big festive meal in mid-afternoon, exchange of presents— "

"With 60 people?"

I smiled. "Everyone picks a name out of a dish, usually at Summer Solstice, and gives to that one person. Mr. Barnard gave me something he'd carved out of wood, a cat, curled up asleep. You wouldn't think that'd be something he'd know how to do, would you? But he said he'd learned whittling from his father, and had taken it up again. Beautiful little thing. Must have taken him months to carve. Or maybe not. Remind me sometime to show it to you.

"Anyway, the day passed." My instinct here was to skate lightly over the memory rather than relive it. I made myself participate in it. A little gift to Dennis Corbin that he'd never know about. "The worst time was that night. I got blind-sided."

Now, carefully. "You have to understand," I said, looking him in the eyes, "that when I came here at age 26, I was very closed-off emotionally." A lot like you. "I was more used to thinking than feeling, and I really didn't trust emotions much. Didn't know how to express them, didn't know how to listen to them and be taught by them, often couldn't even be sure what I was feeling. If something made sense to me intellectually, I listened. If it made sense emotionally, I didn't pay much attention."

A little too abstract: I was losing his attention. "Until I started listening in on the radio in November, 1963, I thought I'd come to terms with being here. Like you, I figured it was just bad luck, but there wasn't anything I could do about it. I did try to escape once . . . [a quick flash of keen interest here, which I saw him instantly suppress] but I found out it was impossible. So then I told myself there wasn't anything to be done, and I told myself I'd accepted it."

I looked at him again, trying to see if he really understood. "You see? I told myself I *had to* get resigned to it, so I assumed I *was* resigned to it, when I was just trying to tell myself what I *ought to* feel. But that all went out the window Christmas night."

Trying to anticipate his reaction, I had to smile. "Probably you will think this is silly, but every so often the monks come together to sing and play instruments and entertain each other. When you are totally on your own, as we are, you make your own routine, and part of any routine has to be a *break* in the routine, if you follow me. So, we have a Christmas program and a Easter program and smaller celebrations throughout the year. Like any community.

"Well, that year I represented spectatordom, as Thoreau put it. Mr. Barnard and me. The others all participated, singing sometimes, forming part of the audience other times. I don't know if that sounds dumb to you."

"It doesn't sound dumb," Corbin said.

"Really, it was very nice and sort of homey. Reminded me of college. Well, anyway, as you can imagine, we had music from all over the world, China and India and all over. And it was interesting, and I told myself that I felt okay, I'd gotten through Christmas. I don't know why I didn't see it coming.

"The third piece was a bell choir. Eight of the monks put on gloves, gathered around a table, and each picked up a single copper bell. And just before they hit the first note, I shivered, and I could feel the hair rise on the back of my neck. *Before* it happened, somehow."

Remembering, even 16 years later, I closed my eyes for a moment.

"I'd been congratulating myself on getting through a difficult day, and then, halfway up the side of this mountain in the middle of nowhere, they started moving their bells, note after note, and they were playing 'Silent Night,' that I'd heard every Christmas night of my life. I sat there and cried, Dennis. First time since I was a kid. I cried and cried, and couldn't stop myself. Didn't even *want to* stop myself. And that was very much unlike me." And you. "It caught me by surprise."

Corbin didn't say anything, but his eyes were brighter than they had been. A little tell-tale moisture? A little indication that I'd cracked his shell?

✳ 3 ✳

Sunnie came out and joined us. Corbin stood up when she appeared, greeted her politely, offered her his seat and in general conveyed by his body language his awareness of her presence. Good manners, I thought at first—then I realized that if Corbin didn't have a steady girlfriend, it wasn't from lack of opportunity. He was a born ladies' man. Even in the presence of a woman 80 years his senior (assuming he believed our story) he automatically kept himself in practice.

"I was just telling Dennis about Christmas of '63," I said.

Sunnie's expression was as serene, as placid, as ever, yet it conveyed to me the existence, if not the content, of some hidden purpose. I prepared myself to follow her lead as soon as I could discern it.

"Anyone here could tell a similar tale," she said gravely. "We all, at one time or another, were plucked from the land of the living and yet were preserved from death. A fate difficult to bear, at times, but not without its compensations."

"A long, long life," Corbin said—and if his shoulders did not shrug, his voice did.

"Long, but scarcely boring," she said. "Life is quite as full of challenge here as anywhere, for the very good reason that life is much the same here as elsewhere." She had his attention, I could see. "It is, you know. We are as near God here as elsewhere. No nearer, no farther."

"Dennis doesn't believe in God," I said neutrally.

"Do you not? Well, at that, disbelief is not so very dis-creditable, provided one doesn't let one's doubts harden into dogmatic certainty about what one cannot know."

I saw that innocent remark catch Corbin on his blind side. He didn't know how to respond.

"I say, you aren't dogmatic about it, are you, Dennis? You do leave room for doubt?"

Corbin was tactful, but not deceitful. "I guess I don't think about it all that much. But I haven't seen much reason to believe in God. If he made this world, he's out of practice."

(Corbin's statement had an unexpected effect on me. Instant-ly I was transported to the world of my childhood. Sometimes we would visit our cousins who lived on the Maurice River,

down near Mauricetown where that placid river starts to become a tidal estuary. Sometimes four of us cousins would take
their wood-and-canvas canoes up one of the tributary streams.
Around us—above us—would be sea oats and sawgrass and
wild flowers. Birds flitted around from clump to clump. We'd
hear the splash of a fish, or the longer, startling splash of an otter
or possum. I'd forgotten, in these long years stranded on a
mountain, the feel of a small boat on the water; how your every
movement shifts the balance, how the swell from passing boats
lifts first bow, then stern, or rocks you from side to side, or,
taken on the quarter, lifts and tilts you and turns you to one side,
then lowers you while turning you to the other. And for some
reason I'd forgotten the look of a light-blue sky, seen filtered
through a perforated screen of green leaves. I'd forgotten the
odd, unbalanced, but not painful or unpleasant, strain on
muscles—unlike any other I could think of—that comes from
pulling a paddle through the water. I'd forgotten how much I'd
loved those excursions. My last was—when? when I was 17 or
so? No, I'd gone out my third summer of college. Nearly a
quarter of a century, a long time to be away from open water.
Odd it never struck me until it was precipitated by some
"chance" remark of Corbin's.)

Sunnie was looking at him quite quizzically.

"Everyone suffers disappointments," she said. "But p'raps
disappointment is merely the result of limited perspective. One
wouldn't expect playwrights and their characters to see matters
in the same light. Not if the playwright is competent, and I trust
this one is."

Corbin smiled. Graciously, but a little condescendingly. No
point in arguing with these people, he said without speaking.
Intellectually they are children.

Sunnie naturally read his expression as easily as I did. More
easily, most likely. "Devising clever machinery is a very useful
life's work, Dennis," she said. "Very much underrated by those
in other fields, I am sure. Machinery has done much to make our
lives more comfortable. Perhaps even more useful, though in
that instance there is reason to doubt. You will find ample scope
for such activities in Shangri-La, both here and in the valley
below. Our lives here are difficult enough to make us welcome
improvements that reduce drudgery. But there *are* other things

to do in one's life, you know."

Apparently the morning had sharpened Corbin's ability to hear things coming. "Such as?"

"You needn't take anyone's word on religious questions. Ask George."

I was still lost in the marshes of the Maurice River. It took me a couple of seconds to come back. "Ask me. . .?"

"Must one depend upon others for the truth about God?"

I hadn't ever put it in those terms. "Well," I said, "I can only speak from my own experience, but it seems to me that when you're talking about religion, you're usually talking about two different things and mixing them up without noticing. I don't mean *you*, Sunnie, I mean people do. You know, in general. There's opinion, and there's experience. If you've had the experience and you're talking to somebody who hasn't had it, you might as well give up. It's the old thing about describing color to a blind man."

Corbin was looking at me doubtfully, but was noticing that Sunnie approved.

"But even if you're talking to somebody else who *has* had the experience, you're likely to get into an argument, because even if you've both had exactly the same experience, it's likely to mean different things to you. You try to fit it into the general framework of what you know."

"New wine into old wineskins," Sunnie said.

"Exactly. So if you're a Buddhist talking to a Moslem, or a Christian talking to a Jew, or a mystic talking to somebody who may not have any religious background at all, you might or might not be able to realize that you've had the same experience, but you sure aren't likely to agree on what it means, and you'll be lucky if you don't start regarding each other as perverters of the truth, or as ignorant, malicious fools."

"Shangri-La excepted," Sunnie said lightly, "because we are so few, and we have had time to learn what each one's words are intended to convey. We have realized that God speaks differently to different individuals."

"And what's nice about it is that there's still room for people like Miss Brinklow, who don't *believe* that."

"Do you understand the implications of George's remarks, with which, by the way, I am in full agreement? We can offer you the experience, so that you may judge for yourself."

"I guess I had enough religion growing up," Corbin said, a bit shortly.

Sunnie considered him gravely. "Your parents mandated your attendance at religious ceremonies, I take it? Services from which you derived no sustenance?"

"You got it." He laughed. "That's an understatement, if there ever was one."

She was still watching him calmly, observantly. "Has it occurred to you that perhaps none of the people in that church had personally experienced the reality, however sincere they may have been? Does it seem at all possible that you have never seen the real thing?"

Judging from Corbin's slightly pensive expression, the idea was striking him for the first time.

"You can find out, if you want to," I said. I don't think he believed me, and even if he did, he couldn't know that I was talking about coming out of the world he'd always known into a new way of seeing, another world.

"For all you know, Dennis," Sunnie said, "it may be that God has in mind for you a career altogether different from what you had in mind. Different, but not less important. Certainly not less difficult, or less interesting."

All true. But I was suddenly struck by a strangely disquieting thought. Why the rush?

It was still considerably less than a day since Corbin had wakened. Already Mr. Conway had told him that life in Shangri-La defied the aging process. Mr. Barnard had told him that he was trapped here. Now Sunnie had told him (hinted, anyway, and pretty strongly) that life here could increase life's depth as well as its length.

All in one day.

Why the rush?

Chapter 13.

Responsibilities

Six weeks later. Early evening. Eight of us sat around a polished wooden table in one of the library alcoves. The two senior monks, Mr. Chin and Mr. Petrov; Mr. Conway; Mr. Herrick; Mr. Chang; Sunnie; Mr. Barnard, and myself. I was emphatically in the presence of my betters.

Mr. Barnard occasionally referred to Mr. Conway, humorously, as Shangri-La's "Executive Director," but I had rarely seen him act in that capacity. The few incidents that disturbed our placid routine were handled in their course by a quiet word in the right place. As the high lama had promised, the burden of leadership there was light.

And never had I sat in on a meeting of the few who represented Shangri-La's guiding hand. They always seemed able to struggle along without my contribution, just as President Kennedy, the Air Force and General Motors always had, back when I was in the States. Besides, Shangri-La has neither the need nor the taste for business meetings. The board of directors, or however they referred to themselves, rarely met. Or so Mr. Barnard said. Ordinarily he and Sunnie, quite as much as I, would be unneeded at any such meeting. Actually, for all I know, they met frequently, if only for the pleasure of each other's company.

In any case, I had no doubt why I had been invited. Items A through Z on the agenda were Mr. Dennis Corbin: progress of and prospects for. At Mr. Conway's request, I told them what I knew of Corbin's motives and beliefs, and sketched his character as it appeared to me. (They'd heard the opinions of Mr. Conway and others, presumably. I suppose they were trying to gauge my biases by weighing my description.) When I finished, there was a small silence, broken by Mr. Chin, the most senior of Father Perrault's disciples, the one Mr. Barnard irreverently, but affectionately, referred to as the chairman of the board.

"You convey the impression that he is unsympathetic to our existence," he said. He paused—and no one moved to break the pause—then turned to Mr. Conway. "Is this impression also yours?"

"It is," Mr. Conway said.

"Is he, then, by nature an unsympathetic person?"

"I think not. He responds well to individuals. But his education and professional training have left him with strong prejudices."

"He as much as called George a reactionary the other day," Mr. Barnard put in.

The old monk's leathery face wrinkled in a slight smile. "It must be most pleasant to be quite certain of the correctness of one's views. I have quite forgotten the sensation." He turned back to me. "What are those prejudices, in your view, Mr. Chiari?"

"He doesn't want to have a thing to do with anything that might have God involved in it," I said. "Just as soon as he heard that this is a monastery, I think he wrote us off to some extent."

"Dismissed us as serious people," Mr. Conway said, translating.

"He thinks religion is superstition. If he humors our opinions, he thinks he's being charitable and generous. He can't imagine how sensible people can believe in a God who concerns himself with individuals. And if you try to talk to him about prayer and miracles, well, he's just got an absolutely closed mind."

"Closed minds may be opened by the proper experiences," Mr. Chang said. "Such, at any rate, has been *my* experience."

Mr. Chin was still looking at me thoughtfully, weighing what I had said, and weighing, it may be, other things unsaid or said previously.

"I seem to recall that you yourself, when you so providentially arrived here, were not untouched by similar superstitions," he said at length. "I recall much talk of bad luck and accidents; much regret over lost opportunity. In what respect do Mr. Corbin's superstitions differ from those you brought here?"

Interesting. If he'd heard "much talk of bad luck and accidents; much regret over lost opportunity," he hadn't heard it from me. In 17 years, he and I had had a few polite conversations, scarcely any of any length. Presumably he'd been talking to those I'd grown close to. In fact (I suddenly realized) perhaps he'd made it his business to receive reports on me at intervals regular or irregular, long or short. But to answer his question:

"We grew up in different worlds," I said. "I was born in 1936, he was born in 1953. I was raised Catholic, he wasn't raised much of anything. His folks were Presbyterian, I guess, but after his mother died I don't think he got much religious training. Anyway, being raised Protestant is a lot different from being raised Catholic."

"Inferior, sure," Mr. Barnard said, grinning.

Not knowing what Mr. Chin might know of my beliefs, I answered as though I thought Mr. Barnard's words were meant seriously. "You know I don't think that. I'm only saying a Catholic school education gives you a structure you don't get anywhere else in the world."

"Perhaps equivalents exist," Mr. Chin said quietly.

I took the hint and did not pursue the subject further. "And then, he's got that scientific training, you know, and I was always strictly liberal arts."

"Mr. Corbin is oriented toward technology and George is inclined toward history and literature," Mr. Conway translated.

Mr. Chin nodded slowly. "I have been told that you write verse, some of which is quite acceptable." I was amused by the careful limits put on the compliment, and astonished that Mr. Chin's briefings had extended so far.

"And, of course, there's politics." I paused, trying to be fair to Corbin without soft-peddling my observations.

Mr. Chin said, "Do I understand that our guest is in accord with the notions of my misguided compatriots?"

That helped nicely to focus my reply. "Well, he isn't a communist, but his attitude toward them is something I just can't understand. He says that our fear of being discovered is the result of prejudice fostered by Cold War propaganda. He says a lot of people—including him, I gather—think the Cold War was just something whipped up by the 'military-industrial complex,' which is a phrase one of our presidents used to describe the relationship between our war industries and the military establishment. He says the cold war wasn't motivated by fear at all, but was a plot to assure that America's economy didn't collapse after World War II because of lack of economic demand. He really believes it, apparently."

["You still didn't break radio silence, even when you knew you had to come down?" Corbin was incredulous. I had looked at him, equally puzzled. "Didn't I already say it? I wasn't about to bring the Chinese in on me, no matter what. I wasn't going to go down in history as Francis Gary Powers the Second." His face revealed that he had suddenly discovered that the gap between us was even wider than he had thought. "Boy, you really bought that Cold War stuff, didn't you?"]

"The history he learned hasn't much in common with what you learned, has it, George?"

"No sir," I said to Mr. Conway. "Like I said, we grew up in different worlds." Which is what I'd told Mr. Barnard a few days before. It occurred to me to wonder if that remark then had led to this meeting now.

* 2 *

I had turned away from Mr. Barnard to look out the window at the mountain across the valley. "No, as far as I can tell he isn't a traitor."

We were in one of the little alcoves that are, to me, one of the monastery's nicest features. I like the bookshelves lining the walls, the sun flowing in through the windows (thick white draperies pulled back to the sides), the dark polished tables, the simple chairs. Ordinarily I like standing at the window, looking out at Karakol across the chasm of the valley. How many hours had I spent here, doing just that, letting the peace of this part of the world flow deeply into my being? Particularly in the first years, I leaned on it for reassurance and comfort. Even the sickness of separation, which had so filled me some nights (looking out at the moon that others maybe looked at, far away)—even that had been easier here. But this day I couldn't feel its support, even as I continued to stare out at the mountain called Blue Moon. I could feel Mr. Barnard's presence, quietly watching from where he sat at the table.

"Don't make much sense?"

Reluctantly. "It isn't that. Things change, even things you'd swear *couldn't* change. I suppose it's natural." I turned to see Mr.

202

Barnard smiling at me. "What's so funny?"

"This is your swearing-in ceremony, I reckon, that's all. I was thinking you'd been with us long enough that you'd earned your wings, but I can see there was one more experience we'd forgot about: seeing the world change so much after you'd got out of it. Everybody goes through it. When you're the last one in, why, the world is whatever way it is when you came; it's natural to you, and all you can see is how different all these older guys see things. Then sooner or later *you* are one of the older guys, and somebody new comes in and all the things that could have been are suddenly dead, and all there is is how things worked out. You can't help thinking about all the things you half-thought might happen, that didn't."

"All the lost opportunities, you mean?"

"Lost opportunities, and worse than that. Watching it all slide. Like, for me, being here in the '30s and then hearing you talk about Hitler and Stalin and the death camps and the war and the atomic bomb and all. You can't help seeing that it didn't need to be that way at all, and you get the news all at once, not a little bit at a time the way news used to come to you. Up till now, George, you were the junior member of the firm, so you were the only one couldn't see things that way."

"Oh, I see it."

"Sure, but you see it a little different today than you did before you talked to Corbin. Talking to him makes it real to you that life is still going on out there."

"Maybe so."

"I don't know as it's going any too well, either," he said.

"Mr. Barnard, it isn't! I can't even talk to him. We don't live in the same world." I left the window and paced a few steps up and down. "You wouldn't believe the crazy stuff he comes out with."

He smiled again. "I wouldn't? How about all the crazy stuff I used to hear from you?"

"From *me?* What crazy stuff did you ever hear from me?"

"Lord, who could remember it all?" He laughed. "It's just natural, George, it's different generations. I'm born one time and I see things the way folks naturally did then. You're born another time and you see things different. How else could it be? People are used to what they're used to. Don't you remember all those arguments you and Herrick used to get into about the British Empire? He grew up taking it for granted and you didn't; that's all that ever amounted to. That, and the fact that you'd watched it fall to pieces, and he hadn't."

"It fell to pieces long before I knew it was there, Mr. Barnard. They lost India before I was a teenager."

"Well, that's what I say. To you, it wasn't ever real, it was just something you read about in the history books. But to him, it was still there, in all its power and glory, right up until you came here."

"Until I—? But there's the radio!"

"Yeah, but hearing it on the radio ain't the same thing as meeting it in the flesh, which is what you're finding out right now. You and me and this Corbin boy are all Americans, and maybe the others figure that makes up pretty much alike. Maybe to them we *are* pretty much alike. Now, the three of us know that America covers a lot of real estate, so we expect some differences between us that maybe the others don't—but even if we all came from Yellow Springs, Ohio, we wouldn't be alike, because we wouldn't really be from the same place at all. The same place, 50 years later, *ain't* the same place."

"Apparently not!"

"What's he saying that's got you so hot and bothered?"

"I'll give you just one example," I said, pacing again. "He says the reason we're afraid of the Chinese finding us is because we've listened to too many years of Cold War propaganda. That's what he called it. Said a whole people can't become villains overnight just because they had a change of government, and we're just behind the times. He didn't quite come out and say it, but he more or less thinks we're a bunch of reactionaries."

Mr. Barnard pursed his lips. "He does, eh?" Absent-mindedly, he picked up one of his cigars from the table, licked it, and put it unlit in his mouth, where he proceeded to chew on it.

"I asked him if he'd ever heard of Hitler's Germany. He said that was different, the *chedrool*."

Mr. Barnard laughed. "The what?"

"Chedrool. You know—a stupe, a dummy."

"*Is* he dumb, though?"

"Well, no, he isn't. But he's *plenty* ignorant! And when he's wrong, there just isn't any use telling him; he just looks at you like you're some moron he has to humor."

Mr. Barnard stood up and went over to the little brazier where the shouldering fire was kept. Bending over it, he held the cigar against the coal, puffing in and out until the cigar drew. He straightened up and replaced the top carefully. For a minute or two he stood there, occasionally emitting puffs of smoke, saying nothing, looking at nothing in particular. "By the way, George," he said after a minute, "I meant to tell you. Herrick says the radio from Corbin's airplane works. Chang and the others are going to put in some time listening to whatever they can find on the military frequencies, see if we're becoming famous with the Chinese Air Force."

"Tell them for God's sake to be careful not to hit the transmit button! That's all we'd need."

"Herrick already disabled it," Mr. Barnard said. Then he lapsed into pensive silence.

"Well," he said finally, "it's the same old story. We've got somebody here who don't particularly want to be here. He don't fit in with our beliefs, he don't see any value in our ways, and he thinks he's smarter than the rest of us because he's read later newspapers than we have." He took a long pull on his cigar. (I wondered, sometimes, what Mr. Barnard would have done if the natives in the valley below had not had their equivalent of tobacco to make cigars from. Would this particular vice have been replaced by a heavier indulgence in the native liquors?) He glanced directly at me. "He's still your problem, I'm afraid. At least for a while."

* 3 *

Still my problem. I looked around me at the other six. *Why* still my problem? All anyone asked me to do was (1) spend time with Corbin, to keep him more or less content, and (2) write this endless memoir. And even Mr. Conway, normally so open and articulate, wouldn't tell me why I was doing either.

"I can't see that anybody sees it as particularly important," Mr. Barnard was saying. "You don't hear about it on the radio to amount to anything. Course, maybe they been talking about it and I missed it, you can't tell."

My mind had been on autopilot while I'd been elsewhere. I played back the recording. They were talking about the revolution in Iran.

"Surely," Mr. Chang said, "the importance of so singular a phenomenon must be self-evident to the well-informed."

Mr. Barnard grunted. "Maybe the well-informed don't run the radio."

"You've all heard Henry say, as well, that the establishment of a Marxist regime in Kabul has also received little attention."

Mr. Chang pursed his lips. "No one doubts your diligence or accuracy, Mr. Barnard. Still, the substance of what you report surpasses understanding. In Afghanistan, Marxist revolutionaries overthrow the king and the West scarcely notices. In Iran, Islamic revolutionaries overthrow the Shah—and the West scarcely notices. And Mr. Dennis Corbin has no resistance to socialism. I trust that everyone here takes the point."

Mr. Conway turned to me. "You can't have followed that, George. You have been kept from knowing much that has gone on. Please accept my assurance that if you've been left in the dark, as you have, it was not because we did not trust you, but for other good reasons."

Mr. Chang spoke. "Nor is this necessarily the time to reveal all that has so long been concealed from you, Mr. Chiari. However, we are being forced to reconsider many things."

I looked from one to the other, and finally addressed Mr. Conway. "I don't get it," I said. "I can see that Iran and Afghanistan and maybe Dennis Corbin are all intertwined in your minds somehow, but I don't see how, or why."

Mr. Conway frowned, an expression rare for him. "We are wondering if it isn't time for us to throw our last ounce of weight on the scales. Before it becomes too late. We see the blind leading the blind, armed with ever more powerful weapons every day. Unless something changes the pattern, surely there can be only one end. If we, here, can help divert the world's suicide course, obviously we must. But it's not at all obvious that we can intervene effectively, and it is of importance that we make the correct decision."

Mr. Barnard responded to my frown of puzzlement. "We all know that Father Perrault had a vision of the destruction of civilization, George. What we don't know is, did his vision include radioactivity?"

Mr. Petrov spoke, and as usual his words were few: "The problem, Mr. Chiari, may be stated so: The world has forgotten who it is. Your America, Conway's England, my Russia, Chang's China—they think they are one thing; they are something else. So they have no peace. Not with one another, not with themselves. They forget who they are, they cannot stand."

I'm sure I looked as bewildered as I still felt.

"Life ain't a matter of what people would like it to be," Mr. Barnard said in explanation. "It's what it is. People that get the wrong idea about their life can't live right. They can't even think right, see right."

"Which is why one's religious ideas are so important," Mr. Herrick said, a little sententiously, as was his way. "One's religious ideas shape one's views on what forces do or do not exist in life."

"And the other way around," Mr. Barnard said.

"To be sure. One's views of what exists shape one's religious ideas, certainly."

"I still don't get it," I said, feeling dense.

Mr. Conway said, "It is a matter of evidence. The West sees two Asian Moslem countries taken out of the Western orbit and transformed: one into the Marxist orbit, the other into something new and unpredictable. It sees, but seems not to notice."

I shrugged. "But what could the West have done?"

"Quite possibly nothing. Quite possibly there was nothing it *should* have done. But it should have noticed. That it does not notice argues a terrible, dangerous blindness."

"Dangerous?"

"Quite dangerous. A society so blind to immediate menace is arguably beyond the point where it can still renew itself. And without the West, where is the world? In our time, and into the foreseeable future, the future is in the hands of the West, for it was in the Christian societies of the West that the individual was nurtured. If the West should fall, what would become of the individual? And without the individual, where are the eyes of the human race?"

I wasn't much further out of the darkness. "Mr. Conway, I can't see why the revolutions in Iran and Afghanistan are so dangerous. But if they are, don't you think the West will realize it sooner or later?"

"Perhaps. And in any event, two instances of statesmen's blindness would not in themselves have roused such alarm within us. I have been close enough to the statesmen of my time to have little faith in their wisdom or foresight. But those examples merely confirm other evidence. Years of Henry's gleanings from radio broadcasts, plus other things I won't go into, plus your Dennis Corbin."

(*My* Dennis Corbin?)

"More specifically, Dennis Corbin compared to one George Chiari. Vintage 1953 as compared to vintage 1936. The comparison is in your favor as an individual, George, but it argues poorly for the trend in America as a civilization."

I smiled, not too convincingly perhaps. "A trend? On the strength of comparing two people?"

Mr. Petrov shook his head slowly, emphatically. "No. You do not know." He raised a hand in a gesture that included his comrades at the table. "Many people watch many years. Blind lead blind." He turned to Mr. Chin. "Conway should tell his dream."

"Yes," the old Chinese said.

* **4** *

Long ago, in the course of introducing me to so many things, Mr. Conway had taught me to take dreams seriously. He and I had discussed many a dream in the process of his teaching me how to hear what they were saying, so dealing with dreams was no big thing to me any longer. So why did the very mention of this yet-undescribed dream tighten my throat and set my pulse racing?

Mr. Conway divided his attention between Mr. Barnard and me, from which I concluded that we were the only two around the table who had not previously heard the dream.

"Some months before Mr. Dennis Corbin dropped in on us, I had a dream in which I addressed an audience in New York City. I think we have been able to puzzle out the meaning." Seventeen years before, I would have dismissed the idea that a dream could have real meaning. "Here's the dream. I was on stage with someone else. We were inside a lecture hall in New York City, but as I looked toward the back of the hall, I realized that it went on and on to the horizon, so that the audience consisted of tens of thousands, hundreds of thousands. We were speaking about the life of the spirit, and they were listening, with attention."

"In New York City, of all places," Mr. Barnard said. "What do you make of that?"

[Mr. Barnard's words made me think how I have never been fond of New York City. Not enough trees, for one thing—and with that thought I was stabbed by a violent longing to see the mixed forests of my youth. Particularly there arose a vision of the marshlands of the Delaware Bay. The fact that I would never see them again suddenly seemed unbearable, even though I knew full well that if I were by some magic returned to that area, and that life, the marshlands would fade, within days or weeks, into the half-noticed background, and I would be longing to be back within this valley, my real home. But to know that did not diminish the intensity of the vision. Sitting in Shangri-La, perched halfway up the side of a mountain in northwestern Tibet, all I could see was marsh grass and isolated pine trees, in early morning, with a blue heron taking wing. In my ears was the harsh cry of sea gulls, and not so many miles away, by car, was my parents' house. I could drive at a reasonable speed and still be there in 20 minutes.]

Mr. Conway was looking at me. "George?"

I pulled myself back to the here and now. "The place to begin, so I've been told," I said, smiling at Mr. Conway, "is with each symbol, and what each symbol means to the dreamer. Your dream had you and another person talking to an audience. How did it portray you?"

"I was in evening dress, with highly polished shoes. That is, my clothing was totally appropriate, even elegant. I spoke confidently, I was filled with energy and conviction, and I could feel that I was carrying the audience with me."

"You could feel it as the character, or as the dreamer?"

"It was the atmosphere of the dream. They were listening with respect and interest and profit."

"Anything else about yourself?"

Mr. Conway was silent, thinking. "It was strange. The

audience and I could see each other, but only through a veil of some sort. It was as if a thin curtain was between them and me; I think that was one reason why it took me a while to see that the hall extended so far out. Until my eyes adjusted to see through the curtain, or veil, I could only see those in the front rows, and those indistinctly. I can't tell you much. I didn't actually *see* a veil, it's more a manner of speaking. *Something* was between the audience and me—but something not tangible. The audience appeared hazy, as if far away, yet they were right there before me, very close."

"And the other person?"

"He was a young man, dressed not as I was, but in everyday clothes. I remember noticing that I was doing the talking, but the audience was looking at him, as though he was the one speaking. In fact, I have the impression that they couldn't see me at all, only him."

"Anything else about the audience?"

"They were a mixed group. Some in evening clothes, looking prosperous and influential, others looking like workmen, some in coveralls. Some in military or police uniforms."

"Any ladies in the crowd?"

"Oh, yes, a thoroughly mixed audience in every respect. I thought they were a good crowd, and I was pleased they had come and was pleased they were listening."

"What does a lecture hall mean to you?"

"A place to communicate, of course. Not much reaction to it, other than that. I was somewhat surprised, but not terribly, to see it extend so far. You know dreams have their own logic."

I knew. "Well, what about New York City? What does it mean to you?"

Mr. Conway smiled with lazy irony. "You may not think this too flattering to your country's greatest city, George, but on my only visit it impressed me as having too many people in too little space. Too much energy, too much money, too much of the sort of power that money and energy bring. Its vitality left one awed—but held something of the inhuman."

"Inhuman?"

"Not the right word, perhaps. 'Impersonal?' Yes, impersonal. The city was so big, and its concern for the individual so small. It tended to leave one dwarfed."

That was certainly true enough. "So there you were, speaking to a crowd of New Yorkers, and getting across to them. You're doing the talking, but they think they're hearing someone else. You aren't even sure they see you at all. You're dressed formally and your partner is not. Do you have a sense of this partner?"

"He is an American, a young American. He reminded me of your doughboys in training with my troops in the trenches in 1918, radiating simplicity and idealism and youthful vigor. They affected many of my brother officers similarly, I know. They were direct, frequently humorous, very cheerful and willing. Very quick with their hands, very full of self-confidence, particularly in matters involving machinery or rifles. They seemed, to us who had been three years in the trenches already, prodigies of youth."

He looked from me to Mr. Barnard and back to me. "The image of America I formed in those years has never dimmed. The two of you share many of their best qualities."

Mr. Barnard and I were equally embarrassed. I think we both considered making a joke, and both decided against it. I asked, "And there wasn't any more to the dream?"

"There was. We had been addressing the crowd for some time, I recall, before I realized the size of the audience. Then we could hear airplanes coming, and I knew they were bombers. We are all filled with the greatest dread, a sort of impersonal dread. Not so much that we feared our own deaths as the deaths of others. Of all the others, somehow. And that's all I remember. The dream did not portray us ending our talk, or coming off the stage."

"What did it *feel* like?"

"I can only stress the *intensity* of the dream, the air of urgency that did not diminish when I awakened. If anything, it gathered strength."

"You take this pretty serious, I guess," Mr. Barnard said.

"Certainly," Mr. Conway said. "Every tradition of this house speaks to the value of dreaming. Even twentieth-century science has caught up with the older wisdom in that regard."

"Well, Joseph, what do you reckon it means?"

It took me a moment to catch the allusion: Joseph, the dreamer.

Mr. Conway generally appreciated Mr. Barnard's sense of

humor. He'd told me once that a sense of humor not dependent on malice was among the most valuable gifts one could bring to a closed community such as ours. He smiled affectionately at him now. "I think the message is clear enough. The dream uses me as the person talking. I doubt the outside world hungers to hear the details of my childhood, or my reminiscences of the foreign service. Surely it envisions me speaking of what is closest to our hearts here. And what is that but the need for the world to find a new way of seeing? I think it wants us to give the world what we ourselves were given by time and reflection."

Mr. Chin said, "Is it not appropriate that this monastery's famous personage should bridge the gap between two visions of the world? I ask myself, indeed, whether this is not why he was led to make his long journey out from here and then back again. That journey brought him fame, which may prove useful now."

"Well, not literally," Mr. Barnard said. "You can't go anywhere after all this time. You ain't 40, remember, Conway, though you look it."

"I haven't forgotten. You will notice the dream has me speaking to the world only through an interpreter."

Mr. Conway turned to me again. "Since, as Henry rightly points out, I am confined by my age to the limits of this mountain and valley, the question becomes: How could I speak to the world if I chose to do so? Transmit over the radio? Not very convincing to the outside world, I should think, nor likely to be long continued. Anything more certain to bring the communists down on our heads, I cannot imagine. Should we invite others here, that they might see and listen? Again, impossible, unlikely to be persuasive, and very quickly fatal. And so you see why you were invited to this conference, George. Not alone for your knowledge of Dennis Corbin's mental state."

I hadn't the faintest idea.

"Your manuscript. The record you are writing of your years here."

This manuscript. I could scarcely believe him. "But—there's nothing particularly great about what I'm writing, Mr. Conway," I said, "you know that. It's just some things I remember. And it's full of side-tracks and stuff that wouldn't interest anybody but my family, maybe."

"Perhaps you underestimate its value as evidence. A personal testimony often evokes response where a formal presentation does not. These past few weeks, I have set several people to writing, not yourself alone. I hoped we would produce some credo, some document that would persuade some in the world outside to look more seriously at 'discredited' remedies for their situation. For this we need not a formal tome, but a reminder, a nudge: Beyond the nudge, I think we must rely upon *spiritus mundi* to lay its thumb upon the scales. I think you have come closest to producing what we need. You are closest to this generation, your own reactions to a new way of seeing are recent enough to be fresh in your mind, and your style is—is, let us say, more in the vernacular than any of the others. I think it may win response."

"You print something that lets the Chinese communists know we're here and you'll win response, all right," Mr. Barnard said. "It'll be the end for us. D' you think whatever good it might do is worth it?" He cleared his throat. "It seems kind of foolish to me, to work like beavers to stop anybody from finding us, then go print an announcement that says 'To whom it may concern, look under the right rock and you'll find us.' That don't sound sensible to me, Conway, and you surprise me. It don't sound just like you."

Mr. Conway looked at me, rather than at him. "Henry has a point, of course, and we have debated it here more than once, these past few months. We have a responsibility to protect this institution, and also, no less, those in the valley below who seem to have been entrusted to our care. But is it enough for us to remain here, anonymously working for the world in ways it would not acknowledge, while we watch it sleep-walk over a cliff? Or do we owe it something more?"

Rhetorical question. No one felt moved to answer.

"We all know Father Perrault's vision of civilization being destroyed by war. We have since heard of Carl Jung's vision, in 1944, of the destruction of most of the world. But they need not happen. They are only possibilities until they are ratified by millions of individual decisions and are frozen into time."

Mr. Chin spoke again. "Mr. Conway's dream invites us to consider how we can best make our weight felt. I take it none would argue that our lives, or the lives of the inhabitants of the valley below, would outweigh the life of the world?"

No one did.

Into the silence I said that in any case I didn't understand how we could get my manuscript—any manuscript—into the world.

Mr. Conway said, "We could get it to the world. But I'd prefer not to leave it at that." He gazed at me somewhat abstractedly, as if he were looking beyond me—the first time I'd even seen him do so—and asked if I thought that Dennis Corbin could be prevailed upon to accompany my manuscript to the outside world and see it through the publishing process.

Corbin?

Corbin?!

The idea was absurd. Which wasn't like Mr. Conway.

* 5 *

In six weeks, I'd spent a considerable amount of time with Corbin. Six weeks may not be much time in the outside world, with distractions and preoccupations and schedules and this and that, but it's a long time aboard ship. Time enough to get to know somebody pretty well, if you want to. Even, almost, whether you want to or not. He'd helped me do chores, and we'd sat around and talked about life in the States, and—just as I had with Mr. Barnard when I'd first arrived—we'd told stories, swapped impressions of where and when we'd grown up, described things we'd done and things we'd wanted to do but hadn't done.

Naturally, we'd wound up talking about who we were, what we believed, what we valued: Thoreau's "where I lived and what I lived for." We had come out of different worlds, and lived in different worlds still. Even if I had never come to this beloved place, he and I would have had little enough in common. As it was. . . .

He and I were hiking, one brilliant still morning, up and back along the ridge where we get our exercise, the same ridge he'd measured with his feet when he'd first been told he couldn't leave. [And how was it that he couldn't leave, and I couldn't leave, and all of a sudden maybe he *could?*]

"There's a lot involved," I told him. "Meditation, visualizations, instruction, the study of texts—and some direct experimentation, too. It's not a matter of taking somebody's word for it."

He wanted to know why, if what we'd found was so great and so "globally applicable" (his phrase), nobody had ever discovered it before.

"Dennis," I said, "that's just the point! *We* didn't discover it, it's been known for thousands of years. You can find descriptions of the process in all languages, in all cultures. We've got lots of those books here, and obviously the outside world had them long before we did. They're available, if anybody wants to take the time to look for them. It's just that so much of the process is non-verbal. It's hard to describe in words. You wind up talking about the way you experienced it, rather than *what* you experienced. The best the books can do is give hints. And anyway, you can't accomplish anything by trying to duplicate the externals of how somebody else woke up. All you have to work with is what's closest to hand at the moment. Fortunately, that's all you need."

"'When the student is ready, the teacher will appear,'" Corbin said mockingly.

I was surprised he'd even heard the saying. "That's right. How did you know that?"

"*Be Here Now*. This is like being back in San Francisco. The Age of Aquarius, and all that."

["Individuals recognize the truth when they hear it," Mr. Conway told me. "That's how the truth makes them free." But it seemed to have left Corbin unaffected.]

"I guess you could find a teacher here," Corbin said. "I'd hate to try it in Brooklyn."

"Why? Is there any reason you couldn't be sincere, and humble, and curious and loving there? Or anywhere? Can't you pray and meditate there? It's just a matter of calming the mind and lessening personal desires, and staying on track. That's all you need. The teacher *will* appear."

But this was all mumbo-jumbo to him. To him the world is luck and chance and struggle and circumstances. He couldn't see that internal and external reality are inextricably connected. Certainly he couldn't see that his view of the world—the Western secular view of the world—makes no sense once you step outside of its assumptions. He'd never done so, had no intention of doing so, and hadn't ever met anybody, before me, who had done so.

I puzzled him. "I don't get it. You have a good mind, you went to college, you were in the Air Force, a flyer—you *know* about science and technology. You know their value. How can you throw it over for this superstition?"

"It isn't superstition. It's experience."

We came to the end of the trial, the farthest point we could reach in that direction. Hardly pausing to look at the spectacular but almost painfully familiar view, we turned and walked back toward the buildings, maintaining our pace.

"Then why can't your experience be scientifically verified? If it can't be verified, maybe it isn't so."

"How can science possibly verify it, when its assumptions rule out what it would have to investigate? Can science measure will, and emotion, and different levels of being? Science thinks of people as if they were interchangeable physical particles— and then wonders why it can't find soul or mind or psychic powers."

"Hold it! That is precisely the problem here. As soon as we start talking about verification, you say, 'Oh, this can't be measured.' But if it can't be measured, why should we take it seriously? They used to say outer space was filled with ether, but when they couldn't find any trace of it, they finally gave up on it."

I walked along in silence for a few steps, wondering if the impossible distance between our assumptions could be bridged. I decided that probably it couldn't—but not the least of Shangri-La's gifts is the time for impractical pursuits. "Spoken like a true materialist," I said. "Mass and volume and velocity measure everything, explain everything, predict everything. The universe is a giant clock, running—running down—all by itself. Tell me, Dennis, did any of your computer programs ever write itself?"

He didn't bother to answer this verbal jab.

"What's left of Newton's clock, Dennis, now that we've discovered that matter doesn't exist?"

Contemptuously: "That's ridiculous."

"Is it?"

Corbin took an energetic kick at a stone. It went clattering over the side.

"That's been done before, Dennis," I said, grinning. "Dr. Johnson kicked the stone. But it still doesn't *prove* anything."

"I don't know who Dr. Johnson is. All I know is that you can try as hard as you want to, but you can't talk matter away."

"I don't want to talk it away, exactly. But it isn't what it looks like. Sure, you swing a hammer and drive a nail. But what's really happening? The hammer and the nail are made up of atoms which are mostly space. And the parts of the atom that aren't space—the electrons, the nucleus, all that—are particles that are themselves mostly space. And so on down the scale, *ad infinitum*, as far as anybody's ever been able to see. Particles aren't bits of something, they're more like patterns of energy, wrapped around nothing. So where is the material in your hand? Or in the hammer it holds? Or the nail it drives?"

"You're playing with words, that's all. You want to see my hand? Here it is. Here's the mountain we're walking on. You can't argue the mountain out of existence."

"Dennis, I know they're really here. But the point, again, is that they aren't what you think they are. We experience them, so we know they exist. But we *don't* experience those ultimate particles of yours. They're just concepts. They don't exist. Physicists says that at low mass and high energy levels, matter acts sometimes like waves and sometimes like particles. So where's your ultimate particle? Out acting like a wave some-where? Seems to me it's more likely that its a wave, acting like a particle. Mr. Herrick convinced me long ago that matter is what he calls 'a purely local phenomenon, confined to certain energy levels.'"

Corbin asked me if I had any idea what I was talking about.

"Yes I do. I'm telling you simply that there isn't the slightest 'scientific' excuse for saying that matter is the realest part of life. We know matter and energy are different forms of the same thing. I don't see any reason to think that mind—spirit, if you prefer—is only a fringe effect produced by matter. I think it's much more likely to be the other way around, if anything."

"Boy, I can tell you were a liberal arts major."

"Yeah?"

"Yeah. Nobody with a scientific background would be caught dead saying stuff like that."

I'd been expecting that. "Ever hear of Sir James Jeans, Dennis?"

"No. I take it he's another crackpot being rushed to your rescue." Despite our mutual irritation, we grinned at each other as we walked, with some difficulty, side by side on the narrow trail.

"Not quite a crackpot. He was a great British physicist of the 1920s. Won the Nobel Prize, I think. Anyway, he once said that increasingly the world appeared to him less as a great machine than as a great thought. You see? Matter isn't any more 'real' than thought and spirit. You don't have any 'scientific' reason to think it is."

"I still come back to evidence," Corbin said stubbornly. "I don't care what it is, anything real leaves tracks. If you can't find tracks, maybe that's because it doesn't exist."

"But you have to be willing and able to recognize the evidence when you see it. There's plenty of it, God knows."

I gave him example after example. Verified accounts of faith-healing at Lourdes and other places. Carefully documented accounts of extra-sensory perception. Modern examples of people under stress performing feats of strength or endurance normally far beyond their powers. I even threw in the example of professional gamblers and others who are naturally "lucky" (not counting the innumerable cheats among them) as people who possessed the knack, conscious or unconscious, of drawing to themselves positive energies leading to favorable results. I also mentioned people who were spectacularly "unlucky" as examples of the same energies.

Nothing shook him. He was convinced that "scientific" materialism was the sole alternative to medieval superstition, and he wasn't about to consider any evidence that might lead in a different direction. It put me in mind of Miss Brinklow. He and she were opposite sides of the same narrow coin.

Corbin, shepherd this manuscript to publication when he wouldn't agree with a word of it? Clearly, the idea was impossible.

Chapter 14.

Messenger

"**M**rs. Bolton," Mr. Petrov said politely. "Your dream. Mr. Chiari, you will listen inside."

By now it was night. The table we sat around was illuminated by the two oil lamps on its surface. The room's walls and ceiling had become shadowy, indistinct. The effect was not one of gloom, but of comfort, the sort of almost luxurious comfort you feel beneath warm covers in a cold room; the comfort comes from the contrast.

In lamplight, people speak more softly, observe each other's faces and words more carefully, penetrate into their own thought, and the thoughts of others, more deeply. At the same time, they are apt to rediscover a part of their mind they normally ignore. As they listen to what is said, some inner day-dreamer goes off on its own quests, and the messages from both parts interact, and reinforce one another.

Not that lamplight will make sages out of dolts, but dolts in Shangri-La are in shorter supply than I remember them being in the world beyond. Or maybe it is that those who seem like dolts are only distracted, and we have fewer distractions here.

"P'raps you should have been the first to hear this dream, George," she said, "rather than the last of those assembled here. It seems to concern you quite closely. As a matter of fact, it centers on you."

It occurred to me that her dream, rather than my acquaintance with Dennis Corbin, might explain my presence at this meeting. Again I felt my pulse speed up.

"I saw you working in a roomful of scholars, translating an ancient medieval manuscript in a forgotten language, which I realized was much older than Latin or Greek. The others in the room were working on treatises on literature, medicine, science, politics, and history. Yours was a treatise on composting."

In my nervousness I laughed, and my laughter rang through the hushed room. "Great!" I said. "My field of study is a pile of manure!"

She smiled. "You had been given that task because they knew you had been reared on a farm. I assure you, your work was held in high respect. They were quite anxious that you complete your work. But their chief concern was that you use darker ink. The copying room was well-lit, but your manuscript was shaded, though there was nothing shading it. Your translation, though, glowed as though lit from within. It was *too* brightly lit. They continually implored you to darken your ink."

"I don't understand," I said as she paused.

"There is more. Next I saw you working in a desert, building a compost pile, adding layers of garbage, and dirt, and manure, and a bit of fertilizer. Every so often you would wet it down and then would add more layers." I wanted to ask where I was getting the garbage and the water in the middle of the desert, but knew not to ask, dreams having their own logic. "You were applying what you had learned from the manuscript you had translated, you see." The briefest of pauses. "A manuscript Hugh had authored. I could hear you murmuring to yourself repeatedly: 'Time-tested. Guaranteed.'"

I cleared my throat to comment, but she forestalled me.

"Then dozens of us were in an airplane, flying high above the earth. Below, we could see vast areas of desert, lit only by a few flickers of light. There were great cities, but the cities were surrounded by desert, and the desert extended into the streets. Those who lived in this area were asleep, and some were dead. It seemed hours went by while we passed over this desolation.

"Then, as we were returning, dispirited, we saw, far below us, as though through a telescope, another compost pile. Or it may have been the same compost pile from the previous scene, grown much bigger. Vegetation was springing up around it, spreading in all directions into the desert. We could hear you, still saying to yourself, 'Time-tested. Guaranteed.' Much time must have passed, for you were very old.

"We continued on our way, and we saw a few other compost piles like yours. Isolated, they were tended by lone individuals, most of them old, working alone, unaware of each other's existence. And each of them was nourishing greenery that was spreading into the desert, reclaiming it."

I had been aware of Mr. Conway studying me closely as I'd listened to Sunnie's dream. "Do you understand the dream, George?"

Well, what is a manure pile but a way of turning refuse into new life? The man who tends a compost heap tends a fire that cannot be seen: dark fire, hidden in the midst of earth. And in this dream I had been studying, and then practicing, the lost art of tending dark fire, working alone to reclaim the desert that was overwhelming the world. Working in concert with other individuals who were also tending their own dark fires, but working essentially alone.

The image made me shiver.

* 2 *

I wondered, in a detached portion of my mind, what Dennis Corbin would have made of this careful consideration of dreams. I knew his tune, but would like to have heard the melody. Corbin, in his moments of outraged defense of science against superstition, could be amusing on several levels.

Who listens to dreams? Primitives. Biblical figures like Jacob and Joseph and Saint Joseph. Not modern man. Not scientific modern man. Or, if he does, he does so only as Sigmund Freud did, to try to catch half-censored whispers from an individual's unconscious self, to deduce what secrets a sick person is trying to hide. There isn't anything *constructive* in dreams, certainly. Nothing objectively real about them. They are not reliable source of guidance, and no serious person would even consider basing his actions or decisions on so unreliable (so "unscientific") a source. Thus Mr. Dennis Corbin, presumably, on dreams. He'd think we were all crazy.

The thing is, we know better. Unlike Corbin, we have had the experience of it. We know reliable guidance when we experience it, and we aren't much troubled by the theory of it. Here in Shangri-La, we are protected (by the closed nature of our company) from the two chief hazards of relying on dreams: fraud and self-aggrandizing delusion. Neither of these corruptions could be hidden from the senior, most clear-seeing monks. Perhaps more to the point, who in our company would wish to perpetrate fraud? Who would wish to linger in delusion once it had been brought to light? Except Corbin, of course.

No, I must be more careful in my judgments. Corbin has many valuable qualities. Frankness, courage, optimism not least. The things that irritate me about him are but the defects of those qualities: a tendency to oversimplification, to rash judgments, and to shallow, complacent thinking. Tendencies easily picked up from the civilization we both sprang from! Plus, he is so young. He and I *appear to be* more or less of an age, but 43 is not 26, and between us it is more or less true what Yeats said: "I am old and you are young, and I speak a barbarous tongue."

I notice that Mr. Barnard does not seem to feel the same strain I do in Corbin's presence. He had grinned at me when I asked if he did. He said Lord no, he'd used up his supply of frustration dealing with me, a dozen years earlier. But when I pressed him, he said he thought the problem between Corbin and me was simply that he and I were too much alike. "He's more your age, he's got more of your reactions—which, you may not care to admit it!—and so of course you find him hard to take," he had said. "With you two, it's like fathers and sons, almost. Him and me, it's more like grandfathers and grandsons. Grandfathers got a lot of patience with grandsons, usually. Probably they learn it dealing with their sons first."

"Well," I had said, "I guess I'll have to wait til *my* grandson drops in. That ought to be in about 17 years, if our schedule holds."

"We waited 31 years for you," he'd said quietly. "Worth waiting for."

The sentiment was so unexpected that I had shot him a quick, startled glance, thinking he might be gently mocking me. But he wasn't. "Worth waiting for," he'd said again. He'd cleared his throat. "I can't remember that you and me ever had words."

I'd been tempted to pretend to misunderstand him and say we'd had nothing *but* words all these years. Instead, I merely agreed that we hadn't. "But I haven't had words with *anybody* here. Why should I?" My heart had been in my throat, and it had occurred to me for some reason that I hadn't told anyone of the visions of marsh and sea and farmland that had been coming to me with some frequency, ever since Corbin had arrived.

* 3 *

"In your time here, George," Mr. Conway said, "which no doubt seems to you a very *long* stretch of time, I have noticed that when on occasion your curiosity has elicited no response, or only a vague, non-committal response, you rarely probed farther. Didn't your mind tease at those loose ends, George? Weren't you hungry for answers? How is it that you did not persist in your inquiries?"

I hadn't ever thought about it. I'd just followed my instinct. "I guess—Well, I don't know. I guess I thought if it was any of my business somebody would tell me." After a few seconds I added, "I've never had a sense that you were concealing anything without good reason."

"In short, you trusted."

"Yeah, I guess that's about it. Why? [I said as a joke] Are you finally going to tell me all your secrets?"

"Yes," he said seriously, "we are. Some of them." And in that lamplit room, with the other monks watching my reaction, he began to tell me certain things I'd need to know, filling in certain blanks that had puzzled me all these years, and adding things I should have thought to wonder about, but hadn't.

For instance, the monastery's contact with the Tibetan rebels. He proceeded to tell me things about the history of 29 years of Tibetan armed resistance to Chinese occupation. [But of this he has enjoined me strictly to write nothing.] In the course of absorbing his précis of various rebel actions over the years, I suddenly realized where his knowledge had to have come from.

"Mr. Conway, you're in contact with the rebels! How else could you know all this?"

"Yes we are," he said. "That's what I want to tell you."

"But you always said you didn't have any contact with the outside world!"

"We implied that, yes. And with good reason. Henry made something of a point of telling you how he closed the supply pipeline 30 years ago. What he told you was true, but it was not the whole truth. What he carefully did *not* tell you was that other, less conspicuous, less dangerous points of contact remained. We were careful to see that they did remain. Even before the Chinese overran this country, it had become plain that isolation would be more dangerous than carefully limited contacts."

He told me some things about the young warriors who carried on guerrilla warfare against their Chinese overlords (things I am not to repeat), and talked of how the monastery maintained contact with them.

"You know our young men who guard the entrance to the valley. For nearly two decades now, they have competed among themselves for the honor of acting as couriers between us and the rebels of Mustang and, earlier, those of Chamdo, and other provinces. They enjoy danger. In fact, they contend for the honor of having performed the most daring exploits. As a matter of fact, we have had to remind them, more than once, that the greatest exploit is not the most reckless but the one that produces the most valuable results." He smiled. "As you may imagine, they tend to receive such advice with the tolerance of the young, showing proper respect, but trying hard not to let their elders spoil their fun."

That cleared up certain points! I had always thought it curious that Mr. Herrick and Mr. Barnard could have been able to keep up with the world outside strictly by listening to the radio. Radio broadcasts are so brief; they assume so much background information on the part of the listener. Could you really make sense of the world over a long period of time by reading the headlines and not the stories? *That's* what I had half-sensed that Mr. Barnard was leaving out. Which told me—

* **4** *

"Mr. Conway, if you can get men to the rebels, you could have gotten me over the border any time you wanted. That means that all this time, I could have been home!"

"That is true," he said quietly.

"There was a girl I could have married. She's in her 40s now, and I've missed her whole life. She probably married this jerk I used to know. Probably has grown children. Grandchildren, maybe." Frustration boiled up within me. "Seventeen years! And my parents are all old now, maybe dead, and my brothers and sisters are middle-aged, and I've probably got nieces and nephews I've never even seen! I've missed a huge portion of their lives. Of *my* life. And I missed having a family of my own."

I paused, but he made no defense of their silent deception.

"Probably they've forgotten me!"

"I very much doubt that," he said. "But it's natural for you to have regrets."

"Regrets!? Regrets?! Mr. Conway, I don't see how you could do that to me!"

"I ask you to believe that we were well aware of what we were taking from you."

"You took normal life from me." Images appeared in the theater of my mind. "I suppose this is going to sound stupid to you, but I missed all those years of going to the shore—the seashore—and eating watermelon and fresh peas in the spring, and fresh corn in the summertime, and going canoeing. And even ice cream! I dream about ice cream, sometimes."

"Lost your career, too," Mr. Barnard said, unexpectedly.

"Yeah, I did. I really loved flying, and it's been all these years since I could go up. If I'd stayed in the Air Force, I'd be pretty nearly retirement age. I've lost half a lifetime of normal, everyday living."

"So you have," Mr. Conway said gravely.

Another thought struck me. "I'll bet some of you have been over the border and back yourselves! And probably more than once."

"No, lad, you're wrong there," Mr. Barnard said. "Too much risk. That's for the Tibetans, or for the real young monks—and you're the only one of us young enough to risk getting delayed. You know how it is: If you go out, you get back inside of two weeks—a month, at most—or you all of a sudden catch up to your real age. Where do you think that would leave any of us?"

Dead, of course. Dead, or suddenly so biologically old that death would not be far behind.

But I could not get over it. All this time, I could have been back in the world.

* **5** *

"Mr. Chiari," Mr. Chin said out of a stillness, "Shangri-La is a place of few regrets. Perhaps this is because time brings clarity of vision, and clarity of vision dispels regrets."

Mr. Chin's face by daylight is all wrinkles. By lamplight his eyes—black marbles—dominate.

"Few have volunteered to enter this life," he said slowly, "Mr. Conway perhaps one-half excepted." There were smiles around the table at this gentle jibe at Mr. Conway's escape and return. "At a younger age, I indulged in the young man's prerogative of rebelling against fate, of struggling against what must be. You will understand, I do not refer to struggle against odds, but of what *must* be. This is a young man's reaction. But time delivers us from such compulsions. We learn to accept life as it comes. Nothing comes to us unmingled, neither good nor bad. Was it not an American poet who referred to triumph and disaster as two impostors, to be treated alike?"

"Hardly American," Mr. Conway smiled. "Rudyard Kipling."

"Near American, anyhow," Mr. Barnard said. "Might as well have been."

"Kipling. Very well. I hope that you, an American, will forgive my thinking an English poet American." His eyes were drawing me into him. Such joyous eyes, luminous with compassion and transcended suffering. ("Their eyes, their ancient glittering eyes, are gay," Yeats said.) "You were called upon to sacrifice your life here. Perhaps you may find comfort, as I do, in the fact that you were summoned here for reasons no one could know."

He paused.

"I have said this is a place of few regrets. I have lived here more years than I can remember, and my regrets are very, very few. However, I now have another. Little thinking that time might fail, I neglected to pursue your acquaintance, and now it is too late." He repeated himself. "'Too late.' Words not often heard within these walls."

Too late?

* 6 *

"As you know, we must send the world a messenger. We have no one able to return to the world but you."

"Me!?"

"You alone are young enough—as the world counts years—to return in full vigor. Mr. Conway, Mr. Barnard, would return as old men. Mrs. Bolton would remain young anywhere [I looked at Sunnie, smiling in the lamplight at her own expense], but she cannot go. Miss Brinklow is quite as old as Mr. Conway, and in any case would make an unsuitable envoy. And Mr. Corbin, as you very ably saw, is too young, too untrained, too little in sympathy with our message to be able to deliver it."

"That leaves you, George," Mr. Conway said. "And I can only say I regret the necessity. But you have it in your power to do much good."

As it turned out, publishing this memoir was not to be the sole task, or even the chief task, entrusted to me. The monks of Shangri-La never thought to save the world with yet another manuscript. And in the end, without much argument, I said I'd do it, of course. There was no one else.

Odd, isn't it? I had just experienced, to the fullest, my regrets at having been held here, apart from the world. And now, as soon as I was told I must leave, equally strong feelings of loss overwhelmed me at the thought of having to leave.

If I had left right away, as soon as I'd arrived, I could have fit right back into my life and never known what I was missing. But now—

"Nearly everyone who comes here learns to find our life very much to his liking—or her liking," Mr. Chin said, with a nod toward Sunnie. "This has been true of you, I know."

"Yes," I said. "I missed a lot in the outside world, but I've been happy here."

"Which is more than you can say for Dennis Corbin," Mr. Barnard said quietly. "It'll be many a year before that boy settles in here. He's going to be a handful."

"He couldn't come with me, I suppose?"

Mr. Conway shook his head. "We considered the idea, George, but we cannot risk it. You know why."

Indeed I did. Dennis Corbin in the outside world would be more dangerous to Shangri-La than Mallinson ever could have been, circumstances having changed so.

"He will find his fate," Mr. Chin said. "You were summoned here for reasons none could know. Now you are summoned to leave, for reasons none can know. If it is one's fate to be a wanderer, that fate will be fulfilled. If not, other possibilities will arise. One can only obey and hold oneself in readiness."

∗ 7 ∗

At length I realized I was expected to respond. My valedictory. I spoke, not knowing what I would say until I had said it.

"I'm getting all choked up," I said. "It's embarrassing." I took tight hold. "I'm not going to make a speech. I can't think of all that much to say. All I know is this. Maybe I *did* sound, a few minutes ago, like I still regretted coming here. But I hope you all know that this is my home. When I go over the mountains, I'll be going to the place I was born, and the people I grew up with, but it would be far more accurate to say that I will not be going home. I'll be *leaving* home. This is where my friends are. You are my family.

"I came here as a kid, living in a shell. I had emotions, but I couldn't feel them. I had abilities that I didn't dream of. I had a hunger and thirst I never could have filled.

"You all—Mr. Conway, especially—showed me another world, and helped me travel to it, and live in it. How could I ever repay that?

"And Mr. Barnard, Sunnie, how could I ever put a price on the time we've spent together?" I felt tears welling up, but held them back. "I know that in a few months I'm going to look my real age, and feel my real age, and it's hard to believe, I've been 26 for so long. So I guess I'll never know what it would have been like to be in my thirties. But what have I lost? If I hadn't been lucky enough [I smiled at Mr. Barnard] to come here, I still would have grown old, but I wouldn't have had any idea how much I would have missed. You've all heard Mr. Barnard quoting that saying of his: 'We grow too soon old and too late smart.' Well: Here, we don't.

"Mr. Chin, you don't have to worry about my having regrets. I do have some, but they aren't important. The only thing I'll worry about it whether I can represent us creditably to the outside world."

I looked down at the table. "If you don't mind, I prefer to say my goodbyes to people in private." My eyes were full of tears.

"You will represent us creditably, George," I heard Sunnie say. "And you won't be alone, ever. You'll carry us with you."

Epilogue. 1994

If my life in the monastery hadn't taught me about chance and accident, my return to the world would have. I could have gotten to Pakistan at any time, weather permitting. But getting home *from* Pakistan, without papers, without money, without a coherent story explaining how I'd arrived there, might have been a trick. As it happened, God took care of the problem. It was just a matter of timing.

Mr. Conway set a dozen monks at a time to copying out my memoir, dividing the job among them, so that the monastery would retain my story after I carried the original over the mountains. (The original, I should mention, is considerably longer than this version. Discretion, necessity, and economic constraints have all mandated that I leave out great slices of my experiences there. I particularly regret having to remove many, many of my conversations with Mr. Conway and Mr. Barnard.) Within days of that final, nighttime conference, we—three young Tibetans and I—were on our way over the mountains.

Even after 15 years, I cannot detail how we traveled. Lives still depend on my discretion. The Chinese still rule Tibet. Suffice it to say that together we made our pre-arranged meeting with members of the Tibetan resistance, and made our way undetected over the border into Nepal. There, after fulfilling a duty laid upon me before I left (a duty that was an honor for any friend of Tibet), we got back over the border into Pakistan. Once safely inside that country, my companions left on their long return journey, and I was on my own. And suffice it to say that getting to Islamabad from the border proved unexpectedly difficult. I arrived November 21, 1979, to find a mob attacking the American Embassy.

Welcome back to civilization, Mr. Chiari.

I stood in the street, dressed as a Pakistani among Pakistanis, watching in dismay and puzzlement as the crowd rushed the embassy I had come so far to surrender myself to. I saw the hysterical mob attack in great surges, beating at the gates. I had a glimpse of a scared young Marine guarding the grounds, and was relieved to see him recalled into the building. Then I realized that, incredibly, the mob meant to burn the building. And I absorbed the fact that there were no police to prevent them from doing so.

I faded out of the crowd, and walked the streets in shock and blankness until I came with great relief to a building flying the Union Jack. This had to be the British embassy; an American would be safe there.

And thus I completed the first phase of my long journey back to the world I had known, and another that I couldn't imagine. I announced myself to a British sentry, rather than to an American sentry, telling a straightforward and believable lie (that I had been attacked in the streets and had lost my papers and almost my life) rather than the clumsier lie (involving an accident in a river up-country) I had expected to rely on. Maybe my earlier lie would have worked. I doubt it. In normal times it certainly would have come under close scrutiny. The authorities frown on people who sell their passports and turn up claiming that they lost them in improbable accidents.

Timing.

Because of the rioting, my story of being set upon and robbed was plausible.

Because the embassy had been burned to the ground, complete with all its records, embassy officials were left with no time, no way, and little inclination to counter-check my claim to have legally entered Pakistan some months earlier.

Because Washington promptly chartered an airplane to bring home embassy dependents and other U.S. nationals, I had a way home without having to provide airfare in cash and without having to provide identification. Thus I was able to get back into the States (under the name Hugh Conway) without attracting official attention to myself.

Quite a lot of compounded coincidence, if you insist on insisting on them. I don't. I may not be the brightest guy in the world, but I can learn from experience.

As I said earlier, publishing this memoir is not the only reason I was sent back to this world. However, even though 15 years have elapsed, I must leave the other responsibilities entrusted to me undescribed. All I can say is that they had two aspects: one public, one private.

The first part of the public aspect seems to have been success-ful to a wholly unexpected degree: The world today is farther from nuclear war than at any time since 1962. But the more difficult, if less immediately dangerous, portion of this task remains before us. It is easier to defeat external threats than internal errors. The private aspect might be described as con-tinual composting. This is as immediate—and as difficult—as it was at Shangri-La.

There is not a day in which I do not miss that cloistered world. That long shipboard journey on the roof of the world taught me what voyagers always learn: we may fill in for one another in role, but we are irreplaceable in essence. Yet I am fully aware of how much I have, beyond those walls. My life has lost length, not depth. God is as near here as anywhere, and my friends are still my friends, regardless of time and distance. My home, too, is still my home, wherever I may be.

It is pleasant, in difficult times, to think of the lifeboat's silent existence. On those nights, at a certain phase of the moon, when Mr. Barnard knows to expect a radio message from me, I can talk, if not listen, knowing my words are bridging the gap opened by experience and geography. Our lives know many endings, but they do not cease to flow along the unending river that is time, and the deeper river that is behind and beneath time.

Of all that cloistered world, what remains to me physically are those companions my friends also see: the sun, the planets, the stars, the moon. Some nights I look up at the moon, as I looked out at it on my long night's homeward flight eastward over the Pacific, or as I used to look out at it from a particular window or a particular courtyard, and sometimes it seems I can almost smell the strong, sharp smell of Mr. Barnard's cigars. I take the moon as Noah took the rainbow: as a covenant. It says to me that the force that brought us together once will bring us together again, in its own good time. Better, it says we are apart only physically. I look at the moon and I know that Sunnie was right: I carry them with me.

Yet it is true that the physical distance between us is a dull ache, sometimes only half-noticed, but never absent. I think, sometimes, of how we parted: Mr. Barnard's fatherly, surprising embrace; Sunnie's motherly kiss; Mr. Conway's warm handshake that, like Mr. Barnard's, had turned into an *abrazo*. And I think of other farewells.

Some years earlier, moved by a similar ache for my family (yes, for Marianne), I had sat up half one night putting my longing into verse. Staring out at the moon that seemed to sit so tranquilly, I wrote of the only bodies that my distant friends could see as well as I.

Connectors

When the silent, watchful lunar face,
From far beyond death-dark, winter-dark,
Evening-dark cloud reaches to your place,
Do you know that I am there?
When afternoon sun descends toward night,
Slowly withdrawing from city streets,
Emptying sky with darkening light,
Do you know that I still care?

When, in strengthening light before dawn,
Pale Venus and other morning stars,
unmoving, remain, though seeming gone,
Know that I remain behind the glare.

Whenever sun, moon, planet or star
Is seen by one, the other is there.
Our earthly distance holds us apart;
No one sees the life we share.

Now I am on the other side of the mountains, in a world that thinks me naive, or superstitious, or merely eccentric. Yet I am back in my native land, the country that shaped and nourished me, that formed my ideals and beliefs, that educated and protected me and opened opportunities for me. If it has gotten so far off the track as to find my way of seeing nearly incomprehensible, that merely underlines the great need, the importance of the effort. In any case, it doesn't depend on me. Miss Brinklow would understand that thought.

Tomorrow night the moon will be full again, and my eyes will automatically seek it out. It will be there regardless what happens to me or to America or to the human race or to the world. As it always has, it waxes and wanes and waxes again, following its cycle as do the planets and the seasons and life itself. And, like life, it never sails through the same space twice, any more than the earth does, for the earth pulls the moon along as it circles the sun, and the sun pulls the earth, and the rotation of the galaxy pulls the sun, and on and on. All that cyclical motion: No wonder we can't ever return to where we were.

Afterword

Fifteen years ago, I was reading *Lost Horizon* repeatedly and thinking about Shangri-La continually. Like Alexander Woollcott so many decades earlier, I had gone "quietly mad" over James Hilton's book, I think now because I was clinging to the thought that somewhere there existed a refuge of sanity.

In September, 1979, I began to write *Messenger* as a sequel. Why? Several reasons.

* To win fame and fortune. (Ask any author you know.)
* To finish at least one of the novels I intended to write.
* To persuade myself that Shangri-La could have survived the coming of the Red Chinese.
* To protest the death of Tibetan culture, and the fact that no one in the West seemed to care.
* To emphasize the importance of individual spiritual development, at a time when all the nation's attention seemed to be aimed outward.
* To express something of what I'd learned about life and meaning, most notably from the work of Laurens van der Post and Carl Jung.

I wrote *Messenger* four times, and each time the focus, the center of gravity, changed, almost against my will. In fact, the only chapters to survive more or less intact through all four versions are the one dealing with Miss Brinklow and the one describing George's—originally Dennis's—first experience of the drunken monkey.

I began the first version at about the time of my brother Joe's sudden and mysterious death. (I have never been able to trace the underlying emotional connection between the two events, but I know it's there.) Dennis Corbin was the protagonist. In that first version, George Chiari was nowhere to be seen. Central to that version was my conviction, fortunately erroneous, of the imminence of the Last World War. Equally central, equally erroneous, was a reluctance to concede that life is to be lived here, wherever we are, rather than somewhere else.

A second version attempted to tell Corbin's story as a flashback after his return to America. I realize now that I was working on returning the focus from far-off Tibet to the world around us. I didn't know it then.

When a third version followed, a few years later, George Chiari entered the scene, complete with as much of my background as I found entertaining to give him. Also, psychic matters and the nature of reality took center stage. In that version, the section called Another World was as long as either of the other two parts. Fortunately my friend Suni Dunbar (whose painting of Shangri-La graces the cover) persuaded me this would not do. "It's *boring*," she said bluntly, and she was right, as always.

Finally, for no reason I could ever figure out, came the gift of the Saturday morning in 1988 when I sat down with a cup of coffee and a pen and a legal pad in my dining room, looking out at the marsh behind my house, and began writing out a new version, beginning with George Chiari's U-2 taking off from Peshawar. As I wrote I could see the action as though I were watching a movie. In fact, as I wrote I could imagine the movie version: silent shots of Chiari being bundled into his airplane in the predawn darkness; the U-2 soaring into the sky; flight far over land, over increasingly rugged scenery, as the credits and titles began to roll. Then — still with no words — a quick shot of his engine exhaust suddenly ceasing; his face, startled, followed by him beginning to flip switches. . . .

I wrote all of Chapter One that morning, as I recall, and the rest of the book followed smoothly and relatively easily. The revisions and changes that have taken place since then have all been minor. *Messenger* took 15 years to write, or took only a few months. I can't decide which statement is less misleading. And although I put plenty of work into it, I'm not always sure who wrote it.

Frank DeMarco
August, 1994

About the Artist

Suni Dunbar says this of her paintings:

"I paint because it's healing — for me and for those who receive my paintings. For instance, a friend who is a doctor commissioned a painting for the room in which his patients receive chemotherapy treatments. I chose healing colors and an impressionistic abstract design so that they could find in it whatever they needed.

"I never plan what to paint. I commune and let it take its own shape and direction. I love the feel of the colors, how sometimes they melt and flow into one another. Other times they make a strong statement.

"I lived in Bermuda and Naples and those colors — sun-washed pinks, strong purples, magenta, the robin's-egg blue of the sky, the turquoise of our balcony, the wonderful balls of orange, lemon and green from the groves nearby — became a part of my being.

"*Lost Horizon* was a special film for me, mystical yet real. One day in 1985 my brush took life and painted what I felt was the essence of this fascinating place. Two years later I met a young man named Frank DeMarco, with whom there was an instant connection. He came to my office and told me about a book he was writing set in Shangri-La. Hanging on my wall was this special painting, and I knew I had painted it for him as a gift. That's why it hangs in his office today, and why it appears on the cover of this book, nine years after I painted it."

Suni Dunbar is president of Suni Enterprises of Virginia Beach, Virginia.